Cumberland

Cumberland

Michael V. Smith

A CORMORANT BOOK

The Canada Council Le Conseil des Arts
for the Arts du Canada
since 1957 depuis 1957

ONTARIO ARTS COUNCIL
CONSEIL DES ARTS DE L'ONTARIO

The publisher gratefully acknowledges the support of the Canada Council for the Arts and the Ontario Arts Council for its publishing program. We acknowledge the financial support of the Government of Canada through the Book Publishing Industry Development Program (BPIDP) for our publishing activities.

Printed and bound in Canada

National Library of Canada Cataloguing in Publication Data

Smith, Michael V.
Cumberland

ISBN 1-896951-36-8

I. Title.

PS8587.M562C8 2002   C813'.54   C2002-900031-9
PR9199.3.S65C8 2002

Cover design: Angel Guerra
Text design: Tannice Goddard
Cover image: Nickolaos Dimitriou Stagias

Cormorant Books Inc.
895 Don Mills Road, 400-2 Park Centre
Toronto, Ontario, Canada M3C 1W3
www.cormorantbooks.com

For the man who'll never read
a book like this.

MID-MARCH

M alouf's was crowded, even for the afterwork rush. There weren't any free tables, which meant people came in and left, while others packed themselves around the bar, standing until they were lucky enough to nab a stool. The spring weather got everyone out of the house. See and be seen, as Bea understood it, was the driving principle for going out — aside from drinking. Women checked themselves in the bathroom, undoing a button on their blouses, or letting their hair down. A few drinks later, they'd reconsider their outfits, making even more changes. When they returned to their tables, they'd claim to be more comfortable and sit next to the man they were after.

Bea saw a lot of that. She knew the tricks. In some way, all they wanted was to be beautiful. Bea didn't blame them for how they felt, though she herself tried to be less obvious. She wasn't a kid anymore, so there was no need to make herself stupid over a man who might very well not be interested.

Knowing this to be all too true, Bea couldn't help noticing that one woman had spent the better part of an hour watching Ernest. She wasn't attractive. She was much older than Bea, with grey hair, and hips so round she looked like she had watermelons in her pockets, but the attention she paid Ernest unnerved Bea.

The woman and the friend she was with, a big guy young enough to be her son, were getting their beer at the bar from Hank, so Bea didn't get to talk to them. They were in the front window. Two decades ago, Bea would have dumped a drink down the front of her, sending her home in a cab, or she'd have whispered something threatening or cruel, but she'd grown out of that. She almost lost a job once being smart to someone. The fighting wasn't worth the reward; she rarely achieved what she'd intended. Instead, when she brought Ernest a beer, Bea touched his shoulder, hoping the woman would see how they were with one another.

"I think you've got a girlfriend," she teased, testing him.

Ernest chuckled. "What do you mean?"

Bea kept her hand where it was, feeling the muscle under his flannel shirt. He was fifty-two, and his hair had gone grey. "That woman, the other side of the bar. In the corner with the big guy in the hat. See her? She's been looking at you all night."

Had she not been touching him, Bea might not have noticed — his expression barely changed, he was still smiling, but his shoulders tightened up. "I don't know her," he said, casual, but dismissive. He picked up his beer and took a drink.

"Maybe she's crazy," she said, taking her hand away.

Two young guys sat down at the other corner by the windows. Bea took their order and, as she headed to the bar, just to be certain she wasn't making things up, she glanced at the woman again. Whoever she was, she gave Bea a definite stare, none too nice as far as Bea could gather. *Maybe she is a nut*, she thought to herself. Bea didn't mind the crazy ones, but she hated trying to get them out of the bar. They were next to impossible to deal with at closing time. Hank gave her the beer, she brought them back to the table, and when she turned around, there was Ernest beside her, two paces from the door.

"I'm going early tonight, Bea. I'm damn tired," he said, tucking his money in her front pouch. He was one of the few customers she trusted to pay at the end of his night. Ernest was a good man. She sometimes charged him a beer or two less, on the nights where she knew he'd lost count.

"Theresa's closing, so I'm off at ten," Bea said, "if you want a ride."

"I'm okay, Bea. Just bagged."

She cocked her head and took a long look at him. He had a hand on the door handle already. What was up? Maybe this woman *was* an ex. Maybe it was his wife, who lived in some other city. "We'll see you later," Bea said. She suddenly felt self-conscious. The other woman was likely watching them both now. Bea told herself she could do whatever the hell she pleased. She straightened her back and squared her shoulders as Ernest winked and stepped out the door.

A good ten minutes passed in which Bea noticed the woman looking at her, the expression on her face mixed. Bea couldn't figure what it meant. Finally, when her big friend got up to go, the woman stood as well and untied her jacket from around her

3

waist. She walked past the bar and met Bea at the entrance to the back room.

She was even older than Bea had thought. Her face was round, keeping her complexion smooth, but her eyes were wet and glassy. The woman leaned in and whispered to her. "I don't want to know what's going on between the two of you, but if you're sleeping with Ernest Mackey, I hope to God you don't have kids," she said coldly. She didn't hold the look. Her expression melted into something more like embarrassment, then she turned as quickly as she could and left.

Bea was speechless, watching the woman walk out the door, until Hank came to the end of the bar with her order.

"Woo-hoo?" he said jokingly. "You napping?"

Nobody knew Ernest. He hated it, hated hiding at home and going to a new bar every few years because someone eventually got to know him better than he liked. He had friends at work, buddies from the bar, and not much else. Anything he had ever loved was in his past.

Sitting at the bar, Ernest had been telling Nick and Figgy about Carter. When he was seventeen, Ernest had lied about his age and got a job apprenticing as a welder for Walter Henley. It was good work for a young guy. He and his buddy Carter used to pick up his pay-cheque on the Thursday and take the car down to the beach with their two-fours in the trunk, one case for each day of the weekend. Ernest was only part-time and had Friday to Sunday off. Carter wasn't working yet. They'd drink from noon till sundown because that was the hottest part of the day. Carter would walk around barefoot and he'd step on a bottle cap they'd tossed by the fire and missed, and he'd just look up and lift his foot with the teeth marks from where the cap squeezed his skin and say, "Damn, those things." He didn't bother to put shoes on though. The more they drank, the more bottle caps he'd step on. Ernest would laugh and say, "Fuck you're stupid, Carter, put some shoes on." Two years running they did that, all summer.

And then Ernest got him a job at the plant the next year. They had to wait till he could pass for older because they only hired students who were at least eighteen, but Ernest got him in. So one Tuesday, Carter comes looking for him. Walter has Ernest working round the front of a pressure vessel while he does his thing on the opposite side and the sparks are flying and some guy has left a bucket of oil nearby and one of the sparks takes a nose-dive and next thing, whoosh, the bucket's on fire.

"Now this ain't pretty," Ernest had said, "so old Walter picks it up by the handle quick as anything and tosses it out the open door of the place, only Carter's come looking for me. You get the picture; there weren't nothing left of him. Only the leather on his boots and belt weren't burnt through. Sixteen. Went up like a marshmallow at a camp roast. That's no way to go — screaming. You think he expected to go out like that? Sixteen?" And then, at that moment, Bea had set her hand on his shoulder. Briefly, he'd felt maybe she knew what was going on inside him. Instead, she was pointing out his ex-neighbour in the front window of the bar.

Ernest had had to leave, he was so unnerved by her. He thought she'd be dead by now, nearly thirty years later. He wondered if she'd happened into the place just this once, or if she'd be coming back. Ernest didn't think he had the energy to find a new bar and start all over again. There weren't many places left in the town to drink that he hadn't already tried. Cumberland was only an hour from Ottawa or Montreal, depending on the direction you drove out of town, but he couldn't move away, not now, at his age. He was comfortable at Malouf's. He liked coming with Figgy after work and setting himself down with Nick for an hour. The man was something to look forward to at the end of the day.

Out on the street walking away from the bar and this ghost of an ex-neighbour, Ernest felt his belly burn with anxiety. He didn't want to be alone forever. This is what he usually thought when he was drunk, heading home. The quiet walk by himself was the worst part of any night, anticipating the apartment being empty when he got there. The cold or the heat or the wet were nothing to the loneliness growing in him, welling up in his chest, his feet pulling it from the ground with each step.

Approaching the corner of Water Street and Johnson, too drunk to care what he was doing, he veered left into the entrance to the civic centre arena and its adjoining park. He was going to delay the feeling, if he could, or cut it short entirely.

He crossed the empty lot. The breeze grew cooler, coming off the river. The St. Lawrence was narrow at this stretch, narrow enough to see the houses across the way, on the island, which was the Mohawk reserve, set in the middle of the river between Cumberland and the U.S.

The strip was deserted. Ernest hung out beside the hockey arena, watching the boats in the marina bob on the water, but no luck. Not a soul was out. Eventually, he continued down the trail that ran behind the arena and then the air force building and on into the bush where the paving ended and the small hiking trails began. By the time he was under the large bridge to the U.S., with its grey metal bulk above him, the large girders and rivets, he knew that nothing was going to happen tonight, especially now, in the cold, when he didn't feel quite drunk enough. He turned towards Sumac, pissed off with the bar and himself, and picked up his pace for home.

⌒

Alphie had been wild when Amanda met him last summer, and she'd liked that. He had a habit of pulling the brim of his ball-cap down over his eyes and looking out at her with a grin, his hand sitting on top of the brim or still grabbing it, and his teeth so small and white. He had a cast the first five weeks they dated so Amanda thought him aggressive the way he'd grab her with his good arm and pull her into him. He smelled of cigarettes and sometimes cologne. The whiskers on his face would burn and scratch and she liked his tongue pushing against her lips and rolling down the underside of her mouth.

He was a boy, and eager. If she put her hair up with bobby pins he'd pull them out and drop them so she'd have scratches from when they made out on the floor. If she worked his cock up and down in her hand he'd play with both her nipples, flicking them with his thumbs, the one arm dirty white and crooked at the elbow. This is when she had him in control most, with her hand upon him and both arms working and he noticeably bent. She'd liked that, the way the cast seemed to make him jumpy with frustration, how he'd be wound up and aggressive and grin at her, eating meals too fast or drinking, lighting a joint and dragging half of it back with the first inhale.

The week the cast came off he seemed just about the same. When he picked her up at the curb after work, he was howling at the moon, he was so happy. He drove them the twenty minutes to the campsites further up the St. Lawrence, with a lot along the river and a tent all set up. Amanda liked facing the tent towards the water, so that the first thing she saw in the morning when she pushed back the nylon flap was the river, and the small islands with pine trees on them.

The first night that weekend, they didn't go in for the usual drinking and carousing, so his friends came by, rattling on the tent flaps and making noises outside as a complaint. They shone flashlights on the canvas. Amanda was sure she made shadows next to it and wanted to stop, or get Alphie to make them go away, but he wouldn't and she felt horrible with her legs hoisted up. She felt cheap. And crazily giddy from it all. Her stomach made somersaults and the sex felt wild and dangerous. She grabbed Alphie's bare ass and hung on with her eyes closed till it was over.

Nothing got to be so reckless or uncomfortable after that, but the feeling stuck with her. She wasn't sure if it was Alphie or just the whole business of that night bothering her. The thing was, the cast hadn't changed him like she'd thought. Without it, he was still wild, still skittery and pent-up. What she'd attributed to his being injured and limited, and so bound to disappear, stayed on and seemed worse. With two free hands Alphie was simply faster, rougher, more difficult. His hands seemed to be everywhere. If she went to sit down he'd open a palm under her so she'd sit on it accidentally. Or he'd pull at her bra strap, tickle her ribs.

This was Tuesday night and they were out at a bonfire. It was early and already he was frustrating her with all his touching and pinches. She'd tried to be sweet with him by curling into his chest so that he'd come round to being cuddly back but he only wiggled a finger down her thigh with the other hand. It inched towards her crotch until she slapped it. Then he started all over. When she'd had enough she told him she was ready to go home and eventually they got in his car and left.

"So what do you want to do?" he asked. He drove them down the old Number Two highway that ran alongside the river.

"Go home."

"I want to drive around for a bit."

"But I'm tired."

"We'll get there. I'm just taking a bit of time to unwind," he said, then added, "Relax, it's early."

He held his left hand on the steering wheel and the right sat on the stick shift. He booted it down the highway so the engine revved up. He jumped it into fourth gear for a few seconds, then coasted in neutral. He drove like this late at night and it made Amanda sort of woozy, but mostly irritable, to be starting and stopping like some damn fool.

"Let's just go home. I'm *tired*," she said again.

"That's where I'm taking you."

"In the opposite direction?"

It was nearly nine o'clock at night and Amanda had been on her feet all afternoon. She only wore a short white top, sleeveless and cut above her belly button, with tights, a cut-off jean skirt and sneakers. Though she was cold and her uniform was in the knapsack on the back seat of the car, she wouldn't put it on. The blouse was getting old and had stains in the front from tonight's shift. Alphie had the blower on and she reached out and turned off the switch.

"What are you doing?" he asked and turned it back on.

"I'm cold."

"You'll be colder if you walk," he said and chuckled, nudging her with his elbow. She didn't laugh. He gave a sigh like he was disappointed in her.

"Why are you driving in the opposite direction?" she asked crossly.

"Because I'm high," he said and his voice sounded like Jack Nicholson in *The Shining*. He revved the engine and jumped it into fourth again. When he came back into neutral he gave a sigh of satisfaction, then put his hand on his lap instead of on the stick shift. They coasted till his hand snapped out and turned the fan off and rested back in his lap again. He eased the car onto the gravel and turned at a driveway that led into an empty field.

"What are you doing?"

"Turning around," he said, without making a move to put the car in reverse.

He looked at her for a while. Amanda thought his face seemed empty, as if he was still stoned (which he couldn't have been by now) or he was dead stupid. She tried not to smile at the thought in case he got the wrong idea. She was angry.

"Well?" she said, trying to sound frustrated.

Though she hadn't noticed him pull down his fly, he began fishing in his pants.

"Oh, Alphie," she said. "Come off it."

He grinned at her, with his swollen dick in his hand. The car was still running and their lights grazed the dried grass of the field.

Her voice was quiet and soft. "Give it up. I want to go home."

Something inside her felt funny. He could be greedy, and she didn't mind that so much if he was pressing down on her, or grabbing too hard, or just grabbing when he shouldn't have been. She didn't mind as much because at least it was about her, and what he wanted. Sometimes the greediness made her feel important. But every now and again he'd do this — whip it out as if it was something she hadn't seen. Or in the middle of sex he'd just stop, pull out, and beat off over top of her until he came, which could be a while. How could she complain? What do you say to a guy who does that, other than *don't*. It never seemed right, but he wasn't hurting her.

"I'd turn the car off if I was you. Someone might pull over to see what's wrong."

He was watching himself now and didn't look up. "If I leave it running I can just back out." His breathing was ragged. He held his balls in one hand and fisted his dick in the other. Occasionally he smacked it against the steering wheel. Amanda thought that was stupid. He looked small and ridiculous. She wanted to get out of the car and walk into the field to leave him to his business but was afraid he'd drive off without her. Maybe she was supposed to touch herself, or watch. She had no idea.

She sat beside him in the car and thought that if she hit him, he might just hit her back. She had to hold her hands in her lap so that she wouldn't strike out and scratch him, up and down his face.

"Having a good time?" she asked dryly. She gave an exaggerated yawn. He didn't answer. Amanda could only guess that he didn't realize what he was doing as he watched his right hand beat himself off, while the left had a glassy bit of precum on its thumb that he brought to his lips and smacked off. "Frig," she said. "Get it over with." She tugged on the loose weave of her skirt, pulling the stray ends off and rolling the white cotton bits together.

After his breathing sped up and the hiccup of his orgasm squirted itself out, Alphie leaned back in the bucket seat and closed his eyes with a long satisfied sigh. Amanda gritted her teeth. She wanted to bite him till she drew blood. Or hammer a pencil in his ear.

"That's it, Alphie. We're through." She felt very satisfied saying those words. She felt suddenly adult.

Without moving his head, he snapped open an eye. "You mad at me?" he asked innocently.

"Yes! Take me home."

"If you're mad at me, we should talk about this first."

With her lip thrust forward and a set jaw, Amanda stared out the side window.

"Come on, baby," he nudged her. "Come on, talk to me."

"Go fuck yourself."

Alphie sighed tiredly, leaned an arm lazily across the top of the steering wheel, and smacked his gums. "Well what am I supposed to do about this if you won't talk to me, huh?" He looked at her, then looked away. "Geez," he said. "You're frustrating me here. What am I s'posed to do? If you don't tell me what's wrong, I ain't cold, we'll sit here all night waiting."

"Nothing, Alphie. Nothing. Everything's fine."

With his voice now full of concern, he asked, "You mean that? You're okay here?"

"Yeah," she said. "Sure. Take me home. Call me tomorrow."

"Maybe you're getting your period or something. Is that it?"

"Yeah, Alphie," she patted his shoulder. "That's my problem."

Aaron hated evenings. He hated his father going somewhere without him, as he often did after work, or supper, leaving Aaron at his aunt's and picking him up when the night was over. As much as he loved his Aunt Lue, he couldn't stand to come out of the school and see her car parked at the side of the road waiting for him as he had today. He and his dad used to play cards, or rent movies, they'd take walks by the river or go for ice cream in the summer when his mother was alive. They would all go.

Neither his Aunt Lue nor Uncle Gary ever mentioned where his father was, but Aaron knew he spent the evenings with friends at a bar. Aaron had been there before, nearly a year ago, and wondered why he couldn't go too. After his mother died, the waitress from there, Bea, came over to the house a few times and she and his dad would sit in the back room and talk with the door shut. Sometimes, when he'd heard the muffled sound of his father crying, he'd turned the TV way up until they'd come out. That didn't happen anymore because his dad spent more time at the bar, so no one needed to visit at home.

When Aaron had nearly finished his supper, his Aunt Lue asked him where his painting was from school. Aaron shrugged.

"Show your Uncle Gary the painting."

"It's downstairs," Aaron said, sounding as if that was too far away to bother.

"Don't I get to see it?" Uncle Gary asked.

He shrugged. "It's not so good."

"Doesn't mean I don't want to see it." Uncle Gary was smiling. It made Aaron angry.

"I can show you later," he sighed, exasperated, hoping they'd drop it.

"Mm," Aunt Lue said, noticing the tone in his voice. "What's it of?"

"A fish."

"A fish? That sounds like fun," she said. "What colour is it?"

"Blue, green and orange." He really didn't want to talk about the painting. He'd forgot it on the clothes pegs at school, but when he'd been about to get in Aunt Lue's car, Trisha Yardley had run towards him with the painting flapping in her hand. Aaron snatched it from her and jumped in the car without saying a word to her, which his aunt hadn't liked.

"You can't keep this up forever, Aaron," she'd said.

He'd looked at her, pretending he didn't understand. She'd smiled sweetly at him, but he knew she wasn't happy. "You know, kiddo? You're going to have to get some friends eventually," she'd said, though she had no idea what it was like for him at school. Being nice to Trisha Yardley wasn't going to help him find friends. Nobody liked Trisha, not even the teacher.

So the last thing Aaron felt like doing was showing his aunt and uncle the painting. "I want to watch TV until my dad comes."

Aunt Lue was going to say something but his uncle spoke first. "Sure, kiddo. I think the remote's on the floor. Don't step on it."

Aaron got up from the table and took his dirty dishes with him. His uncle messed his hair as he passed, but his Aunt Lue didn't say anything. Placing his dishes carefully in the kitchen sink, he had the urge to drop them, and call it an accident, but it was too late. He'd already set them down.

In the den, he turned the television on, but didn't really watch it. He sat on the prickly carpet, his arms stretched across the coffee table holding the painting. He could hear his Aunt Lue running water, then the dishes bumping together in the sink and the sharper clinking sound as they were placed in the drying rack. Other nights, he helped her with the dishes. She'd call to him to come help, which he liked, because they'd paint bushy beards and eyebrows on each other with the bubbles. He knew she was upset with him, for some reason, because she didn't ask him to come up.

He didn't know why she was angry with him. Maybe because he wasn't nice to Trisha Yardley this afternoon, though that didn't seem fair.

Aaron took hold of the painting at the top edge and pulled in opposite directions, slowly so as not to make noise, splitting the fish in two. The paint was thick. Small bits flaked off like scales. He tore the page again, and again, watching the paint crack, then chip and fall in his lap. When the pieces were small enough, he tucked them in his pocket and brushed the scaly bits from his pants.

Bea knew better. She was forty-three and had lived with a real bastard for six years and was all the wiser for it. While she'd been sick of him it wasn't enough to end it because it kept her busy — moving inside all that hate and loathing and trying to make do — but one day she woke up and realized she didn't give two shits for him anymore and kicked him out. She wasn't so bad off. She was just over thirty then. Now her hair was growing in grey and looked a bit more frazzled with the grey ones coming in thicker and kinky but she dyed them and still made a good blonde. Her figure was decent, her clothes clean and simple and not too showy, if a little mismatched. Bea didn't care so much because she'd settled herself into being single and had planned to stay that way. She really couldn't care less what people thought; as long as she was clean she didn't think twice about all the rest of it.

And then, to her surprise more than anyone else's, something changed. She met someone, and he was interested in her, and the thought of him didn't displease her, or make her uncomfortable. The first night she'd caught sight of him, it had been a long shift. Bea's feet weren't sore too often because, apart from buying good shoes, she'd been working standing up for twenty or more years and barely noticed anymore, except that that particular weekend her shoes were new and Saturday had been a busy day so she could feel the skin of her soles. They felt hot and flat, as if two coins were pushing into them. The sweat collected under her arms and dropped occasionally down her shirt or ran into the curve of her elbow. She remembered the day was that hot, and her feet stinging, and an hour or so left to her shift when this man came in and sat himself directly at a table. She hadn't seen him before, but he walked in as though he knew the place already; he didn't stand in the doorway to look around. He was a stocky guy — broad shoulders and thick arms — in a short-sleeve cotton shirt with two buttons undone from the top. The hairs on his head and chest were all grey, though he didn't look very old. He wasn't a senior. She guessed him around fifty, and thought maybe that that was too old as well.

What struck Bea was how tired he seemed. It was midnight on a Saturday. She'd been working seven and a half hours already, her hair out of whack, beer spilled down the front of her and sticky on parts of her legs, most of the customers bombed or carrying those too drunk to get to their cars or cabs. But this man, sober, clean, his hair combed back, and buttons undone, looked tired in a way Bea wasn't. Like she hadn't dared see this kind of tiredness before because it filled the room. Everyone, when she looked around, carried a piece of it. All the bodies moved slowly the way this man moved, they all lifted themselves with the same precision and difficulty, drank with the same need, filled themselves with what they could and looked empty. For a second, the sight of him sickened her and she felt herself sink a little into the floor, her knees going soft.

She did her work and came around asking what he'd like and when he looked at her, the feeling left. As quickly, and as easily, the air was light again with smoke and the noise from people and the jukebox.

Nothing remarkable happened, he said very little and what he did say was polite, if brief. He was a guy. They were in a bar, and she was tired. He left, without ceremony, about two minutes before closing. It was when she'd locked up with Hank and he walked her to her car that she felt it again. The heaviness in her knees. Like he was around the corner and she could feel him there, walking home after one thirty in the morning, with her hand on the door to her LeCar. Sometimes it came back when she saw him. Not always, but it was there when she wasn't expecting it. This man was Ernest, and he became just one of the faces in the bar that she happened to like, compared to those she could do without, but every now and again, out of the corner of some place he kept hidden, the heaviness would spread itself out and colour the room, muffle the music and the people until it tumbled away and dissolved.

She liked him. She'd admitted that to herself after he'd come in a few times. He was quiet enough, though he had his moments of boisterousness. The evenings with Ernest were usually engaging and playful in a quiet way. He was a decent-sized man with large thick hands he'd worked with so many years, and he knew how to tell a good story and how to ask or answer a question. There were nights he didn't do so well, where he was almost morbid, and in the last few months they'd increased in number, but Bea liked him for the respect he gave her. He flirted, he wouldn't have been a man at that bar if he didn't, but it was friendly, and he shared it with her. He didn't make like he owned it, he simply brought that playfulness out of the both of them and turned it around and handed it back to her to use as she wished. Not like some of them, who were clumsy or rough with the feeling inside them, their words harsh or the look of them too screwed up or deflated. She liked Ernest. He knew how to treat her and treated her that way always despite his mood, unless it was low, and then they both left each other be.

Sometimes she'd give him a ride home if he seemed too drunk or it was too cold to be walking, but not often. Having a man in the car was a luxury she'd once taken for granted and now could appreciate again. So she kept it seldom, lest either of them grow too attached to the idea; not that Ernest ever asked for a ride, he always said no the first time she offered and then seemed thankfully surprised when she asked again. It was herself she didn't trust so much.

And then one night last month her car made a racket when she was taking him home and he said it was just the muffler and he could cut her pipe shorter if it wasn't too bad, and the next day he walked over to the apartment with his hacksaw and did it. Free of charge. He looked sexy walking off with the hacksaw in hand. What could she think of that? Amanda giggled at her and Bea felt embarrassed, though she didn't know why, really. It wasn't anything out of the ordinary.

When the buzzer from the hall went off, Bea noticed she was thinking again of Ernest. For a second, she half-thought it might be him, but Ernest wouldn't be coming by her place after ten in the evening. It was Nick, who Bea had talked to for a few months after his wife passed away. Bea had made herself available because, at a time like that, you needed someone, and Nick hadn't been talking to anyone about it, that she could tell.

She was a little concerned when she saw him at the door. "Everything okay, Nick?"

"Yeah," he said, cheery. "But you forgot this." He pulled a large can of maple syrup from behind his back. She'd forgotten it after he'd brought it to the bar for her. "I figure you've paid for it, you might as well have it," he said, smiling.

She thanked him and invited him in for coffee.

"Tea'd be nice," he said, stepping through the door frame.

"Sure," said Bea and turned for the kitchen. As she unhooked a cup hanging inside the cupboard, she called out to him, "Ernest left in a rush tonight."

"Wellll, it wasn't a good night for him," Nick answered.

"No?"

"He was talking about a buddy he saw burned up at work."

Bea came around the corner. "Today?" Nick was on the couch, bent forward, with his legs spread and his arms resting on either knee. His brown hiking boots were by the front door.

"No, no. When he was a kid. Thirty years ago. Some kid working at Combustion. Ernest and he were buddies and he saw the kid burn up at work. A bucket of oil on fire. Some guy shot it out the door as the kid was walking in and 'Whoosh,' Ernest said, 'Like a marshmallow at a camp fire.'"

"God that's rough," Bea said, pausing. The thought travelled through her veins in a chill. She went back to the counter for the teabags, gently changing the subject. "I wonder where Amanda is. Have you met Amanda, Nick? She's the girl that lives with me." Bea didn't like it if Amanda stayed in her room when Bea had company. She worried Amanda didn't feel wanted. Bea hoped she'd come out if she heard her talking about her, partly because of this, and partly because Bea didn't want Nick to feel like she'd orchestrated their being alone together. She liked Nick, he was a good guy, but she wasn't interested. He was a man from her work who turned out to be the cable guy. So they kind of knew each other better than most people from the bar knew Bea.

"Don't think so," Nick said.

"Oh well, you will. She's come into the bar to drop stuff off a couple times. She doesn't stay. She's just seventeen."

"Oh, yeah," Nick said. Bea could tell he was curious why the girl was living with her. She peeked around the corner again and whispered to him, "I'll tell you later," with a little nod.

The door to Amanda's room opened just then and the girl almost caught her whispering.

"You are here," Bea said, looking up the hallway to see Amanda in a jean skirt and tights, with her hair tied back.

"Mhmm. I just got home before you. I was listening to music on my headphones." When she walked to the end of the hall she stopped just short of stepping into the living room.

She looked at Nick. "Hi," she said.

With a quick nod, he answered, "How are ya?"

Bea introduced them and offered Amanda tea too.

"Only if we have cookies," Amanda said and went to get them. She brought the bag into the living room and set them on the coffee table.

Bea poured the tea and brought them out each a cup, then got hers and set it down. When she noticed the bag of ginger snaps on the table she went back into the kitchen and came out with a plate.

Amanda had taken the chair next to Nick so Bea sat on the other side of the couch. She opened the bag of cookies and arranged them on the plate.

Amanda asked, "So where do you work, Nick?"

He picked up his tea and leaned back, cradling it in his lap. "Rogers."

She looked blankly at him but he didn't add anything else. "Oh," she said.

Bea piped up. "TV. He hooked up our cable."

"Oh, right," she said. "Of course." Then she offered him a cookie.

"I bought a big tin of real maple syrup for us. Nick was at McAllister's today."

"Great," said Amanda. "You drive, Nick?"

"Yup." His mouth was full of cookie.

"What do you drive?"

"A Range Rover. I got some insurance money last year so I spent it. She's a nice vehicle."

"I love those. Lots of room in the back."

Bea's teacup made a clatter when she set it down. The girl could be so obvious. Why the heck would she be hitting on Nick? He was nearly old enough to be her dad.

"Not bad," Nick said. "Eight cylinder, four wheel drive."

"Do you camp?"

He shrugged his shoulders. "Yeah, sometimes."

"I bet it would be a great truck to go camping with."

"It's not a truck," Bea corrected.

"Range Rover," said Nick with a chuckle.

"Whatever. Truck, Grange Rover, I know. What colour is it?"

"Green."

"Dark green?"

"Pretty much. You like green?" he asked, picking up another cookie and smiling.

"Definitely. I'd get a green if I had a car. You should've got a green car, Bea."

"I got mine second-hand. As long as it runs smoothly. Fine by me." Bea couldn't stop herself from sounding curt, but she tried to smile. "You'd like the maple syrup camp. They have a horse there, I think."

"Do they?" Amanda answered, and turned to Nick to explain. "I rode horses with my mother's boyfriend a few summers ago. I was pretty good. He said I had great form."

"Do you still ride?" Nick asked.

"Not there. My mother dumped him."

"That's too bad for you."

"Not really. He was gross. I never liked spending the day with them much. He'd feel my ass when he pushed me up in the saddle."

"Didn't you tell your mother?" Bea asked.

"No. I didn't want to make her feel bad. He did it to her too and she'd giggle. It was really gross."

Nick laughed and picked up another cookie. "Does she still live near here?" he asked.

Bea looked to Amanda but the girl didn't take her eyes off him. She didn't so much as blink.

"River Heights," she said. The tone in her voice dropped as she reached out and touched Nick's sleeve. "We don't talk to each other any more," she said, trying to sound mature.

Bea wanted to help out, but couldn't think what to say.

"It's a good thing you've got Bea here to talk to. She's got a good head on her shoulders," Nick said.

"Yup." Amanda smiled.

"So how about if I make pancakes tomorrow, Amanda? Will you be here in the morning or are you going back out — tonight?"

There was a pause. Bea almost said *with your boyfriend* but decided against it, though she wanted to, and Amanda seemed to notice. She leaned back into the chair, then pulled part of her hair out in front of her face to see how healthy the ends were.

"Don't know. Maybe Nick will take me for a ride in his Grange Rover."

"Could do," said Nick, smiling again. Bea could tell he thought Amanda was cute. He watched her separate the strands of her hair. "I've got to pick up my kid at his aunt's so I can't be too late," he said, "but I can take you for a spin if you want."

"Great," Amanda said, dropping her hair. If she'd heard the part about his boy, Bea didn't see her let on.

"Do you want to come along, Bea?" Nick asked.

"No. Thank you, Nick," she said too politely. "But say hi to Aaron for me."

Again Bea wasn't sure if Amanda had heard her as the girl ran into her bedroom for her keys.

Bea looked at Nick. He smiled at her, a little awkwardly, so that she didn't know what was going through his mind. *Be careful* she wanted to say, but didn't dare. It wasn't her place to be saying anything. He was a grown man and knew what he was doing. But Amanda. Bea knew better. Amanda was wild yet and didn't seem to understand certain things about the world. Then Bea thought that maybe Nick didn't know the girl was seventeen. Bea considered saying it again, only Amanda reappeared. After Nick thanked Bea for the tea and put his boots on, off they went.

When the door shut, Bea stacked their cups, picked up the plate and cookies and carried them all into the kitchen. She threw the teabags out, poured the excess down the sink, picked up a washrag and walked to the table in the living room, wiping up the last of the crumbs they'd left behind. By then, she realized there was something she needed to do.

When Ernest got home from Malouf's, he kept drinking. He didn't mean to have more than one but he did. By the time he'd nearly downed a six-pack, the television was turned to a police drama. The night was wasted. He half-wished he'd have stayed at Malouf's with Nick, but he wasn't in any mood to go back. And Nick was likely home by the time Ernest got to thinking about it. It was late.

That woman was on his mind. Ernest felt vaguely ashamed of himself, as he often did when faced with everything that had happened, which meant, again, he was trying not to think about the park now that he was home.

When he did stumble along the trails feeling drunk and lonely, when he got off either by himself or with the help of someone else, it was brief and silent. He never spoke, and was reluctant to even look his partners in the eye. Most often he was drunk enough that in the morning he remembered very little about them — at once a blessing because he wouldn't suffer embarrassment if they met on the street, and a fear that he would one day be recognized.

So each morning, he started fresh. His nights in the park were foggy and removed from the everyday. Flashes of memory. A hand or smile, a particular smell, sometimes a kind of car that had pulled up and passed him as he swerved off the grass and headed for the marina, which was the beginning of the path snaking along the river as far as the power dam.

It was after eleven o'clock at night, and Ernest was almost passed out on the couch. His cat Brutus lay all curled up on the end of his bed in the other room. Every now and again Ernest would look over and see her there and call to her, but she wouldn't stir. Her ear would pull back when he called her name and occasionally the eyes would open slightly but she wouldn't look up. Ernest had been married, and this is how his wife had been in the last months before she left. Seeing Brutus act like this tonight only made Ernest sadder, and drink more. It seemed Brutus knew all too well how Ernest was feeling and she didn't want anything to do with him either.

His wife's name was Claire. Ex-wife now. They were married a dozen years. Ernest loved her still, he loved her a great deal and didn't know what to do with his love now that she was gone. He had no place for it in his life since she'd left, and he had no other place to put it. Sometimes he wished she'd come back to him, but he knew she wouldn't. She didn't know where he lived any more. Nor his phone number. Since she'd moved back to Hawkesbury she'd stopped keeping in touch. They agreed this was for the best because Ernest would call her when he was drunk and upset them. He'd embarrass her new husband and himself when they hung up on him.

He'd called repeatedly, partly because he couldn't see their lives as separate and partly because he couldn't stand to lose her too. Even now, so many years later, he still thought of Claire as his wife, despite knowing that she was married to someone else. Greg. That was his name. He was a nice guy. He treated her well, she said. He was very kind. Yes, she was happy. That's all Ernest wanted to know. Then he'd ask if they had children yet or were planning on it and he'd start to cry and either Claire would hang up or cry as well, at which point Greg would come over and talk to her softly and click the receiver down. Then Ernest would wait as long as he could, for weeks or months even, before having to call again.

When they'd served him the divorce papers the first time,

he'd torn them up, even though the day before he had promised to sign them. Then she had to talk to him all over again, and a few weeks went by that they were still married and Ernest got to thinking the more he talked to her, the harder it would be for her to serve papers again. She would call when he got home after work and ask how his day was. Things didn't seem so lonely then for those few weeks. Ernest stopped going to the bars after work so that he could be home in case she called. He drank less, knowing that if he was drunk she wouldn't talk to him as long. But eventually she asked him again, and then she brought the papers over herself. The bundle sat on the kitchen table in front of Ernest for a long time while he and Claire talked. Ernest held the papers in front of him, threatening to tear them up again, but couldn't do it. He couldn't bring himself to do it in front of her. So he signed them. She said thank you, hugged him quickly, and left soon after.

That had been a hard week. Ernest couldn't focus at work and drank a good deal at home to forget what had happened. He tried not to call her, but failed, so a week later, she telephoned to say they had changed their phone number, and Ernest wasn't to have the new one. He never knew her address in Hawkesbury, and now she had an unlisted number. Which meant he didn't cry as hard, or as often.

That was years ago, but Ernest still missed her, and wished he wasn't alone. He wished Brutus wouldn't ignore him like that and remind him of her. So when the phone rang and he picked up the receiver and it was a woman's voice at the other end, he couldn't help but think it was Claire. She said hello and Ernest asked her how she was.

"Not very good," she said. "Can I come over? I could use the company."

Ernest was drunk and wanted to ask where she was calling from but realized it wasn't Claire, she wouldn't have his number to be calling him. "Who is this?" he asked.

"It's Bea," she said.

With his head swimming, Ernest processed that: this wasn't his wife, it was Bea, who'd been in the bar tonight and had seen his ex-neighbour staring at him, until he'd left. He was home, and feeling pretty awful.

"Ernest? It's Bea," she repeated.

"Oh, oh. Right. How ya been, Bea?"

"Were you sleeping?"

"No. I was just sitting here watching the TV." Ernest tried to sound alert. "What can I do for you?"

"Think I could come over?" Bea asked.

"Sure, Bea. You got a problem?"

"No. Well, maybe. I'm a little teed off right now." Ernest waited as she paused. "Hey," she said more brightly, "you left early tonight. You okay?"

"Sure, Bea. I'm fine," he said, his stomach settling with relief. Bea sounded friendly and warm, meaning she mustn't have heard a thing. "You come on over. You know where I live?"

"I've driven you home before."

"Oh, yeah, right. Right. Come on over."

Ernest hung up and walked into the kitchen for water. He poured a big glass and drank it and filled his pitcher up again. Then he walked to the bathroom and took a leak. He felt better. It was after eleven at night and Bea was coming over. He went out on the front step to take in some air and try to wake himself up. The wind was picking up. His feet were cold on the small wooden porch. Why would Bea be coming over to his place? What could be wrong with Bea, Ernest thought, and what could he do for her? Though the fresh air helped, he still wished it was earlier in the night and he wasn't so tired. The stars were out behind some of the clouds and the wind was strong enough to blow his hair up at the back. Things were really quiet in the city. The roads were deserted. Ernest stood like that until Bea pulled up in her LeCar with its white headlights sweeping up the siding on the house and blinding him for a second. His apartment was in the rear, with the door and a small canopy extended a few feet out from the side. She parked. As soon as she got out Ernest said hello to her and invited her in.

She was wearing a brown three-quarter-length coat with big brown plastic buttons. The coat hid her body but brought out her blonde hair that seemed suited to the colour of the material. Her hair was done differently from earlier that night and she smelled nice, it was faintly like pot pourri or something flowery.

"So what's the problem, Bea? You want a drink?" he asked as she sat down on the couch. She had a jar of something in her hands that she'd taken out of her coat pocket.

"No, I'm fine. I brought you some maple syrup. Nick picked some up for me today and I thought maybe you could use some too. I bought a big can."

Ernest didn't eat pancakes or French toast but he thanked her like he was real pleased. His mother used to give him a bowl of real syrup with bread and he and his sisters would tear bits off and dunk them.

Ernest sat down on the couch beside her, then set the Mason jar of syrup on the coffee table. She looked at him a second before she began. "What do you think of Nick?"

"Nick?" Ernest said. "He's a good guy. I like him, Bea," he said, feeling more vulnerable than he should have for admitting that. He could see Bea collecting her thoughts.

He looked around at where they were and found the living room smaller than usual. He had to burp. He lived in a small place, he realized. There wasn't a lot of room for two people.

He let out a slow quiet belch, tasting the beer.

"Nick dropped by with the syrup tonight and we had tea."

"So why're you here Bea?" Ernest couldn't keep himself from asking.

"He didn't go home right away." There was a pause while she considered something and Ernest thought it meant they were sleeping together, she and Nick, and he hadn't had a clue.

She asked again, "What do you think of him?"

"I don't know if you want to be telling me this, Bea. I mean, I don't know . . . What business is it of mine what you do? You know what I mean? I'm not one to be giving advice like that."

"No, Ernest." A look of concern wrinkled her brow, and then he noticed her get something, and she smiled at him, warmly. A heat flushed through his bones. "I'm not interested in *Nick*," she said softly. "The girl I live with. Amanda. He's out with her, driving or something."

"Oh," he said and seemed hoarse. He cleared his throat. "Does that bother you?"

"I'm not sure if it should. That's sort of why I'm here. Maybe I will have a drink."

"I got beer. You want a Blue? Or orange juice."

"A Blue."

Ernest went to the kitchen and got them each a beer, and her a glass. When he came back in she was settled into the couch, a little more comfortable. She looked tired to Ernest and he felt bad for her. He felt very tired as well. The thought of Nick was heavy in his arms and his legs.

Handing her the glass, Ernest sat back down, twisted the lid off one beer and handed it to her, then opened his.

"It's not that I don't trust Nick. I sorta don't trust Amanda. She's only seventeen, and she doesn't really know what she's doing. She's a good kid, but I don't know what to do about her. It's hard, it's very hard living with someone young like her and seeing the things she gets herself into. I don't want to be putting her out, you know. She's got nowhere to go and I'm it for the girl. I'm it. I'm all she's got to come home to. I can't say as I blame her for wanting a man of her own, but he's newly single, and old for her. It's the way she goes after them. She's bound to get herself into some kind of trouble, chasing after men the way she does. How do you tell a girl a thing like that and have her listen to you? I've tried, but she doesn't understand. God knows what she's up to tonight. God knows what trouble she'll try to cause for poor Nick. I just hope she doesn't try anything stupid. For his sake, I hope she doesn't."

Ernest had half his beer gone by the time she was done. He wanted to go to bed with his arms wrapped around a pillow. He was sitting on the left-hand side of the couch with an arm along the back of it and his beer in the other hand.

"Don't worry none, Bea. Nick's a big boy. He'll be fine with that Amanda. She's just a girl. He's not stupid, Bea. Don't you worry."

Ernest looked at Bea with her head resting against the back of the couch, the beer in her hands and little TV sets reflected in her eyes. He knew what she was waiting for. He couldn't say why he was doing it other than that's what was expected of him — they both wanted something, didn't they? — as he leaned forward and kissed her. It was easy. He kissed her and she kissed him right back, with her soft lips, and the thin smell of her perfume rising in his nostrils. Ernest loved the sweetness of kissing a woman again. She was soft against him, and breathing nicely. He could taste the beer on his breath was stale compared to hers, her whole mouth was full and fresh, with its teeth and slender tongue. Ernest felt his heart go bang in his cock. As drunk as he felt, his cock throbbed with the smell of her against him.

Together they leaned forward and set their beer on the table. When Bea's hands were free she wrapped them behind Ernest's neck then ran them down his chest and over his arms. Ernest felt like he was broken and she was checking out the spots where he'd fall apart.

There wasn't much to do. She undressed them on the couch and manipulated him until he was hard and wanted it. She breathed in his ear. She made noises he thought might be words but couldn't tell what they'd be so he didn't stop. Her hair fell on his face. She grabbed his arms, she kissed him steadily and pressed herself against him.

When he entered her, she made a small noise, which Ernest loved. It was her body responding. As much as she was pre-pared for him, her body still cried out with surprise, as his did, his senses jumping alert. He thought less, his mind quieting down, feeling her surround him, smelling the perfume, tasting the sweat on her neck as they worked themslves closer, trying to make the space between them disappear.

The moon was bright behind the clouds. It was still pretty chilly out, despite the truck being so much nicer than Alphie's Chevy. At first Amanda was wishing she'd brought a sweater, but as they drove for ten or so minutes, the truck warmed up and she decided it was worth it to have been a little cold. She liked this blouse and how thin her waist looked. Amanda was glad that she'd thought to put on something nice and see who it was when she'd heard Nick come in. She'd only been home a few minutes before Bea, and then the buzzer had sounded.

He was a hot guy, with his thick forearms and the sleeves rolled up. He had a wisp of wiry brown chest hair peeking above the V of his shirt. He was totally solid, no-nonsense, no stupidity, with a big truck.

They drove alongside the river, which Amanda thought romantic, only he hadn't put the radio on. They didn't say much. Amanda was trying to figure out what to talk about when Nick asked how she liked living with Bea.

"She's alright."

"Yeah, I like Bea," he said. "You still in school?"

"Mm, no. I have one year to finish. I might take night school in the summer. I'm too busy working. I have bills to pay."

They passed the golf course on the left, with the greens lit up, though it was still too early in the season to start. There wouldn't be grass for another month, at least. Nick asked if she played.

"Sometimes," she lied.

"Maybe we can play this summer. We'll get Bea out, and one of your friends."

Without blinking, Amanda said, "Bea doesn't golf. She hates golfing. But I'll go."

"Hm. We'll have to convince her, won't we?"

Amanda didn't answer. Pulling out a pack of Dentyne, she popped a stick in her mouth and offered one to Nick. He declined.

"You have a boyfriend, don't you?" he asked.

"*Had.*"

"Oh. You broke up."

"Yup," she said. It wasn't a lie. She had no plans to call him back after tonight.

"So that's a good thing then?"

She sighed heavily, "Alphie's immature. He's just a kid."

Nick said, "I see."

Amanda wasn't sure what that meant. Nick was playing it very cool, which began to frustrate her. Bea, Alphie and school were the last things she wanted to talk about. The ride wasn't proving as exciting as the promise of being out in a stranger's car should have been. He hadn't tried to touch her, and they didn't even put the radio on, let alone blast it.

When they reached the big stone church in Glen Walter, not far out of town, Nick pulled into the parking lot. Amanda got her hopes up, with butterflies in her belly, until the truck didn't stop. He pulled around, out onto the road, heading back.

They were quiet again until passing Grey's Creek and entering the city limits. Amanda straightened herself in her seat. She smoothed her skirt.

Nick cleared his throat. "So how do you like the truck?"

"It's awesome!" she perked up. "It drives real smooth. I love all the buttons." Then, with a start, she added, "Hey, we didn't put the radio on."

"Go ahead," Nick said.

The scan button turned to half a dozen stations until a breathy guy sang something about a wishing well. Amanda kept it there. "This is pretty."

"Sure," Nick said, putting his blinker light on. He turned the truck up Leonia, a tree-lined street with small bungalows and duplexes split into two apartments. The truck pulled over in front of a house with red siding and stucco. "I just have to stop here. I've got to pick up my boy."

Great, Amanda thought dryly, *that was quick*.

෴

In less than a half-hour from when it started, they were finished. Ernest was finished. He felt exhausted, and drunk, and had to sleep. "You wanna stay, Bea?"

She lay against him on the couch. Her breath tickled the grey hairs on his chest.

"I don't think so, Ernest. Not tonight. I'm sorry."

"No, no, that's fine. That's fine. You do what you have to. I'm fine here."

Bea sat up and looked him in the eyes. She kissed him. "I should get dressed. We'll catch pneumonia sitting here all night."

Bea checked the floor for her clothes, separating them from the tangle they made with Ernest's. She slipped her bra back on, then the rest of her clothes, without saying a word. Ernest pulled his jockeys on when she was almost done. They stood and walked to the door. Bea took her brown coat and slid her arms into the sleeves so that Ernest couldn't help but think how much she looked like a movie star with that hair and the woolly collar. When her shoes were on, she turned to him and gave a laugh at the sight of his jockeys.

"You can't keep that in your pants, can you, Ernest?" she said with a quiet giggle.

Her hand touched his penis that lolled out one side as she tucked it back behind the material. It was a harmless gesture given their night but Ernest was struck by how easily she touched him. Everything that had changed between them was in that one gesture, and she'd thought nothing of doing it.

✧

Aaron was awake.

Often in the evenings he'd pretend to be asleep so his father would have to carry him to the car. Sometimes he really was asleep and didn't wake up, but sometimes he faked it for the warm feeling of his dad cradling him. He liked the jostling, and the way his dad and his aunt would whisper to each other. He liked the attention; he could soak it up and not have to do a thing but lay there.

His father came in late tonight, later than usual, which had made Aaron cranky in anticipation, especially when his Aunt Lue had sent him into the room to rest. When his dad finally got there, Aaron was frustrated, and relieved, and pretended to be asleep because he didn't want to talk to him.

He was sprawled out on top of the bedcovers. He could hear his dad breathing as he bent over to pick him up. Lifted off the bed, his back was cool in the air except where his father's arms held him. His face rested on his shoulder, breathing into his corduroy jacket. It smelled of the cold outside.

"Do you have his shoes?" his aunt asked quietly.

"Right here."

"I'll get his coat."

They walked down the hall and into the living room. The light was on in the kitchen, making it harder for Aaron to pretend he was sleeping. The bright lights made him want to squint.

"Are we going to put it on him?" his aunt asked.

"Let's just drape it over. I'll hold it." Aaron felt his coat on his shoulders as his dad readjusted the arm across his back.

"Okay, Lue, thanks. I'll see you tomorrow?"

"You guys coming for supper?"

"Maybe," his dad said. "I'm not sure what I'm doing tomorrow night . . . Aaron'll be here, though."

"Nick . . ." His aunt's voice was tentative. Aaron tried to lie perfectly still, with his mouth open, pretending. He knew what tomorrow was. His mother was dead. Tomorrow was the day they buried her, a year ago. His Aunt Lue tried again, whispering even more quietly. "You can't keep doing this, Nicky. And of all days you should be home . . ."

"What? You tell me what I'm doing wrong."

"You can't keep dropping him off here every night."

His father didn't answer, walking them over to the door. Aaron felt his chest grow tight. His throat burned. He felt the cool outside air wash across his face.

"I mean it, Nick. I don't want to talk about it when you come for dinner. It's not an easy day for any of us. Let's talk about it now and get it over with. I'm suffering too, you know. We all are."

Aaron wanted to hit her. He wanted to jump out of his dad's arms and slap her in the face and yell, *Why don't you love me anymore?* His aunt didn't want him with her, and his father couldn't come home after work. Everyone was turning against him.

"I'll figure something out, Lue," his dad said. "Don't you worry. He's not your problem anymore." And they charged through the door and let it swing behind them. Aaron waited for the crash against the doorframe, but Aunt Lue must have been there to catch it, because there was no noise from the house as they crossed the lawn.

∽

Amanda watched as Nick came down the walk with the woman standing at the door watching him. He didn't look happy.

She absently chewed her fingernail. The window had fogged up a bit but now that Nick was in view she didn't want to wipe the glass. He came to her side of the truck, with the boy curled over his shoulder. Amanda could tell he was heavy by the way Nick walked.

Trying the door handle and finding it locked, Nick gave a light tap on the window, though she'd already started to reach round and unlock it.

"Is he sleeping?" she whispered when he set him down.

He clicked the seat belt shut and adjusted his coat. "Sort of," Nick answered. "He's always in a dull haze when I get him up to go home, aren't ya buddy?" The boy didn't respond except to blink and squint. Nick came round the car and climbed into the driver's seat. He turned the stereo down and took a last look into the back. "He should sleep the rest of the way home."

"How old is he?"

"Almost nine."

"He's *cute*." Seeing Nick smile at the boy made Amanda realize she didn't know about his wife. Maybe that's why he was so distant. He could still be married for all she knew, though that didn't seem likely if he had her in the car with his kid, but it was possible. As he shifted into gear and put his hands on the wheel, Amanda glanced at his ring finger. Sure enough, dammit, he had a gold band on the left hand. She hadn't been with a Man-man before, anyone really old enough to be married, for her to be used to paying attention to that sort of thing. When she had a guy sitting at a table alone and being too fresh at work, the girls always told her to look at his ring finger. If he was married, they could be twice as cheeky. He wouldn't be one to complain. It meant better tips if they played him right, but Amanda hadn't got in the habit yet.

The closer to home the more the ring bothered Amanda. His little boy was in the back seat. He *had* to be divorced, or at least separated, or why else would he be so casual in the car if his son was in the back seat and a girl was in the front? He couldn't count on the kid being *that* sleepy. So if he wasn't with his wife, why did he still wear the ring? And why didn't he try to make a move on her? She concluded that he must still be married and he had been torn between whether or not to go for it with her, and that he had decided not to, that's why they picked up the kid.

"You want to get anything for tomorrow while we're out?"

"Huh?" Amanda asked. Busy in thought, she was only half-paying attention.

"Do you need anything while we're out? Otherwise I'll take you home."

"Oh," she said, curt with disappointment. "No. Thanks." Clicking the electric switch of the door panel, she put her window down. The wind made a racket as it whipped through the compartment.

"Are you hot?" he asked.

"No," she said.

"It's a little breezy for Aaron back there."

Pulling a ribbon of hair out of her face first, she tucked it behind her ear and said, flippantly, "Okay, I'll put it up then." With her finger on the button, the pane slid back into place.

"Thanks," Nick said.

Amanda drummed her fingers on her knee, then stopped that

to check if her earrings were both on tight. "So where's your wife tonight?" she finally asked. "Is she out of town?"

There was a pause before Nick answered. "No."

By the sound of his voice Amanda knew she'd said something wrong. Immediately she felt a pain of regret in her stomach.

"My wife died a year ago. We buried her a year Wednesday, actually."

In her head, Amanda swore. "Aren't I the idiot," she said aloud.

"Don't worry about it." He checked his mirrors and glanced at her. She tried to give him an apologetic smile, but he looked away too quickly.

"Her sister's a good egg. She helps out quite a bit, looking after him."

To make up for the blunder, Amanda offered to baby-sit too, if he were ever stuck. Nick thanked her. "He's cute," she said. "He can't be any trouble at all, with a face like that." Nick chuckled like he had before, making Amanda feel better.

When she was getting out of the truck she thanked him for the ride and told him once more that she'd love to baby-sit if ever he needed someone. He seemed surprised that she offered again. "Maybe," he said. "I have trouble after school mostly, and his aunt told me she's getting pretty busy."

"I got time then, now that my boyfriend's history. You let me know. You need my number?"

"No, I've got it. Thanks for the offer, Amanda. I appreciate it."

She gave him a big shy smile. "My pleasure," she said, and shut the car door, satisfied.

⁂

It was cold against the vinyl of the car. The drive was short enough that the heater wouldn't pick up before she pulled in to her driveway, so Bea didn't bother turning it on. After she backed out of Ernest's and onto Sumac, she looked at him standing in the doorway, exhausted and what she thought of as small. He was like a kid, in his jockeys, and the expression his body had. There was something sweet about him, something very small and vulnerable inside the man. His dick and balls and the wiry hair on his chest, and running across the bridge at the back of his neck, all of that was the full-grown man, but it told nothing about him. Not like the way he stood there as she pulled off, waving, and he not responding if he saw her, which he likely didn't.

The car engine ran high in the cold air. Bea could see mist collect on the window with each breath she exhaled, and tried to breathe more shallowly. No one was on the streets. The gas station at Eleventh was closed for the night. Most houses had their porch lights turned off, and none on in the house, save the odd glow from above a kitchen stove. Bea drove down Sumac feeling she was the only person left alive in the world. It had been a long time since she'd made love to a man. Her thighs hurt from the exertion, and her insides still throbbed some. When she got home, she'd take a hot bath to warm up and relax her muscles.

Each streetlight she passed pooled into the body of the car and swept across her. Light after light, she blinked from where it glared in the rearview mirror. When she stopped at Ninth, she pulled out a cigarette, partly to warm her hands from the cold steering wheel. A police car drove past while she waited. The two officers looked over as they drove by and made Bea smile. She was beautiful in the way you only can be when you've left

a lover, when you're driving home in the middle of the night
and no one's there as witness but yourself.

The first thing Amanda wanted when she woke up was a cigarette. If she had a joint, she'd have that, but she settled on a
smoke. The pack was on her bedside table. She propped herself
up in bed, pulled a cigarette out of the package and flicked her
small pink Bic lighter. She fumbled the childproof switch and
cursed.

"Stupid fucking thing," she mumbled. Pushing the safety
button back up on the lighter and reflicking its grooved knob,
she got a flame going. She lit the end, taking a big drag. A dusty
tingle ran down into her lungs.

Amanda sat in bed looking at her room. She felt disgusted
with the place — more for the look of things than the state they
were in. Her room may have been a mess, but it was how everything seemed ugly that bothered her. Her bedspread was old
and worn, the dresser along the wall at the foot of her bed had
scratches on the drawers. The metal plates holding each handle
had pink flowers printed on them that were supposed to seem
pretty but only cheapened them. The nightstand was a match to
the dresser, with its own scratches and a dirty white surface, and
its handle replaced with a white knob. Over the window were
orange curtains that didn't quite meet in the centre when you
shut them.

She took another drag of her cigarette and looked for something to butt the ashes into. She couldn't find anything nearby.
Stretching her arm out, she tapped the ashes over the edge of the
bed. She'd vacuum later.

It was such a rotten room, she thought to herself. When she

was living with her mother, things were better. There wasn't the noise of neighbours in the building to contend with. She had matching curtains, and furniture, and a carpet that was plush and clean. Bea's apartment had grey brushed carpet in every room, except the tiled kitchen and bathroom. And at her mother's new place, Amanda had her own bathroom since her mother and Georgie had a master bath off their bedroom. It was a new house on the recently developed streets off Westgate Road, in the east end of Cumberland called River Heights. They were big houses, and it pissed Amanda off that she should be stuck in another shitbox like the one she grew up in when her mother was across town sitting pretty.

It wasn't her fault they couldn't get along. Why'd she have a mother like this? Why'd her mother suddenly get so stuck on herself, and leave Amanda behind? She didn't act like she cared, despite coming behind her and running her fingers through Amanda's hair and saying she did. How could she believe her? It was too hard to really believe, what with her tantrums, her sudden rules and new curfews. No shoes on the couch, no food in the living room, no boys in the den or the bedroom, or after eleven, or after her mother and Georgie had gone to bed. Don't sing in the shower, Georgie gets irritable. Don't talk so loud on the telephone, Georgie's napping, or her mother has a headache. This wasn't the life she'd had, and Amanda couldn't stand the changes that came along with Georgie and his money.

They weren't so different. When her mother was younger, she had her fair shake of boyfriends and lovers. Amanda was a bright girl. She recognized this and it made her sick. She hadn't liked thinking of her mother as cheap, but how else to think of her when she'd trotted out the door in her lipstick and nylons and come home late at night with her hair undone, and the lipstick gone or smudged? Amanda knew better. There was no way she was going to let herself bump along putting out for dozens of guys only to be disappointed when they didn't return calls in a few weeks' time. Amanda wouldn't have that sort of bad luck. You make your own luck, like you make your own bed, and she could keep the sheets clean.

Before Georgie, she and her mother had loved each other and complained a great deal. Why do you wear so much make-up? What do you have to wear that for? Why are you going there? And with him? The script was the same for each of them. It wasn't perfect, but it had worked, and they kept each other in line. When they needed sympathy they could get it. And when their lives got too small, they could always look to each other to broaden them, or be grateful they didn't suffer what the other one did.

With only Amanda's last year of school left to go, Georgie had come into the picture. Georgie had money and a big place in his heart for Amanda's mother. He would show up early for every date, take her to Ottawa and buy her presents, or theatre tickets with dinner. They went skiing in the States and made plans for a trip to Florida's Disney World that Amanda wasn't a part of.

They met in the summer before school, and things weren't so bad in the fall, except Amanda was busy and stressed with classes and had to fend more for herself. By Christmas, though, she had problems with the whole affair. The phone calls, and giggling. The attention her mother paid to Georgie that had been hers. Usually after a few weeks, or months at most, a relationship would drop off and her mother'd be back to cooking and worrying about her and arguing and all the rest of it. But Georgie wasn't going away.

After only seven months, they'd announced they were moving in together. Amanda would follow with her mother, of course, but she couldn't feel wanted, really. Georgie and her mother Estelle were a couple and she was the unmistakable third wheel. It only took a month — February, the shortest of the year — for Amanda to be thrown out of the house. She'd been doing more drugs and started dating Alphie, who supplied her, and she quickly decided school wasn't worth the work. Not right now. Not with the adjustments being made at home and the attention she'd lost, the dynamic.

Had she thought about it, she'd have known it was stupid of her. In the back of her mind she could hear herself saying it was stupid to skip out on school just when things were going better for her, when someone would be there to pay for college if she decided to go to St. Lawrence in Kingston, or, better still, to university. But the voice said everything her mother did, and when she tuned the one out, the other followed.

Bea was a nice lady and Amanda was glad to have a decent place to stay. If she'd taken Alphie's offer to move in with him, she'd have been screwed now that she'd dumped him. Amanda was thankful for Bea, and her generosity, though she didn't know how to show it without feeling like she owed her something — and maybe she did, but what did Amanda have to offer back?

The best thing Amanda could do was to not think too far ahead. It was too painful if she did. There was a lot of pride she'd have to swallow. After all the terrible things she'd said to her mother, and especially to Georgie who she hardly knew, and who wouldn't be as inclined to forgive her, or understand, she couldn't consider the prospect of going back.

Yet, still, Amanda wanted the obvious things. She wanted comfort and security. She wanted to feel loved and have someone hold her again and tell her things would be all right. That's what was driving her with Nick the other night. It grabbed her, that feeling. It jumped up inside her and made her heart burst and pound. Nick was a decent man. He was decent, and that meant a lot. Besides being handsome — broad in the shoulders, round butt, even stubble — he'd talked to her like he thought she was worth something. He didn't dismiss what she had to say, or just not listen, or make like she was too young to understand. He sat on the couch and listened. It had thrown Amanda off when she first started talking to him, and she liked it, and found it relaxing, which only piqued her interest more.

How old was he? Thirty. Maybe older. She knew he was too old, but how would she find a man like that who was under twenty-five? How would she find a guy who was clean, but not the prissy sort of clean? Though he'd smelled of sweat just slightly below his aftershave, which itself wasn't strong, he was the sort who showered and combed his hair and wore clean clothes after work. He wouldn't have the same underwear or socks three days running like Alphie did. He wouldn't be the type to pick his teeth at the table, or walk through the house with his work boots on. Under twenty, men who were soft like Nick were geeks and she wondered what he'd started out like. Maybe it was his wife that had taught him, or maybe he'd been a geek and then lost all signs of it.

She wanted to see him again. Smoking in bed, thinking how gross her bedroom looked, and how cheap, she had this great urge to run out and wrap herself around Nick and feel his big muscled arms squeeze her tight. She wondered briefly if Bea felt the same way about him. It seemed reasonable. Tapping her ashes over the edge of the bed again, Amanda decided to get Nick's number and call him. She'd offer to babysit, but if she worked it right, maybe they could go to a movie, or maybe he'd ask her over for dinner. She'd like to meet his kid, and see how he took care of him. Amanda gave a little unconscious nod, satisfied, imagining he looked after him very well.

༄

The morning had come fast. Ernest had woken up at six, tired and pasty. He'd drunk a large glass of water in the kitchen, showered, made two eggs for breakfast and been on the curb by seven when his ride came for him.

Ray picked him up most mornings. He was a young guy, and didn't really know much of what he was doing, which the management liked. His old black Ford pulled over and Ernest jumped in.

"G'morning," he said.

"How ya doing, there, Ernest?" Ray grinned at him, which let Ernest know he looked as tired and worn out as he felt.

Ernest gave a groan. "Oh, it was a rough night."

"We'll take it easy on you today, then." He glanced at Ernest's clothes. "You're not wearing any green?" he said.

"Green?"

"St. Patty's day today."

"No," Ernest said, trying to stretch the tiredness out of him. "I don't bother myself with that."

"Me neither. But I'll drink their beer. A little green beer never hurt anyone."

"Except last night," Ernest said. He looked out the window as Ray turned the corner onto Ninth.

"What's that? Did you get yourself into trouble?"

"Nothing I can't fix. Maybe it isn't that bad. I don't know. What the fuck's a guy to do, eh, Ray?" Ernest tried to sound cheery.

Ray laughed. "Do I know her?"

Ernest's voice dropped as he let out a slow, "Yeessssss."

"Oh, really? Who's the lucky lady?"

"Bea."

"Bea? From-your-bar Bea?" Ray chuckled and blew air out of his cheeks. "Well, it's not like you couldn't see it coming. But hell, yeah, that changes things some."

"Yeah, I guess so," Ernest said. He looked out at the trees along Marleau, starting to bud. Both sides of the road were a weaving of bush from Iroquois to Industrial, about eight blocks' worth. This was the nicest part of the drive in the morning. Trilliums came up every spring just off the roadway.

All day at work Ernest heard Ray's voice saying, *That changes things some.* It rang in his ears above the noise of the machines and their engines, the grinding and clanging of gears. It wasn't that he didn't like Bea, but she wasn't Claire and he couldn't help but want her to be. He couldn't keep his mind from seeing the two of them side by side and knowing she wasn't his wife, and thinking she never would be. Ernest knew this wasn't fair to Bea, and to him, and somehow wasn't fair to Claire either, but at the same time he liked how Bea reminded him of her. Ernest felt human again that morning; he was a person in the world. Having sex with Bea was real. He could talk about it with Ray, or the other boys at work. He could tell them he had sex and who it was and how he felt about it, had he cared to. It was something they all shared, and which Ernest liked feeling a part of. Even when Figgy came into the lunchroom, Ernest was alone and had the brief urge to brag because he could. But he reconsidered when he saw the look on Figgy's face.

"So are you celebrating tonight, Mr. Martin?" Ernest asked. "You coming to Malouf's for some green beer?"

Figgy poured himself a cup of coffee and sat down. He was a small slim guy, a couple years older than Ernest, with deep wrinkles running down his cheeks. "I don't think so, Ernest," he said. "I'm not up to it."

"What do ya mean? It's St. Patty's day," Ernest said, with more enthusiasm than he felt.

"I got nothing to celebrate, Ernest. I ain't Irish."

"C'mon, Fig."

"Ahh," Figgy said and waved a hand in the air. He set the paper coffee cup gently on the table. "I'm sick of the whole goddamn business, Ernest. The whole damn works in this city. I ain't going out spending my money in it for no stupid green-shit holiday."

Ernest paused. "Okay, Fig. Fine by me. Suit yourself."

"I'm sorry, Ernest. I just want to get home, you know. I've got a lot on my mind. Things ain't so good."

"Trouble with Eva?"

"No. Sort of. We're thinking of moving or something. I don't much want to, but Eva's been after me to move."

"She restless or something?"

"Maybe. I can't say. Just don't ask me. I just can't go out drinking for a while till we figure out what we're doing."

A couple guys came into the lunchroom then and Figgy got up to leave. "I'll see you later, then, Ernest," Figgy said, trying to sound better.

"Take it easy, Fig."

"I'll drop you off at Malouf's tonight, though, but you'll have to find your way home after that."

"Sure, sure." Ernest grinned as Figgy turned and went out the door. He didn't know what Figgy could be thinking. Ernest sat in the lunchroom with his sandwich between his hands. He tried to imagine picking up and moving but couldn't. No matter which way he turned the idea over in his head, he couldn't see himself anywhere else. As much as he'd have preferred to think it was the opposite, the city owned him. Everything he did was because the city allowed for it. And what he couldn't do was because this place didn't provide. He used to see the Leafs play the Canadiens in Montreal because he lived close enough that you could drive the hour home afterwards. He could fish off the docks but not in a boat on the river, or not outside of Lancaster unless someone brought him because even if he could afford a small boat for himself, he couldn't afford the cost to moor at the marina in town, or the car to tow it home and back, or to get him out of town to where it was cheaper to moor. With the union broken, he didn't make as much as he used to.

Ernest knew that if he were to move to a different town he'd be lost. He'd be without friends, or anything familiar. There'd be nothing resembling his life. There was no way for him to leave. He'd buried family here. He'd buried blood. Most days out of the year he wouldn't admit the city owned him like that, but inside himself, the feeling was fixed tight that he wasn't in control of his life. He was responsible for walking the streets and shopping at the grocery store and going to the bar or a Junior A game inasmuch as the city provided him with the opportunity to do that. How Figgy could leave, Ernest didn't know.

It was a long year. Aaron had heard his aunt Lue saying that to his father a dozen times this last week. And now again, tonight at dinner, the second night this week he ate at his aunt and uncle's place, she'd said it a couple of times. Aaron sat across from his dad, with his aunt and uncle at the ends of the table. They had a large roast of beef in the centre that his father carved with the electric knife in the kitchen and brought out on the platter. As each piece of meat was lifted Aaron saw more and more of the floral pattern underneath. He tried guessing what would come up after each slice — leaf, petal, stem — though parts were still partially distorted by small leftover bits. And they had baby carrots, cabbage, and potatoes cooked in the roasting pan. Apple pie from the Loblaw's for dessert, with ice cream.

Aaron couldn't pay much attention during supper knowing what night it was. He kept thinking about the night a year ago before they'd buried his mother. He held it in his mind like a book on a shelf. Like a room he'd never left.

It was, and had been, March 17th. St. Patrick's Day. His family had come to bury his mother.

He remembered everything as though he were still there. In the middle of the night, he had left his bedroom and come down to stand alone on his back porch. He rested a hand lazily on the top of his head, feeling the material of his ballcap fit into the curve of his palm, his other hand in his left pocket, while his mother lay in a light-brown coffin across town. The yard was covered with a dusting of snow. The light from the street only vaguely filtered into the back yard, the occasional snowflake lifting in front of his face, or catching in his hair below the edge of his cap.

The yard had felt full in the night, though he only saw a hint of trees or bushes, their wide shape, with the insides solid black, or as if there were no insides. Everything seemed hollow to him, his own shoes black and disappearing. He wiggled his toes to feel them inside the leather casing.

He looked for his fence surrounding his yard. It was wood, dirty white, about three feet high and older than he was. He couldn't make the individual boards out at the back but he saw them stretch along on either side of him in the light from the street. The slats darkened as they receded until they made up a wall he imagined you could walk through, it seemed so dark and thin.

Years ago, the small garage at the end of the driveway had been painted white too. The outer pane of glass on the side window had broken and was never replaced. Glass had sat in the sill up until he'd tipped over playing soccer in the yard and had reached an arm out to catch himself, opening a long arc of blood in the heel of his palm. His father had driven him to the hospital and the glass had been cleaned up when he'd got home. His mother had cleared away the glass.

He remembered knowing on the porch how the next day would be a worse one. The next day it would be finished while right then it still wasn't over, people would still be wearing green socks and hats and ties until they went to bed. But the morning had come and everyone went to work, and to school, whether they knew what had happened or not.

Tonight, again, the dinner was for his mother, though they hadn't said that. He was at the table with his aunt and uncle, and his father, and himself, end of list. It was a holiday and none of them dressed up in green, no one mentioned the fact of what day it was, one way or the other, and there was none of the green beer his dad usually passed around which he'd make in their basement with a big bucket.

"We're going to your aunt's for dinner," his father'd told him earlier in the week, and that was enough to let him know, just the tone of voice, just the flatness of it. They were at dinner for his mother, who wasn't there, and wouldn't be. In Aaron's mind, that day wasn't over, the day when they buried her. In Aaron's mind that day would never be finished because he could hold it open like that, waiting for him to walk in and make it fill out and breathe. He couldn't forget.

His uncle talked about cars at the shop and how his dad would do well to bring his Range Rover in for another check-up, it had been some time since he'd had anyone look it over. And his aunt talked about the biscuits she'd cooked. They seemed awfully flat, and dense, maybe her baking soda wasn't right anymore, she'd bought it bulk, and she apologized for them being so hard.

Aaron watched his father eat and nod his head. He took seconds of the roast beef and potatoes and asked Aaron to carefully pass the gravy over to him, which he did. Then he ate that up too. Aaron wasn't hungry. He ate only half his plate and hoped he'd still get ice cream and pie. His father, when he was done, offered to clear his plate for him too, and then they'd have dessert.

He passed his plate over and watched his father take each bite till the food was gone. His dad stacked the two plates together and said he sure could do with a smoke. He excused himself and went outside for a cigarette.

After his father left, his Aunt Lue looked at his uncle and smiled weakly. His Uncle Gary looked back at her. "What's that all about?" he said. Aaron thought he meant his father going for a smoke but he didn't.

"I was just wondering . . ." his aunt said.

"Yeah."

"About last night. He still hasn't told us who she was."

"None of my business. You're not his mother." Gary

sounded rigid, as though suddenly it was hard for him to talk though he'd had so much to say earlier.

"I was just wondering, that's all."

"He was out with a girl," Aaron said.

"What girl?" Aunt Lue asked, and her tone of voice made Aaron regret saying something. His dad didn't know he'd been awake, or sort of awake. He'd drifted in and out the whole ride home.

Trying to cover, he shrugged. "Maybe I dreamt it."

"No, I saw her in the car. Did you know the girl, Aaron?"

"No," he shook his head. Tears were starting to burn in his eyes and he didn't know what was causing them. He felt trapped by the table.

"Aaron, why don't you get us the ice cream, eh?" Uncle Gary said. "You like to dish it out, don't ya?"

He climbed off his chair and went into the kitchen. He had a hard time finding the dishes because his eyes were still full of tears. His aunt told him the bowls were on the countertop already, by the stove. He couldn't reach into the back of the freezer though and she came and pulled the carton out for him. When his father came back into the dining room, Aunt Lue stayed in the kitchen and helped. She ran hot water for the spoon, then cut the pie and served it while Aaron dished out helpings of ice cream for each.

When they were all seated again at the table Aaron saw his aunt gesture to his Uncle Gary. She motioned with her head towards his dad, who didn't look up from his plate.

"So how've you been, Nick?" his uncle asked.

"Good. You know, fine."

"You have a good time last night?"

"Yeah," his dad said, looking at him, "I guess so."

His uncle took a bite of pie. He dribbled a bit on his chin and wiped it off. "It was a late night, wasn't it, Aaron? You nearly fell asleep on the couch downstairs?"

Aaron ate his pie and ice cream. He wanted them to talk about his mother. Sometimes he thought they didn't want to remember, that he'd be the only one left who would. He was itchy with the need to have them just say something about her.

"I was out," Nick said. "I had a good time. I was with a friend . . . driving around."

"Some new friend of yours?" Uncle Gary pushed.

"No, not really."

Then his uncle ate another bite of pie. "This is good pie, Lucille," he said.

Aaron had a mouthful when he piped in with, "I love it!" trying to cheer up. A few flakes flew off his lip as he spoke. If they noticed, nobody laughed.

His aunt pulled her fork out of her mouth and turned it over, looking at it. "So you had a good time, Nick?"

"Yeah, Lucille, I guess so."

His dad looked over at him, so Aaron said, "I fell asleep with my hat on, like I used to."

His dad gave a small laugh. "You did, did you?"

Aunt Lue tilted her head. "You going to see this friend again?"

"What do you mean?"

"Well, you can always bring friends over here, you know, Nick."

His dad just shrugged and looked quickly around the room.

"Why's it a big secret?" Aunt Lue asked his dad. She put her fork down and folded her hands in her lap, though she hadn't finished her pie. "If you've got a new friend, we'd like to meet her."

"It was just a girl I met last night, through a friend. I took her for a ride, that's all."

"Sure," said Gary, ready to drop the subject. "Sure."

"Where'd you meet?" Aunt Lue asked.

"At a friend's house, Lue. We met at a friend's house. She wanted to go for a ride in the truck so I took her out." His dad pushed the last piece of pie into his mouth and looked quickly to Aaron, then over at Lue. "She's just a girl. She's seventeen."

"Seventeen?" Aunt Lue's voice came out like a quiet hiss.

"Yes. I'm not stupid, Lucille," his dad said.

Aaron's uncle stepped in. "If he says it's no one, it's no one."

"But seventeen!" She pushed herself away from the table. "No wonder you haven't brought her in."

Then his dad was angry, holding his fork and knife aloft. "I just met her last night, Lucille, through a friend. There's nothing going on. And I certainly don't want to talk about this today. That's it," he said as he slammed the utensils down on the table.

They were all finished eating, whether they had pie left or not. Without a word, his aunt picked up their plates and went into the kitchen. She began doing the dishes. She didn't offer coffee and didn't ask Aaron to help, as she'd promised.

His father looked from him to Gary and gave a sigh. "What do you say, kid?" he asked.

Aaron shrugged.

"You want to help your aunt with the dishes?"

Aaron didn't want to, but said sure to avoid any more talking. He got up from the table and sauntered into the kitchen. When he left the room, his dad and uncle started whispering.

Aaron tried to remember hearing the girl's name the other night, but couldn't. Now he regretted not trying harder to stay awake. He knew she was babysitting him afterwards, but he hadn't dared say anything. He thought, though, that if he had her name, he could tell Aunt Lue, who was slapping the dishes into the sink. She sniffled, with her face turned red. He took hold of her rubber-gloved hand. "I miss my mom too," he said.

With a weak smile, his aunt softened and squeezed his hand back. "I know. You don't have to tell me, Sweetie," she said softly.

He'd called already to have her over. Not a day had gone by before Nick asked to have her babysit for him, that night. Obviously, he liked her. Amanda was all set to go when the buzzer for the front door sounded. She took a last look in the mirror — grey tights, short black skirt, slim red v-neck top. She raced through the kitchen as the buzzer sounded again.

"Hello," her voice was just slightly sing-song.

"Amanda, let me in."

"Alphie?" The enthusiasm was gone. "Oh, Alphie, fuck off." Nick was going to be here anytime now.

"Let me in, Amanda. I got to talk to you."

"I'm busy." She heard a bang where he hit something.

"Open the door," he shouted.

"Why the hell do I want to let you in when you're like this? Call me if you want to talk. Then I can hang up on you right," she said and clicked the intercom off.

The buzzer sounded again. She crooked her lips to the side considering what to do. Again, the intercom let out a buzz, only it held much longer.

"What, Alphie?"

"Let me in."

"For Christ sake, fuck off. I don't want to see you."

"I'll stand here all fucking day pushing this thing, baby. You've got to let me in."

Though she didn't know how she'd get rid of him, it seemed smarter to get him out of the lobby before Nick showed up. She sure as hell didn't want Alphie there when Nick pushed the button to her apartment. There would be no contest if Alphie jumped him. Nick could kick the shit out of him, though he likely wouldn't, and Amanda simply didn't want to run the risk of them meeting. Alphie was nothing to be proud of.

"You got five minutes, Alphie. Five." Pushing the release button, she heard through the intercom the click of the front door opening. Alphie's feet pounded up the stairs and in seconds he was at the door. She swung it open before he could knock.

His face was pale, with reddened nose and eyes. He wore a green ball cap backwards because he clearly hadn't washed his hair. "I brought you flowers," he said, standing in the entrance with a bunch of six red roses extended.

"I don't want them, Alphie."

He stood dumb. She wanted to slap him for being so weak. Why couldn't he do things right? Seeing him this raw and vulnerable only made her want to hurt him more.

"Well, don't just stand there, come in," she said sourly. "You've got five minutes." Amanda turned her back on him and walked into the living room, gathering up her wallet and lipstick. She tucked them into a small black purse.

"Where you headed?"

"Out."

"With who?"

"With whom," she corrected.

Alphie's face shrivelled. "Well, *whom-the-fuck* with?"

She strode past him and hung the purse on the doorknob to the closet facing the door. "It's none of your fucking business, Alphie."

His voice hardened. "Someone screwing you already?"

"I really don't need this," Amanda said tiredly. "I don't have a lot of time. If you've got something to say, say it. Otherwise, get out."

Taking a step towards her, he held out the flowers again. "I brought these for you. I'm sorry. I came to say I'm sorry and get back together."

"Alphie," she said, her voice softer, "Don't. It's not gonna work. It's over."

Seeing that she wasn't about to take the flowers, Alphie set them gently on the coffee table, then tried to hug her. She took his hands and stopped him.

"Don't," he said. "I just want to hold you."

"No, Alphie."

"I just want to hold you, baby."

As soon as she let his hands go, he stretched his arms out to hold her again and the cycle repeated itself.

His voice grew small. "Don't, baby," he whispered. "Don't, baby, don't," he began chanting, only the buzzer cut him off.

Amanda's heart jumped. *Fuck*, she thought.

"Amanda, don't. Don't," he mumbled, following her to the intercom.

"Stop it, Alphie. Be quiet," she said, but he persisted. He had a hurt look on his face. "Shut up. Shut *up*," she said exasperated. Finally, she held a hand across his mouth, forcing his head against the wall.

"I'll be right down, Nick. I'll just be a second, why not wait in the Range Rover," she said, relishing saying the name of the truck in front of Alphie.

As soon as she released the intercom button, she let Alphie go. He promptly announced, "I'm going to meet him," and opened the door to the apartment, testing her.

Amanda ran out first and put a hand on his chest. "No, you're not."

"Yeah, sure. I want to meet him."

"No, Alphie."

"Why, are you afraid I'll kill him?"

"Go out the back door." She pushed him towards the rear of the hall and the second set of stairs. Grabbing her shoulders, he pushed against them, making her shout with the effort to resist him.

He bellowed, "I'll fucking kill him!"

It was all show, Amanda knew that, but she had to match him or he was going down the front stairs. She slapped at his face, pulled his hat off and tore his hair till he stopped moving.

"You show your face down those stairs, Alphie, I'll never talk to you again. You hear me? I'm going out the front door to meet him, and you're going to wait here till I'm gone or you're as good as dead as far as I'm concerned. Or you're dead," she said, poking a finger at his chest. "Okay?"

She took a breath.

Alphie's face softened and fell. "Is he so fucking good?" he choked.

"Come on," she gave him a push towards the apartment. He stood in the doorway as she grabbed her purse off the closet door handle. Locking up, she said, "I'll call you tomorrow. You wait here for me to leave and I'll call you tomorrow."

Alphie's face was red and swollen with tears welling up in his eyes. "Is he so fucking good, then? He's too fucking good to meet me?"

"Oh, Alphie. Grow! Up!" she yelled and raced away with the clip of her heels on the stairs. She listened for sounds of his following her, but he didn't. She only heard him as she opened the outside door.

"He's no fucking good!" he bellowed. "He's no fucking good either!"

Bea worked five days a week. She worked noon till eight on weekdays, with the other girl coming in around six and closing up with Hank. Now and again if they were busy, or if Theresa had something else to do that night, Bea would close up shop. Which meant she saw Ernest most days of the week, and then some weekends, depending on how her shifts fell and if Ernest could get himself to the bar.

All afternoon Bea felt light on her feet, watching the time every few minutes. She tried not to look and couldn't help herself. She watched Hank dye the kegs, which always amused her. It was a good day of the year to work because the bar would be full all night and everyone wanted the green beer, which was an easy order to get right. People came in and out like crazy, which had Bea looking to the door each time it opened. When 4:30 rolled around and Ernest still hadn't walked through the door, Bea knew he wasn't coming in. He was done work an hour ago and there was no sign of him.

She told herself she wasn't going to be pissed off. Hurt, sure. But Ernest was allowed to do whatever the hell he pleased. Maybe he needed time to think. For all she knew he could be out getting her something. Or there might very well be a message at home waiting for her, with an apology, or an explanation. Though, really, when was the last time he hadn't come in after work? Months ago, when he took a sick day.

Finally around 8:00 Nick came into the bar and Bea instinctively looked behind him for Ernest. The door swung closed. Nick was alone. He waved at her with a forced smile, which made her think that Ernest had talked to him already. Maybe he was here to let her down easy. Ernest had told him they'd made a mistake. Would he send Nick in to check out how Bea was feeling? She wasn't so sure what to expect from Ernest. As far as she knew, he hadn't dated in the year she'd known him. She had nothing to go on to gauge what was up.

Nick didn't sit. He chatted with Hank at the bar until she'd dropped her beer off at a table in the back and then approached her. "Guess who's at my place?" he said, smiling awkwardly.

Bea's stomach jumped. "I don't know," she said.

"Your roommate. She's looking after my kid."

"Oh," said Bea, trying to hide how disappointed she was.

"There's nothing wrong with that, is there? She's a good kid?"

"Oh yeah, of course. Amanda's a sweetie. She's a little rambunctious; she's seventeen. But she's pretty grown-up considering."

Hank had her next order ready, wiping the bottom of the mugs across a rag on the counter. Nick looked around the bar, clearly wanting to say something else, but he was hesitating, like he didn't know how to start. Hank gave Bea a curious look, but she grimaced to make him go away. He set the beer on her tray and took a cloth to the other end of the bar.

"Hey," Nick said.

Bea didn't think that if she spoke her voice would come out

right, so she raised her eyebrows, questioningly.

"Have you seen Ernest?" he asked.

"No," she said flatly. "He didn't come in today."

"What?" Nick said. "Really?"

"No," Bea answered. "I thought you knew where he was. Maybe he's home, sick."

"I don't know. I haven't seen him since yesterday," Nick said, making Bea a little less worked up. She felt very highly strung.

"I might go see if I can find him," Nick said, tapping his hand on the counter.

"Sure," she said, awkwardly. Should she tell him herself? They were kind of friends too, weren't they? Maybe he'd have some advice for her. If she told him, just his expression might say what he thought her chances were. But really, he was Ernest's friend, and she had no place telling him their business.

Nick looked at the beer on her tray. "I should let you get back to work, Bea."

She said her good-byes and he left and she delivered the beer. Hank was waiting for her at the bar when she came back. "What was up with him?"

Bea realized she hadn't given his mood a thought now that she was in the clear. When she shrugged, genuinely puzzled, Hank shrugged back. With Nick going out to find Ernest, she knew there was no point in calling now. She wouldn't get him alone. "Hey Hank," she said, "I'll stick around the rest of the night. Theresa and you could use the help, and God knows I got nothing better to do."

The dream again. Ernest stands on the cold cement at the bottom of the basement stairs. A dank smell has crawled from the walls and corners to hang in the air around him. He's sweating with fear, staring at the closed door above him, light spilling around it. There's nothing else in the basement but him and the smell and the dust that has settled from the beams. Every night he spends a long time waiting, and he knows he'll wait. He knows he'll stand there staring at the door, waiting for the inevitable, hoping for a change in the plot, some intervention, some change of place even, without the slightest release. In the dream, Ernest can think of nothing except the wait. There's a tension between the anxiety for something to happen to break the painful monotony, and the horror of what it will eventually be.

After what seems years, like the time measured in a hospital waiting room when a loved one is bleeding, Ernest sees a shift in the light from under the door. A shadow. Click, the door opens. A body is thrown forward down the steps, tumbling like four sticks in a sheet. It drops bloody and limp into his arms. The face is a bruised peach. Blood at the lip. Blood on Ernest's shirt. Blood on his hands.

Finally, it's ended. It's happened. It's over again. What's he to do now? The body is small but very heavy in his arms. Should he climb the stairs? Bury the body under the concrete? Leave it in a corner, bundled up in its clothes?

Then the light shifts. Someone stands at the entrance above. He knows he should identify them, but he can't look at the person who did this. What if they come down the stairs after him? What would he do with the bloody body in his arms? Throw it aside? He wouldn't have time to set it down anywhere. He's about ready to make a decision as to what to do next, and clank! The door slams shut.

Ernest snapped awake. He was on the couch. It was Wednesday. The apartment was cold in the chill of the spring night; the heat had been turned off for the season. He lay on the couch with its arms in tatters from where the cat sharpened its claws. Synthetic stuffing fell out from the holes in wisps like cotton.

Sometimes Brutus would walk through the house with fuzz stuck to her face. The fuzz would bounce on the end of a whisker as Brutus stepped around and didn't know any better than to take it off, or wasn't able to, occasionally batting a paw in front of her face.

Ernest lay watching a lousy program on Channel 13 because the local news had ended and he didn't want to get up and turn it off and didn't have cable to change it to anything better. A man was telling his wife he loved her. Over and over he said it in different ways, the way he looked at her and grimaced when she made a joke. She was angry with him and deliberately making him feel bad. She'd told the redhead, her best friend, that she was going to do this, and Ernest couldn't figure why this was funny. He knew it was supposed to be because this was a sitcom, but Ernest didn't like the show, or the woman. He thought the best friend was cute. She wore yellow pants with her red hair tied up on the top of her head.

With the door shut Ernest couldn't see out into his driveway, so he didn't notice anyone until there was a loud knock that made him jump.

There was a ball cap on somebody's head in the three windows at the top of the door.

Ernest opened it and his heart seized inside him. He could still feel the sweat inside his shirt from his dream. "Hey, Nick," he said with a surprised tone in his voice, "What are *you* doing here?"

"Wondered where you were, Ernest. Thought I'd check up on you."

"Oh, yeah," he said. "Come in, come in. Can I get you a beer?"

As Nick took off his boots and jacket, Ernest walked into the kitchen. "Sit yourself down, Nick," he called out.

When Ernest came back into the room Brutus was sleeping on the chair. Otherwise he'd have sat down there. He was forced to sit on the couch beside Nick. He never disturbed Brutus when she was sleeping. In the middle of the coffee table was a big ceramic ashtray with a marble design. It was full of butts, all of them Craven A's. Next to that was the jar of maple syrup, and Ernest's bottle of beer.

"So how are ya?" Nick asked.

"Oh, I'm fine," Ernest answered, like the idea that anything else could be the case was ridiculous.

"Bea says you weren't in the bar today. I thought something had happened to you." Nick gave a little chuckle.

"No, I haven't been feeling that well, you know, a flu or something. I've been laying in bed."

"Neo Citran," said Nick.

"Right."

"That'll make you feel better." Nick took a sip of his beer. "You got any?"

"Eh? No," Ernest said. "I don't need any a that."

"It's good for you, Ernest. Honestly, it works."

"Yeah, maybe. I'm feeling better," Ernest said. Then, his voice cheerful, "I'll be seeing you guys tomorrow. I'm fine. How's Figgy? He still saying he wants to leave?"

Nick looked surprised. "No."

"Oh, I think he just did himself in a little too heavily the night before or something. Trouble with Eva maybe. It was nuthin'," he said and looked to the TV.

The jar of maple syrup sat at the bottom of his vision. He could see it there as he watched television and he wished that it wasn't sitting out.

Nick leaned forward on the couch, resting his arms on his knees. He sighed and opened his mouth for a second, and paused before continuing. "It was a year ago Barb died," he said. He gave a look at Ernest and let out a quick nervous smile. "The boy and I went to my sister-in-law's for dinner. We used to be cramped at the table after we had Aaron because there was an extra person. Barb would sit next to him on the one side and I'd sit facing them on the other. I think it's hard for Lucille, her sister. We all fit now, at the table." Then he said, "I don't like having that extra room," and took a swig of beer.

Ernest wanted to wrap him up in something nice, some nice idea, or a blanket, to console him, but he couldn't think of how to do it. "That's hard, Nick. Life's shit sometimes," he said, but knew that wasn't the sort of thing he wanted to tell him.

"Yeah, well. I got Aaron still. Count your blessings."

"Right. Right." Ernest took a swig of beer and wished he hadn't then. It seemed cold to drink now, but he was uncomfortable and wanted something to do, something better to say. He drank another gulp.

Times like this, Ernest felt like an idiot. He babbled, and ran on at the mouth. Though he felt there was more that needed to be heard, he'd repeat stuff, just because no other words came to him.

"I don't want to get you down, Ernest. It's hard sometimes, you know. I can't go to the cemetery. Haven't been there since we buried her. What kind of husband is that, eh? She deserves better than that."

"You do what you can, Nick," Ernest said.

"No, Ernest, she deserved better than that," he said slowly. "She was so beautiful," and his eyes got wet.

Ernest put a hand on his shoulder. "Hey, it's not a crime. That's understandable. That's understandable, there, Nick. You know . . . That's nothing to be . . . that's nothing to worry yourself over. You go when you can."

"I should be bringing my boy there. I shouldn't let him forget her. I shouldn't just up and forget her. But I can't do it, Ernest. I can't go down there and see that earth all dug up. Or there'd be grass now, wouldn't there?" He looked to Ernest like he was waiting for an answer, but Ernest knew to wait. He held back from saying something stupid.

Nick sniffed and wiped his eyes. "I don't even want to go home anymore, Ernest." He shrugged. "Maybe I should move. My sister-in-law's tired of me dropping the boy off at her place and she's right, but dammit, I can't go home anymore. I took us all the way out to the maple sugar farm the other day just so's I wouldn't have to be in that house. That ain't fair to the kid, but I can't help it. I can't be there alone all the time." Then he straightened up and sniffed once more and took a pull on his beer. "I'm fine. Every once in a while, you know. It was a year yesterday, and it sneaks up on you. After dinner tonight, I couldn't go back to the house. Aaron's sleeping in bed waiting for me to be there in the morning and I don't feel like I can go back. Maybe I gotta move out."

"That's not such a bad idea."

"Yeah," Nick said slowly, thinking it over, "But there's the kid to think about. That's all we got left. And I don't want him to move schools. Or find new friends now. He needs all the stability he can get. But a lot of fucking good I'm doing." Nick took a deep breath and let it out. "I'm better now. Sorry, old man. It creeps up on me and I just gotta get it out or I go crazy. I talk to Bea sometimes, but she was funny tonight. Just busy, I guess, but I had to talk to someone."

"That's fine," Ernest said, his heart racing. "It don't matter none. I'm glad you came."

Nick stood up. "I gotta use the men's room."

"You know where it is," Ernest said lightly.

Nick set his beer on the coffee table next to the maple syrup and went through the kitchen and into the bathroom. Ernest heard the door shut, and a few seconds later the sound of Nick peeing. His legs ached to pick himself up off the couch and hold Nick. He wanted to make the man feel better. If only they could hold each other and feel better, Ernest thought, though he knew it was crazy. He felt a chill run down his back as the sweat dried off his skin.

Looking at the coffee table in front of him, Ernest felt he should move the maple syrup, but Nick's beer was right beside it. If he moved it now, Ernest figured Nick would notice. It should have went in the kitchen yesterday after Bea left. Why'd he feel so reluctant to put it in his cupboard? He regretted it now. Nick would know where it came from, and though he wouldn't care, Ernest still felt he'd done something wrong by taking it. He didn't like maple syrup and doubted if he'd eat it. He just wanted it out of sight now.

Nick flushed, and the door squeaked open before he came back into the living room. Picking up his beer, he walked around the coffee table to the chair and set his bottle down on the table there.

"Who do we have here, eh, Brutus? You look damn comfortable there, don't ya?" he said and picked her up in his arms. She let out a tiny lazy meow. Sitting down, he held her against his chest up the crook of his arm and petted her behind the ears.

"You're the little queen of the place, aren't you? You've got it awfully good here, I'll tell ya. Not a care in the world, eh? Yeah," he chuckled, "I guess so."

Trying to be comforting, Ernest said, "You ain't the only one to ever lose anybody, you know, Nick," though he couldn't get his voice to sound right. He could tell Nick thought it was a judgment on him.

When he set the cat down on the floor, Nick said, "Yeah, you're right." He looked out the door and sighed. "Well, it's getting pretty late. The kid's going to be in bed already."

"Yeah," Ernest said. There was a moment while he tried to think of something to add to change what he meant, though he had meant it, but not how Nick had taken it. Ernest had lost far more than Nick over the years, but here he was, still going on, not complaining.

"I'd best be getting back." Nick threw his coat on and walked out the door with a wave, saying cheerfully, "See ya tomorrow, maybe?"

Ernest wished he could have said something to make it right. He wasn't frustrated because Nick was still mourning and feeling lost. That was only natural. He was frustrated that they were both feeling lonely and didn't have to be.

Aaron lay in bed, staring at the lines the street lights made above him. Occasionally a car would drive past and another light would spill through the crack above his curtains and slide up the walls and across the ceiling, changing shape. He spent a lot of time like this, staring at the dark, waiting. He was alone at night.

He had the blankets pulled up tight below his chin so only his head peeked out. He could just barely hear the TV. Amanda was downstairs. She was a teenager, with boobs and nail polish and pretty hair that had made him feel small and silly around her. She talked to him nicely, as though he wasn't a young kid, which made him like her. He hoped, on the days his dad wasn't coming home right away, maybe she'd babysit him after school. He pictured going with her to the mall, or buying ice cream up the road, or swimming in the summer in the park. They could do all sorts of things. They could listen to her music on their stereo in the basement. Amanda could make them supper so that his dad would have to be back after work. He hated his aunt for saying that she didn't want him there anymore, but there was a big advantage to Amanda looking after him instead. He'd be at home. And his dad would know he was there, waiting for him.

Bea spent the whole night at work thinking and rethinking the same thing: she had lived alone long enough. She had hated it for so many years that she had taken out an ad and found Amanda. She moved her into the extra bedroom where she'd been keeping the spare bed.

Amanda was seventeen and Bea knew what it was like to be seventeen and without anywhere to go. Only Amanda wasn't being smart about it and Bea couldn't decide what to do to smarten her up. She wasn't her mother, she wasn't even a legal guardian, so Amanda didn't want to listen as she should. Bea knew more than she was getting credit for, didn't she understand that? Amanda would pick up a glass of Freshie and drink it with her head tipped back and her eyes closed while Bea talked to her. Bea would stop until Amanda had swallowed and opened her eyes and then try again, softer in her coarse voice and yellowed fingers from holding DuMaurier's all day without taking as many drags.

Bea knew what Amanda was up to. The girl woke up around noon and poured a cup of thick coffee left warming from eight or so that morning when Bea got up and made it. She'd have to be at work for four so took the time in between to get ready, barely eating — Bea rarely saw her eat — and then at midnight or one she'd be met at the curb in front of Giorgio's by Alphie and his SupeMachine. It had that written on its back windshield in red lettering, SupeMachine, though it was only a Chevy. They'd go to the quarry or the campsites depending on whether they felt like smoking up and doing hot knives or getting drunk. Bea knew kids smoked at the quarry because they could drink at the campsites. And either way Amanda and Alphie would come careening down the highway and rip into Bea's apartment lot at six or seven in the morning and neck another few minutes before Amanda would step out of the car and watch its tires spin as it raced backwards out the driveway.

This was the type of living Bea worried about. Amanda was seventeen and slept five or six hours a night. She was thin and tired and over-sexed, that Bea could tell by the empty boxes of condoms she'd leave in the bathroom waste-basket. But wasn't Bea over-sexed at her age? Was she? For the life of her she couldn't remember just how often she and randy Randy did it but surely it wasn't as much or as reckless as Amanda. It wasn't as bold either; Bea had parents to answer to. And that was the difference. Amanda had no one to wait up for her. It wasn't Bea's job and if she was going to let out the spare room it wasn't her place to interfere in the life of whoever paid to stay there, even if the girl was only seventeen. Even if Nick was much too old for her.

It was a damn busy night at work and Bea didn't need to be so preoccupied. When she went for a pee in the back, she had a moment's rest, sitting on the cold toilet. Amanda was still in her head. She saw the girl flirting with Nick, moving on him in that way young girls have. Shameless, Bea would think, but she recognized that that wasn't quite it. Not embarrassed. Teenage girls weren't embarrassed showing the big scary feelings inside them. Amanda wanted Nick to like her. Big deal.

Really, Bea thought, what was so worrying about Ernest not coming into the bar? Bea would have to wait for him to call her. Or she would have to call him. And there was her fear. That she'd show herself to like the man. That she'd have to admit it. Well, look at what had passed between them. What was the harm, she thought, in being forward now? She could go after the man, however more subtly than Amanda would, or she could let it all go to hell because she felt too scared to try.

When she'd put Aaron to bed, Amanda had noticed Nick's bedroom door was ajar. She saw the only photo of her in Nick's room, from a distance, passing the open door. The picture sat on the other side of the bed, on a table in a corner of the room so anywhere you'd stand in it you'd see them — Nick and her all dressed up on their wedding day. She had a string of blue flowers in her blonde hair, and curls falling down in front of her ears. Aaron and his mother had the same look about them, the same nose, and skin, and hair. Maybe he'd grow into his father's looks when his jaw widened and he began to shave, but soft as his features were, as a boy, he was his mother's son. Amanda felt sad seeing the photo, and pulled the door closed.

Finally, though, the door having been open was too tempting. It was just another room in the house, she told herself. She checked that Aaron was asleep, which he was, and approached Nick's bedroom. She stepped inside. The carpet was thicker than in the hall but not as thick as in the living room. Nick had made the bed, and left a large pile of change on the dresser top. He had a big glass bottle with pennies in it sitting beside that, and various scraps of paper littered about. Amanda stepped around the bed. She picked the frame up and looked at the young faces and their smiles. Nick's face was a little thinner, and he had a moustache that didn't suit his mouth or his age. He was wearing a bow tie and tux, but since it was a bust shot of the two of them, Amanda didn't know what her dress looked like, or where the photo was taken. The blurry background was blue, so she couldn't even tell if it was a real sky or some backdrop indoors.

Setting the frame back on the table, she made sure to put it in the clean lines where there wasn't any dust.

She looked up and turned to go, then jumped at the sight of her reflection in the mirrored doors of the closet. Her heart raced for a second, in a stranger's house, in the room that felt forbidden. She felt guilty, and caught, even by herself, staring back from the mirror. Wiping her hands on her jeans, she calmed herself and looked again at her reflection. She was so young, even younger than Aaron's mother in the photo. It had been a long time since she'd felt like a regular kid, like a teenager. She worked at her job, and made money. She had sex with guys. She paid her rent, and her bills, and bought groceries for herself and Bea, but she was seventeen, and had scared herself baby-sitting like any other girl would have.

She left Nick's bedroom and went back to the living room to try and find something on TV. She flipped three times through all the channels, and saw the Ottawa news anchor with his bad salt-and-pepper hairpiece. There weren't any videos worth watching on Much Music, and only a stupid B-movie of an albino Sasquatch that ate people. She turned the sound off and watched the young woman running through the woods, followed by the hairy white suit. It was ridiculous, but she couldn't shake the feeling of being spooked. The house was too quiet. Occasionally it let out a creak or two, or a click as the furnace turned on.

She walked back to the hall, and stood in Aaron's doorway. He'd thrown the covers off and was half-over the edge of the bed, one leg and arm dangling in space. Amanda wanted to grab hold of his hand and see if he'd squeeze like a baby would, but she didn't dare disturb him. Instead, she walked softly over and ran a hand across his forehead, brushing back his hair. It was fine, and soft, and smelled like apples. She couldn't believe she'd been this small. Kids were so easy to love. Nick must be crazy about him, she thought, he's so cute and vulnerable. She wondered when she'd lost that. She'd been supporting herself this past year, since she was sixteen, which wasn't very old at all, really. When would she ever feel loved like him again?

The early morning was cool. For whatever reason, Ernest woke up at 3:00. With his old job at Dominion Technical he'd be up at this hour, with its thinner air and quiet streets. He'd throw on the work clothes, eat breakfast with a big cup of coffee and be out the door before the rest of the working world was awake. Those were good mornings. Claire was still with him then. With her warm body under the covers beside him, he'd have to force himself to get out of bed. *I'll count to ten*, he'd think, then count another until there was no time left to wait. One morning he'd watched the light from the clock radio bounce off her skin in the dark until he had to skip breakfast to get to work on time. He'd loved her a great deal then, and couldn't tell her what his heart felt, or how sick he was for sometimes hurting her. His thoughts seemed clearer those mornings than they did nowadays. Those were the best mornings — with the streets empty he felt like he owned the city, driving down the roads and barely a car passing, and the air so cool without the sun up yet to warm things.

He couldn't fall back to sleep with all these thoughts in his head, and knew he might regret it come the end of the day. He spent the morning and afternoon doing what he did, breakfast, ride to work with Ray, work, lunch, two breaks, then Malouf's.

He was fully prepared to go alone today and meet up with Nick, and Bea, who he decided he was ready to see — she hadn't called him, and that made him feel better, that she hadn't crowded in because some women call the next morning, and then you know you don't want to see them again. But Figgy offered to give him a ride.

"You sure, Fig?" Ernest asked.

"Yeah, I can spare a few minutes today," he said with a small grimace. Things still didn't seem so good with him.

They walked out of the plant and over to Figgy's blue Datsun with the rust marks and the two cracks in the front windshield. His wife drove the nicer car, though it was six years old now too, with a bit of wear. Figgy opened his door and climbed in, setting his lunch box on the back seat. The passenger side door was locked so he leaned over and undid the latch, then scooped up the papers on the bucket seat and threw them in the back too.

Ernest climbed in with a small grunt. "Oh, it was a long day."

"It doesn't get easier," said Figgy. The engine whined a bit before it turned over, then roared and choked as Figgy pushed on the gas pedal. "I got to warm this up first. She stalled on me this morning, in the middle of Ninth and Pitt. I was worried she'd died for good."

"Ah, you'll get a few more years out of her," Ernest said. His breath made thin swirls of mist on the windshield.

Ernest had had a car, living with Claire. When they were first married, they drove a white Monte Carlo. Coming home from a New Year's Eve party that first year, he'd felt sick. Claire told him to sit forward with his head between his legs because they were almost home and he'd better not throw up in her car. She wore white fake patent leather shoes that looked amazing with her ankles and the inside upholstery. He thought he was leaning forward to put his head down but lost control of his stomach along the way. Their first car, and it was white. He tried to apologize but she wouldn't even look at him. She drove the last two blocks home without a word for how he was, and then he began sobbing with the beer in him and the fuming smell of vomit all over his pants and he couldn't forgive himself for that.

Figgy turned the blower up and pulled out of the parking lot. They both waved at a trucker pulling in.

When they got out on Boundary and turned down Water Street, the plant was out of sight. Figgy switched the blower down. "Things aren't so good here, Ernest," he said.

"How do you mean?"

"You can't say a thing, now, or I'll be in a pile a shit to my ears."

"Sure. Right," he said.

"They're moving everything to the States."

"You're kidding."

"The whole fucking works."

"You're fucking kidding. Oh, no, Fig," Ernest's voice dropped. "Don't tell me that." He was talking in a whisper. "Oh, no. Now don't tell me that, Fig. You're fucking kidding."

"I ain't to say *any*thing, Ernest, so I gotta ask you to keep this shut up tight."

"I know. When they closing up?"

"Late next week. Friday, if we get the next load of stuff through on schedule. They're just coming in and locking it all up on Friday like normal, handing out thanks, then *See ya — and don't come back on Monday.*"

"Oh, fuck."

"I'm sorry, Ernest. I'm not supposed to tell a soul, but I couldn't keep it from ya any longer. A man's got a right to know. Severance package or not, they should be giving everyone notice ahead of time."

"Well, I don't blame them. They aren't going to put the place at risk," Ernest said, "or stick their necks out any. Some of them guys'll be pissed off enough all right to do something stupid, given the chance. But next fucking week."

"I wanted you to get a jump on things. Nobody knows, so you go down to the employment centre and see what you can do."

"You been there?"

"Eva wants us to move to Kingston. Or Belleville."

"Belleville's not much better," Ernest said, his voice still quiet.

"You don't need French there — and she can't find nuthin' here. I don't know, Ernest. It's all shit nowadays."

"Ah damn, damn," Ernest said to himself, mumbling under his breath. Figgy turned the blower back up so the car filled with the noise of the warm air whizzing out. Ernest didn't know what else to say. He sat there quiet until they pulled up to Malouf's.

"You coming in?" Ernest asked.

"Don't think so. Want a ride home instead?" They were sitting in their separate seats with the engine rumbling.

"I think I need a beer after that," Ernest said. "Thanks for the scoop, eh, Fig? I appreciate it a lot."

"Wish I coulda told ya sooner, that's all."

"No problem, Fig. What can you do?" Ernest opened the car door and got out. "You take care of yourself. Say hi to Eva. Things'll be fine, eh, Fig. Don't you worry none."

Figgy nodded. "See ya, Ernest."

"See ya, buddy," he said, and pushed the door closed with his hand. He patted the roof and Figgy drove off.

Ernest watched the little car recede, then stared down the street for a few more minutes after it had turned a corner. There were old-fashioned lampposts all along either sidewalk that the city had installed several years back to help improve the look of the street. It used to be one of the main shopping strips decades ago, but stores closed up, and second-hand shops, tattoo parlours and arcades opened in their place. Things were picking up slowly, here and there, though a few restaurants opened and closed down again. A man walked past Ernest and stared at him, wondering what he was looking at.

Ernest took a deep breath and smelled sulphur from the paper mill. And car exhaust, and his own sweat from work. He was tired from waking up so early. Facing the front entrance of Malouf's, he saw Bea through the glass window. He wondered if she'd spotted him on the street yet. It didn't seem so. God, she looked decent. Her hair was tied back with a tiny black bow. And she wore her apron tied in the front, with the long slim order pad hanging out and flopping as she walked. The woman has energy to burn, Ernest thought. He was sad that he was getting older, with his pot belly, and grey hair, and the wrinkles on his forehead that made him look meaner than he thought he was.

Ernest stayed on the street. He walked to the edge of the window and looked for Nick in the bar. He wasn't there yet. Ernest didn't expect him for another quarter hour or so, and was glad he wasn't there to tempt him. Not tonight, he wouldn't go in tonight. He'd call Bea up when he got home, maybe, and leave a message, or phone from his break tomorrow morning.

Quickly, not wanting to run the risk of getting caught out there now that he'd made up his mind, Ernest faced home and began walking. He walked for hours, a great number of hours that began from the bar and took him to his door, but still left him unsettled when he was inside and warm. The rooms seemed narrow and cluttered with furniture. Ernest tried turning the television on, then sitting by the window and sleeping in the chair with Brutus, but he couldn't settle himself, until he stood and slid on his coat and the walk began again with the click of the lock on the apartment door.

He headed south along his block towards the river. He passed the neighbour's dogs barking through the open screen door. Ernest sniffled and looked up into the dark sky swelling with its clouds pale and billowing above the lights of the city. At the corner of Eleventh, he walked past the gas station that was already closed with its pump lights turned off. Only half the overhead halogens were left on, and the interior was dimly lit. The neon at MacFinn's billiards blinked its crazed dance of red and blue as he passed on the other side of the street, passed the fire hydrant, the tree half-cut-down from earlier that day and the limbs lying at the curb next to it, the street light at Eleventh, a butcher shop there, the gravel yard no longer used since the company went bankrupt so many years earlier, south still he walked following the houses, then the cemetery from Sixth to Fifth, and more houses facing the tombstones on his side of the street, framing the tombstones behind and beyond. He walked three more residential blocks, crossed Second Street with rowdy Baker's Dozen on its corner, all the teenagers hanging off the hoods of their cars spitting Coke onto the pavement, the girls singing, and the cracking bass sounds of the car radios all turned to the same station. He passed the Cumberland Legion and its parking lot opposite, then the heritage house on the other side of the lights and one last block of houses, once solid and upright when they were built with their wide proud porches and thick oak doors from the early twenties now sunk and bent or slipping on their hinges, this last block before the park. The park at night, the river with its second moon and city lights reflected across its surface, smooth tonight and unsettling, the path leading to the power dam and the dark, if he could follow it.

Ernest stood on a small patch of grass at the edge of the road facing Lamoureux Park. Cars passed on Water Street behind him, and he thought he saw people on the paved paths walking by the river. He stuck to the side of the road and passed the RCAF building with its mounted airplane lit from below, flying into the light, or out of it. He kept going, away from the parking lot behind the building which wasn't as tempting when he was sober, and moved towards the civic centre at the far side of the park, its paths winding over the hill, down along its water-front, and to the doors, front and back, of the building. He stayed to the south of the sidewalk and passed right behind the building and found himself, as he did so often, staring at the boats moored in the marina, the only one in the city. His hands were cold and he put them in his pockets and sniffed again. The smell of fish was stronger here. Each boat tugged on its rope or chain gently with a creak and the soft lap of the nighttime tide. Together the ropes and cords, the water and hulls quieted Ernest. His body relaxed and already his fingers felt warmer tucked in the front of his belly. He left the boats and walked back to the sidewalk of Water Street, passing the old arena where he'd once played three seasons of hockey and where his best friend Carter had lost three teeth in a fight, passing The Colossus restaurant open till four a.m., the latest food and beer in the city. He walked the entire stretch of Water Street till it became Montreal Road and walked that as well, with the hundred things they held and didn't seem to offer, the restaurants and bars, the churches, the one dance bar, cobbler, tailor, movie theatre, even Malouf's again, so he was back where he started, though didn't stop, and moved on past doughnut shops and the college, the weaving mills closed decades earlier and the mills that replaced them closed only months ago, the abandoned bicycles and fence-posts and animals and garbage and the smells and sounds of the city, he passed and was passed by traffic, he walked until the city that was around him moved to behind his back and it was his choice when to stop, his choice how far away he would get, how far into the night along the highway he'd walk before he'd choose to stop and turn, and before he'd go back.

LATE MAY

B ea woke in the morning with the sun on her face. All the rain from the night before still covered the window in distorted dots she could barely make out from the glare. Her face prickled. She thought she could feel the exact spot where the sun stopped across her arm and shadow began. Her breath was stale, her body rested but strained, and her bladder very full; laying in bed long wasn't an option, though she didn't want to get up right yet and get going. There wasn't much to do on her day off except chores.

Brushing the hair out of her face, she noticed her hands smelled of sex and stale smoke. Ernest had spent a good part of the night until he climbed out of bed around four and put his pants on. The rich sweet smell of him made her think back to high school, and what it was like as a teenager. She used to be afraid of that smell, how it lasted, and she would worry that her mother would notice it on her, or that, as she returned from whatever boyfriend's house, the people sitting beside her on the bus ride home would look disapprovingly at her. That seemed so far away, that sort of feeling, and it made her smile to think of it.

Bea had been good to Ernest. For three weeks running, she'd invited him for dinner every few nights, making roast pork and potatoes with baby carrots, and spaghetti on weeknights, meat loaf and scallop potatoes and casseroles. At the end of the night, she'd hand him a smaller dish all wrapped up in Saran Wrap so he could throw it in the oven the next night. She worried he wasn't eating well now that he was out of work, or wasn't cooking much for himself, though he did fine, as he told her, he looked after himself.

She began driving him home more regularly on the nights he stayed late at Malouf's, then every night if he cared to wait for her, which he usually did. People at the bar noticed the change. Ernest came by much like he always did, only he stayed later and drank more and left last with Bea, after everyone else had picked up and said their good-byes. Bea tried to come into work looking good, with a twist in her hair or a new blouse, a skirt, or her make-up done just a little differently. She felt happier. She was lighter on her feet, which matched the warming spring weather.

Only, Bea knew she was waiting. She and Ernest had gone for pool, and darts, they'd shopped for groceries so Bea could give him a ride with his stuff and Ernest could carry in the two cases of diet cola she got each week. She'd bought shirts with him at the K-mart, cat food in ten pound bags from the Walmart on Westside, cheese from the factory out in Ingleside. One Tuesday night she'd even talked him into a movie at the cinemas only he couldn't see the screen too well with his eyesight and wouldn't say anything. Bea had caught him squinting and wouldn't dare ask him again to save him the embarrassment.

All this they'd done, all this Bea did for Ernest hoping to win him over. She liked the way he climbed on top of her at the end of the night and grabbed her by the ankles when the girl was only in the next room, she liked how young he made her feel, how reckless and foolish and luckier she was than Amanda. It was ugly to be so happy that she had Ernest while Amanda was without a boyfriend, but Bea couldn't help see it as sweet that a pretty slim girl half her age spent her nights alone, while Bea, single so many years, wrinkles where she never knew they grew, could still attract a man, and keep him.

And Ernest was impressive. Bea had seen men at the bar, newly unemployed, come in more often, looking for distraction. They laughed louder. They played songs on the juke box and sometimes sang along. A few would cheat on their wives and this too Bea had to watch. The flirting came out of nowhere, from a desperate need in them to be occupied with something, even if that meant trouble. She served them the beer that got them drunk, and made them forget, or, sadly, remember even more. She watched the weeks go by, when they came in for longer bouts, and dressed more shabbily, faces paler, waistlines growing larger. A couple months out of work. That's all it took for a man's life to change.

The younger ones, eager and ready, with high expectations, she'd even say more optimistic, they fell quicker, despite having fewer difficulties on their plates. Without families to keep them in check, to make sure the bills were paid and the money went for food and decent clothes, there was little to keep them on the straight and narrow. The married men took longer, and the older they were the more they knew what to expect. Most guys had been around the block a few times — they knew what it was like to look for work, and to look for new ways to pay bills. The lucky ones seemed to be the men with connections to smuggling, so that they either started carrying, or storing, or selling. A few would start growing pot in their basements or garages, though people only found out after they were caught. The men without jobs who still had money, and some had lots of it, they didn't spend a hell of a lot of time in the bar. They were making deals, and hanging out with the other guys who did, somewhere else. So Bea only saw the sorry side of it, mostly. Which meant she knew a lot. She could recognize the signs.

That's why Ernest didn't worry her. He hadn't known the layoff was coming, and hadn't time before it hit so he wasn't prepared for this sort of thing, but he weathered it well. Sure, he was down in the dumps about not working. News that came out of left field like that was bound to set him on his ass. Bea understood that. And she could understand if it made him more sullen than he was naturally, but Ernest had a good heart. He was a single guy making an effort to stay chipper. Bea knew he was too tough, and smart, to let himself slide.

Maybe because she saw more of him, or maybe just with the weather warming, she noticed her whole body seemed to need him. In the middle of herself she was anxious as an empty jar. Each night, when Ernest touched her, he put the lid on. He was as close to love as anything she'd had.

Perhaps she was crazy — it was still early, she didn't know that much about him — but she wanted him to move in. She liked having someone to cook for, someone more reliable than Amanda, and more thankful. The chores would be the same. The company, better. They liked spending time together, they liked the same TV shows, though Ernest read the paper through the sitcoms — he only paid attention during the game shows. They hadn't been sleeping together much more than two months, but she still thought it a good idea. Ernest paid more rent at his place than he should, whereas Bea's apartment was reasonable. Between them, they'd have a decent amount of money.

When he came by one night for supper and was clearly pre-occupied, she assumed it was work getting at him, finally, and she tried to cheer him up. They were having meat loaf and scallop potatoes with tomato slices. Ernest was on his second helping. Amanda was out shopping.

"I don't get why they closed down," Bea said. "Why didn't they just upgrade the machines if that's what they needed to do? They've got an empty plant this way. There's too many shut down out here for them to think they can sell it."

"They don't give a shit about the building. It's a write-off for them. Taxes."

Ernest was looking at his plate instead of her, so she pressed further. "But what about the machines? They're going to waste sitting there. Can't they sell them?"

"They'll come by in a year or so and take the machinery down south too, or sell it in the U.S. or something."

"But if you say they make a better product up here, why move at all?"

"Cheaper. It's cheap enough now, they don't need to care about quality." He set his arms on the table, with a fork in one hand and a knife in the other, and looked at her directly, engaged, finally. "Listen, Bea. Why would they pay a guy 20 bucks an hour to do a job some other guy will do for half that in the States, or a tenth in Mexico? They got it all figured out. What they save on wages, they can put to upgrading their other plant. They were happy to put us to work up here with the exchange on the dollar, but if they aren't paying tariffs now, why not keep the money in their own country and sell it here? The country's fucked itself. We've fucked ourselves royally. Ottawa don't care. What do they care about some assholes in a mill, so long as they get to push paper and buy houses and take their trips all over hell's half acre to make deals like this. They're all business guys in the government. Mulroney was a lawyer. Who was he going to help? The suit who put him in the government, or the guy in some small town somewhere who pays his taxes? And that's about the length of his support? You can't blame them. They're all a bunch of fucking assholes but they ain't stupid." Ernest scooped potatoes into his mouth, scowling.

Bea wasn't getting where she wanted. Clearly, asking him questions wasn't going to help. She thought she could convince him he was better off not being taken advantage of, but maybe he wasn't. She tried a new tack. "I haven't asked you how you're feeling about all of this."

"Oh, I'm fine. What can you expect? It's Cumberland. Nuthin' stays open here for long any more. You gotta expect that."

"I'm sure it'll get better."

Ernest stopped eating again and gave her a look like he thought she must be fooling. "What makes you think that? It's been a hell of a long time now. They had thirty mills a year closing down eight years ago, and Ottawa didn't lift a fucking finger here. It's slowed down now. They're just getting comfortable. We round out the figures."

Bea sighed. "You don't sound too optimistic today."

Finally, that sank in. Ernest looked a little softer and lightened up. "Ah, what's it matter? I could be worse off, eh? It's not like I'm going to be walking into the lake like Gerry Poirer."

"What do you mean?"

Ernest gestured with his fork. "He filled his pockets with rocks and walked into the lake up by the power dam."

"When?"

"Oh, a month or so ago."

"I didn't hear about that."

He cocked an eyebrow at her. "Did you know Gerry?"

"No —"

"— Well then why would you have heard about it? It's not like they put that stuff in the paper."

"They don't?" Bea asked, confused.

"Well, no," Ernest said, mildly exasperated, playing it up. "They'd have no room for the news if they did. People are walking into the lake or jumping off the bridge all the time. They gotta keep morale up. Too many people out of work and depressed already. They don't want you taking shotguns into the McDonald's."

"Oh," Bea said. "Was Gerry out of work?"

"No, he had a good job."

"Then why'd he do that?" She felt she couldn't keep up.

"Because he wanted to. He was depressed, I guess." Ernest shrugged like he had no idea, then added, "His wife died of cancer that month."

"Well that'd do it," Bea said, looking down at the table.

"Yeah, I guess. Gerry went to visit her one day and drove

himself over to the lake after. The family didn't know where he was for a week or so. His wife kept asking about him."

"You mean she hadn't died yet?"

"Well, no. She passed away about a week after they found him."

"At the dam?"

"That's where he went in, but you don't come up there. The river takes you. He knew what he was doing. You get too close out in the lake, they've got this big intake pipe sucks all the water in to turn the combines in the engines. It's hydro-electric. That's how it works. You get close enough, it does all the work. There's no turning back."

"But how'd they find him?"

"He surfaced after a few days. The pumps must turn off at some point, I imagine. The current took him out to Alexandria. Some guy out fishing caught him, I guess. He'd be an ugly sight."

"But his wife wasn't dead yet?"

"No," Ernest said, like it should be obvious, "She was in the hospital."

"How'd you know this guy?"

Ernest answered, "I used to work with him," as though it should be obvious to her.

Bea didn't like his casual tone. "Did you go to the funeral?" she asked and saw something inside Ernest snap alert.

His voice became defensive. "No. I didn't know him that well. I wouldn't've known anyone there."

"But you worked with him."

"That was years ago," he said, with a wave of his hand. "His wife wasn't there, she couldn't go, and I never met his kids. What am I going to say? There was no reason to go. Gerry was dead. He wasn't going to care if I was there or not."

"But it was his funeral, Ernest."

Ernest leaned into her over the table and stared into her eyes, his voice grown hard. "I don't go where I don't want to go and I ain't never going to another funeral."

Bea felt a fear whistle down her spine, not from his flash of anger, not from what he said, but his tone. There was something else going on here. Something horrible. She felt frightened, more for Ernest than herself. She was hungry inside to take care of him, if only he'd let her in, if only he'd trust her not to hurt him.

"Sure," she said, holding up her palms. "Okay, Ernest, whatever." He seemed to relax. He gave her a half-smile out of embarrassment and sniffed. She hadn't meant to upset him. Why had she pushed? There was no mentioning a move-in now. Maybe later, before she drove him home, unless she could at least get him to stay again tonight.

"So are you going?" Missy asked.

Amanda picked a swimsuit off the rack and checked out the price tag, then glanced at Missy. "I told him I'd think about it."

"Yeah, but are you gonna go?"

"I'm *think*ing about it," she said, hanging the suit back up and moving to the next rack. Missy followed. They were shopping in the afternoon to kill time before Amanda had to babysit again. Nick had her over nearly every other day. She'd started trading late shifts at the restaurant for lunches, which made the new girl happy.

"I don't know why you'd consider it if you guys are broken up and you don't want to go back out. You said he was a dink."

"Well what am I supposed to do? He's in *love* with me."

Amanda spotted an orange suit with red trim. They were in Walmart, which took over from Woolco a half-dozen years back when the Westside Mall started to flounder. Everyone thought having a mall at the base of the bridge to the U.S. was a surefire thing, but they built a larger shopping centre over the border, with a merry-go-round, just outside Massena, which cut a lot of business. That place even had a skating rink. It was early Friday evening, which was gross because Amanda couldn't stand shopping with other people around. She hated to see anyone she knew from high school. "Well," Amanda said, "think what you want, but I'm not cruel. Me and Alphie can be friends, can't we?"

Missy shrugged. She picked up a blue one-piece cut low in the chest.

"Um, no," Amanda said, "not that one."

Missy dropped the suit back on the rack. "Well, have a good time, I guess. Tell me all about it."

"You're not going?" Amanda pointed to the change rooms and they walked over.

"Campsites," Missy said.

"Again?"

"That's all Chris ever wants to do. He likes it in the tent."

As Amanda went into a stall to change, she wondered if she was stupid for going. She'd only agreed to a date to get Alphie off her back. The general idea was to look so damn good and treat him so miserably that he would realize she wasn't good for him, and he not good (she tried not to think "good enough") for her, that he would finally let her alone. She just wanted him to drop off the face of her life. If he knew where she lived and wouldn't stop calling, surely she was entitled to be mean about the thing. If he wanted to drive her to that point, he deserved the consequences.

She'd been practicing all sorts of things to say: "You're not still at that job, are you? My friend Nick works for the cable company. You should see his house. Men under thirty don't understand how to treat a woman. I can't believe I never noticed how bad your table manners are. I almost called the other day, but then I thought, Why bother?"

Besides, Alphie had tickets to Blue Rodeo and she wanted to see them. Hardly anyone came to the civic centre to play, no one good anyway. Why shouldn't she go if he was asking? He knew where he stood with her. And once they were out, she'd make sure he was only more clear how hopeless they were together. In the long run, she was doing him a favour.

The swimsuit looked terrible. It made her chest look puffy. What a rotten place, she thought, that she could never find anything nice to wear. Once she was dressed, Amanda marched out of the change room and over to Missy, announcing, "I'm going. What's there to stop me?" and placed the swimsuit firmly on the rack.

Ernest couldn't believe she'd asked him. He had a few beers too many at Bea's after supper and insisted on walking home instead of sticking around. She wasn't too pleased, but he told her he'd come by tomorrow. She had another day off. She was working a double the day after that. Ernest was heading south to the Sand Club, a small bar on First, only three blocks up and two over from Bea's, thinking he'd have just one more beer before packing it in for the night. He couldn't face the empty apartment and couldn't stand to spend the night with Bea.

Ernest's insides were shaking. He felt he'd been slighted, but didn't know how. What was she thinking? Did she really want him to move in with her? He'd done that already and it was a disaster, though she didn't know the half of it. Ernest couldn't handle the thought of telling her. Just mentioning Gerry Poirier's funeral was enough to set him off; he didn't know how he could find the words to say something. There was nothing to say. He had no way of telling her what he'd done.

Once inside the small bar, with its pine walls and three customers, he drank himself silly talking to the bartender. He was trying to explain why he hadn't yet applied for his employment insurance.

Ernest told him he knew why his company was closed down, why they moved elsewhere, why the whole fucking city was closing up shop, why the government couldn't, or wouldn't, do squat for them, why the mayor was fucking everyone over with all the smuggling shit he was stirring up. He understood all that, but he couldn't get it into his head that he was really unemployed, again. He was fifty. He wasn't going to get snatched up any time soon.

Ernest also explained who the assholes were and why they were being assholes. It was a matter of perspective. Men who had any sort of position were on a ladder, with guys like him at the bottom. And everyone was looking up, so while the men who made decisions were kissing the asses of those above them, Ernest was privy to the same view of every last one of them. It was only when you were up a step that you could look back and see the poor schmucks below you. They'd be a comfort; there were men worse off than you.

That's exactly what the guy at the employment office was like the last time Ernest was laid off. Ernest had tried to get on a retraining program, because he could see how the industries were closing down. He'd known what was coming.

Despite Ernest requesting that he do otherwise, the guy insisted on calling him Mr. Mackey. People didn't call him that and, if they did, it only meant he didn't trust them. Who were they if they didn't know his first name, or wouldn't use it? If they wanted his respect they wouldn't get it by being all formal and mannered, he distrusted that, distrusted what wasn't familiar, or more to the point, what refused to be. Both times Ernest had gone to see the guy, he'd smiled at Ernest with his mouth full of white teeth and a mole set an inch off from his nose.

The agent's name was Maurice Piché. Ernest asked the bartender if he knew him. When the guy said no, Ernest nodded like he approved. He felt like he was on a roll.

The first time Ernest called him Mo the man looked blankly at him, a little confused. When Ernest said it again, the guy sort of flinched. His face looked like an animal clenching to shit.

When he spoke, the guy smiled like a hypocrite, saying, "Well, now, Mr. Mackey, what other options have you explored" or "Yes, Mr. Mackey, I understand your situation" or "I see, Mr. Mackey" or "Certainly, Mr. Mackey, but . . ."

After each "Mo" came a "Mr. Mackey" and Ernest couldn't help but feel put off. It bothered him the way the man's mole bothered him. Because the guy seemed uncomfortable, as though he didn't want to admit Ernest was there. He was Mr. Mackey and never Ernest, and they weren't the same person at all. Ernest had known and worked with a few Mo's before. They were all French where he worked, or half of them were, and they were guys like any other, but with accents. Ernest didn't give a fuck if they spoke French or Swahili or whatnot, so long as they did their work.

Ernest put his glass on the bar, emptied.

"I've known a few fucking Maurices and every last one of

them were called Mo, so why did this guy think his shit didn't stink?" he asked.

The bartender said he didn't know.

"Because he had his nose shoved too far up the ass of someone above him. Plain and simple," Ernest said, nodding good-bye. He opened the door to the Sand Club and stepped out, drunk enough, finally, to leave.

⤚

Though she felt a wee bit guilty, which made her belly tingle excitedly, Amanda went looking for the dress. Nick left the house saying he'd be out till midnight or whatever, as per usual, with the boys, and Aaron played a couple games of Go Fish with her, then amused himself with SuperNintendo until she put him to bed. He was always out like a light within minutes. Amanda read part of her *Jane* magazine, realizing she'd rather have longer legs, but thinking her arms were a good length. They were long and slim. If her legs were as well-proportioned as her arms she'd have it made. Then she got bored in an article about Making Boys Behave and decided it was time to go looking.

She found it in the back of Nick's closet. He had his six or so good shirts at the far right, but behind that was a small set of clothes which were mismatched. He'd likely given some of it away, because surely this wasn't all she wore. This looked to be the worst of it. At the very back, hanging on the rack just waiting to be found, was the dress, in a transparent plastic covering.

Amanda took hold of it and laid it down on the bed. She shimmied the plastic up and ran a hand across the material. Silk. Yellow silk.

In a matter of seconds, she had it on. Except for being a bit loose in the waist it was a perfect fit. The hem could have been above the knee, but it was retro this way, unless it was shortened. And the zipper scratched her. Of course it would have been worse for the mother if it fit more snug — how did she stand it for a whole day? — but Amanda didn't think she could wear it without doing something to fix it. Why didn't she have it covered, or the zipper replaced? And yellow? A yellow wedding dress. Why would anyone wear yellow on their wedding day? The whole point was to wear white. It was like men in kilts instead of tuxes. Amanda didn't understand that.

She closed the closet door to get a good full look in the mirror. She looked great, better than she'd expected. Picking her hair up, she gave it a twist to see what it would look like all done up, then dropped it over one side, then shook it out and turned sideways, with a sultry look over her shoulder. She half-closed her eyes and squeezed out a kiss. It was a great dress. She felt like she belonged in a movie. If only she'd had heels with her. Sliding open the door again and climbing into the back of the closet, she rooted around for matching shoes, without any luck. She couldn't much hope for them to still be around, or to fit.

What would Nick think if he saw her in here, wearing the dress? Her stomach was fluttering with the thought, a kind of excitement born from fear. It was a great feeling. Her face felt warm, her hands too. She pressed them to her cheeks. All the blood in her body ran quicker at the thought of getting caught. Half-wanting to sit out in the living room waiting for him to come home, she glanced again at the wedding photo on the night stand. With a flash, she imagined Nick's expression as he saw her. He'd be mortified, if not furious.

His wife was staring at her in the photograph, severe and accusatory. Amanda's stomach fell about a foot in her abdomen. With a quick zip, she undid the back and turned towards the closet to take it off.

But there she was in the mirror. She looked good. Guilty, but good. It was so silky against her skin. She felt like a million bucks. Maybe, she thought, maybe he won't want to keep this anymore. What use could he have for it, except as a gruesome reminder?

One last look, and she slipped the dress off her shoulders, rolled it up carefully from the bottom, and packed it into her book bag.

Aaron spent a lot of time at school alone. His father had to be at work for eight-thirty and Aaron couldn't be home by himself. School only started at nine, which meant he had to waste forty minutes or more hanging out. Luckily it was late spring — last winter had been freezing, although sometimes if a teacher had seen him out in the yard they'd let him come into their class-room until more kids showed up outside. It didn't used to be like this. His mother had always dropped him off because she worked at nine, which meant he had less time to waste. And he hadn't had to walk.

This morning, for some reason, his dad offered to drive him. Aaron thought maybe it was a new routine. When they got there, no one was in the yard. There was only one car in the parking lot. It belonged to the janitor.

Aaron jumped down out of the Range Rover and said bye to his dad.

"Have you got your lunch?" he asked.

Holding up his bookbag, Aaron said, "It's in here."

"Okay, kiddo, you have a good day." He winked, which made Aaron smile.

"Are you gonna pick me up after school?"

His dad gave a slow shrug. "I don't think so. Not today."

Aaron held the Rover's door open, waiting in case his dad changed his mind.

"I gotta go, Aaron. I'll be late for work."

"Is Aunt Lue gonna get me?" he asked, hoping his dad would say no. Aaron missed her — she hadn't picked him up after school in weeks — but he liked the fact that he was at home instead of across town at his aunt's. He thought it made his dad come home quicker because he was paying Amanda to look after him.

"No, not tonight."

"Are you cooking supper tonight?" Aaron asked.

"Yeah, I think so. Is that enough questions? I've gotta go to work, buddy."

"Bye!" Aaron shouted enthusiastically. He swung the door to the truck closed and stepped back. His dad pulled forward to the gateway and stopped, looking for traffic. As he drove out into the street, he beeped the horn twice quickly and waved. Aaron loved that part. He watched the Range Rover turn the corner and disappear out of sight as it passed the Beer Store.

Aaron ran to the swingsets right away, which was his favourite part of the school ground, while there was no one around. He could go as high as he wanted to without worrying about someone pulling him by the feet, or trying to take his shoes off.

All the swings had been wrapped up around the pole above, though one in the middle was still hanging fairly low down. It had only gone around about four times. Aaron grabbed hold of the rubber seat and gave it a heave. It only made it up partway and fell back at him, catching him in the shoulder. He grabbed it again and swung as hard as he could, then ran out of the way. The seat flew up into the air and passed the post, dropping down on the other side with the metal chains rattling against the bar.

Again, he gave it the best throw he could, but it didn't make it. With the chain longer, it was harder to do. Remembering the trick, Aaron took the seat in both hands and stepped back a few paces so that the swing was over his head. He had the chains fully extended. He jumped up and, as he came down, whipped the seat forward. He spread himself flat against the sand with the sound of the chains banging overtop of him. When he looked up, the seat was wobbling around, low enough to swing decently. He didn't need it any lower.

Jumping onto the seat, Aaron pumped his legs and pulled on the chains until he'd worked himself high enough to feel his stomach drop. Hanging tight, he pushed his ball cap further onto his head, leaned himself back and looked up. The view went from sand below him to grass then trees then clouds. The sky was super blue. Aaron pumped his legs, with his body still stretched back, so that he wouldn't lose the height, until he got tired and stayed resting on the weight of his arms as the swing slowed down. He wondered what it would be like to fall asleep like this. It was very relaxing, watching the sky come in and out.

When he'd nearly come to rest, his head was tingling and his arms were sore. His bookbag was very heavy on his back. He could hear kids playing by the front property. He sat upright, dizzy, with his belly fluttery too.

On the side yard, half a dozen boys were playing football like they did most mornings and lunchtimes. Usually Aaron wasn't interested. He'd make up games for himself, like climbing the monkey bars, or playing with the ants that came in and out of their hole in the concrete. He liked dropping big crumbs from his lunch and watching them try to carry them home. But maybe he'd play football. One of the boys was laughing as he ran with the ball upfield, towards Aaron. It was Mike Fletcher, the big kid who'd failed a grade. The other kids were racing after him, Aaron realized, because he wasn't on the playing field anymore. He'd taken off with the ball, which, by the look on his face, he thought was very funny.

Aaron jumped up from the swing and ran for Fletcher, thinking he might be the one to catch him. He pumped his arms, running so hard. When he saw Aaron coming for him, Fletcher veered to the side, well out of reach. Aaron changed his course, but Fletcher was just too big. He outran everyone. The other boys stopped chasing him, one by one returning to the field, until Aaron was alone, running across the grass. He was far from catching him. Fletcher got so far ahead he was back on the field before Aaron was much more than halfway there, which made him feel stupid. He walked the rest of the way and stood at the side of the grassline, imagining he was one of the boys scoring a touchdown, throwing his arms in the air and wobbling his knees back and forth.

Last night was no different from most others. Ernest knew the longer he was out of work the more he got in the habit of drinking. It wasn't just in the evening or weekdays and the long days of Saturday, with his Sunday rest, because he had nothing left to do, it was most afternoons. He'd go for a drink wherever it was closest if he weren't already at Malouf's.

For the first few weeks, he found himself sitting in the apartment watching soaps and recognizing all the plot lines and felt himself silly. A grown man with a body that could still work hard hours had no business sitting on the couch watching soap operas. The closer summer came, without alternatives he could think of, the more time he spent drinking, meaning the more likely he was to end up in the park. He never intended to go — he still wouldn't think of it during the day if he could help it and made every effort to keep it out of his head — but drunk and sloshing home on the nights Bea wasn't there to take him, he would be out on the street with his feet moving in the direction of the marina.

Something rode in his belly those nights. A lightness, like the first time he'd kissed a girl and he almost threw up he was so nervous. The first time he'd had an orgasm was like that too, only he'd felt calm afterwards. The girl had rubbed him through his pants and he thought he might be sick with the feeling. He was sweating and shaking and couldn't stop his body from doing what it was. He thought he was sick for sure until it was all over. There was a wet mess in his pants, but his muscles relaxed, and his head felt heavy and clear. His bones had a heaviness in them as well.

The nights in the park were like that.

The air would be cooler than during the day and too damn cold some nights in the early spring. The full force of the breeze would hit him off the river. It was always windier by the water, and the air colder. The new recreation centre would be lit up on the reserve across the river. On the cooler nights, when the skies were clear, the moon off the water glared, a white flashlight. The world was larger, with all the tiny houses across the water, their porch lights on, and the cars driving by on one of the roads — it made things seem very far away, as though the landscape had grown immeasurably over the night.

In the later summer heat the smell of dead fish would be everywhere along the waterfront. Ernest would feel it stewing in his nostrils. But during the spring it was the cold that bothered him, and occasionally the heavy sulphur smell of the paper mill. He slowly walked the gravel path right close to the building so he could keep an eye on the other men as they approached him. Until they were within ten feet or so, their bodies were nothing more than dark blocks of shadow moving towards him. Then Ernest could tell the shape of them and get a better sense of size. Their hands became distinct, and the lightness of their faces above a dark shirt or the wide white torso made by a T-shirt. Their bodies came in parts like this, depending on what they wore and how bright the moon made things. Some nights it was only when they came right up to him that he could make out facial features, the cut of a jaw, or the setting of their eyes, the shape of a nose or cheekbones, or a haircut.

The first thing they did was extend a hand like they were going to shake, but instead they would cup his groin through his pants. Every man did this. It was how they said hello before they spoke, if they did. Ernest would hear them breathing, and smell their breath, either beer or onions or toothpaste. And cologne sometimes, and sweat. In the summer it was always the smell of river, and fish, and sweat, but even in the cool spring nights a man could be nervous enough to sweat through his shirt. Or sometimes a man would come by in the middle of a jog because it was the way out of the house without the wife knowing what he was up to. A man could shower when he got home and no one would think twice, or want to go near him till he had. That was a trick one guy told him, though Ernest had no use for it at the time.

Some men would want to kiss, but Ernest wasn't comfortable feeling their bristly faces, or having their tongues digging into his mouth. They were so close then. He tried not looking into the glassiness of their eyes. If the men took a step forward and tried to kiss him, he'd look down, to indicate he was only interested in what their hands were doing, or what more could be done to him. Some went to their knees right away, unzipped him and went to work. Others waited till Ernest pulled it out himself and that wasn't the best way. He preferred to lean back against a picnic table or tree and close his eyes so his mind would swell and sink in the beer and not have to deal with the men talking to him. He'd hear the water running in the river and the traffic not far off. He'd smell the river's dead fish and weeds, and feel cool, except where the hands and mouth of the man were placed. The night would spin in his head. His body would feel full and anxious and ready to give way.

In the park, Ernest was nervous. But he loved it. The queasy feeling in his gut would wobble every time men came near him, and burn when they touched him. So many hours out of the week he was with men and couldn't feel this way. He couldn't think of their hands and what they'd feel like. He couldn't think of their mouths and their thick lazy tongues running over him. Any time he shut his eyes he had the person in mind he wanted. Nick was there. It was Nick talking to him, asking him questions, taking his own hands in his and moving them over his body.

He was always disappointed when he opened his eyes again and it was a man taller than Nick, or smaller, or darker. A man with an accent, or clothes nothing like what he'd imagined. Ernest would pick himself up and zip his fly. He'd step away brushing his hands across the seat of his pants and not look back. Inevitably, he'd be more sober afterwards, either from the time it took or the effort, but his body would be tired and that compensated some. He could settle into the feeling of his muscles emptied of energy and his legs cramped with exhaustion. The walk home was glazed with fatigue; his mind would be dulled as much as the rest of him. With the first step away from the men there, he lost the feeling in his gut. He calmed right down.

But this morning, with the sun pouring in around the sides of his blind, Ernest pulled himself out of bed, pissed in the toilet and splashed his face with water from the tap in the bathroom sink. He wiped his face on a towel, opened his eyes fresh and looked at himself anew. It was late morning. He'd slept well, his head felt clear and painless. Perhaps that helped the situation, perhaps it pushed him into a mind-set he couldn't fool himself out of, but he spotted a ruby mark on his neck the size of a nickel and he couldn't get rid of it. He couldn't get the mark out of his head, nor the sight of the man who put it there. The *man*. Ernest had a mark on his neck from a *man*. He kissed that man and together they did countless other things Ernest couldn't stop himself from remembering. Just look at it, he told himself. Just look at the size of it.

Look there, cocksucker.

He could hear the ugly words for what he was in his head and they meant something to him, he understood them for what they were, he understood them as acts he could relate to, things he'd done, words he'd become.

Ernest had a woman he couldn't love, whom he mistreated regardless of how he tried not to, he had no job, nor any prospects of one. He was fifty, without money in the bank. With the only living to speak of coming from an envelope the government sent every two weeks, which he still hadn't applied for. He was a failed husband and father, a drunk, and likely the cause of a few bastard children he didn't care to know about. All that he could live with. All that rolled off his back. But this small spot of darkened skin on his neck shamed him.

As his knees gave way, he grabbed the edges of the sink to hold himself up. And wept.

"I'm sorry. I'm sorry," he cried into the sink.

The whole night flooded from his body and into his mind. The man's hands on his cock, his mouth, the tone of his voice and its inflection. Their smell, the feeling in his groin when he first spotted him and the words he said to Ernest as he came on his knees at Ernest's feet. There was no more denying the sex he had. The lie could no longer be hidden away in his head like a room he never entered. It was daylight and he could see for himself what he had become.

There was one thing to do.

He showered. He washed inside his ears and between his toes, he clipped the wiry hairs of his sideburns that straggled out. Two splashes of cologne, his good shirt, and the cowboy boots he kept in the closet nowadays. It was Saturday afternoon. The door clicked locked behind him with the summer heat worming itself into his skin. Everything was bright. The dog next door yelped at him as he passed. The cars on the roads glared sunlight off their hoods and windshields. Every house looked solid and square on its block. The city was so obvious. The city was simple and laid out neatly with lawns and stairs and windows and two doors each, one in the front, one at the side or back.

He walked at a steady pace the eleven blocks south and two east, then turned up the asphalt parking lot, rang buzzer 201, took the stairs two at a time and kissed Bea on the lips when she opened her door.

୶

"What's this?" Bea asked. "*You're* in a good mood."

Grinning, Ernest stepped into the hall and Bea shut the door. "Why not?" he asked.

They moved into the living room, Bea running a hand down her hair as she went. When she offered him coffee, he spread himself across the loveseat, saying he wasn't in need of a thing. Something was up. Ernest wasn't this lively. He'd left so firmly last night and was back this afternoon already.

Bea took a seat next to the patio doors to sit in the sunlight. She took out a cigarette. "How about one of these?"

"Sure," Ernest said, jumping up and reaching across the coffee table.

Bea handed him a smoke and a pack of matches. "I wasn't expecting you here this afternoon. What's the occasion?"

Ernest sat back on the loveseat with a flop. "I'm moving."

"Oh." She stopped short.

Leaning back further in his seat, Ernest put his feet up on the coffee table and smiled more softly. "That is if your offer still stands."

"Here? Well, of course," Bea said, trying to hide her surprise. She'd expected him to say he was leaving town. "You just say when."

"Tomorrow?"

"Tomorrow! Tomorrow?" Bea thought he'd gone crazy. "Not at the beginning of the month?"

"Maybe," he said, "or how 'bout the weekend?"

"I should clean up first. I don't know? You sure you want

here that quick?" He couldn't really want it to happen so fast, could he? She'd put the idea out there thinking it'd happen in a few months by the time they'd sorted out the details.

"Well why not? If we're going to do it, let's do it. Why waste time?" Ernest slapped his hands together.

"You mean it?" Bea asked. She began to feel the excitement rise in her belly, making her giddy.

Reaching out for her hand, Ernest moved onto the couch, pulled her towards him with a growl and lifted her onto his lap. "Now," he barked. He nuzzled her neck with small bites and tickles. Bea shrieked with laughter. She squirmed and wriggled on his lap and felt his cock grow under her. With a twist and a push, he bounced her onto the couch so he could climb on top of her. She grabbed his wrists and kissed him but he only wanted to tickle her. They laughed and howled and made themselves sweaty with struggle until Ernest fell on top of her, letting his weight just go. He was heavy.

Bea could feel his breath on her neck, and smell his cologne and sweat. He was very fresh today. She nibbled on his ear for a while as they rested, then, shifting to the left a little, she pulled back his collar to kiss his neck. A mark was there. For a split second Bea thought it a large blemish, then realized her error. It was a hickey. Ernest had a hickey.

Maybe he didn't know he had it. Kissing his neck tenderly, Bea checked his breathing to see if it had changed and given him away. He lay there unmoving, resting on top of her, so she couldn't tell if he knew, not really, not without seeing his face. Bea stretched her arms around him and squeezed tight. *That's okay*, she thought. Maybe there'd been another woman he was dating, which could explain his lack of enthusiasm the night before. He'd been confused. *But if he had someone else and came to me this morning,* Bea thought, *then he knows what he wants. He wants me.*

༄

That afternoon at lunch hour, Aaron was with a few dozen other kids in the far back corner of the schoolyard, down at the concrete culverts, watching Carrie Kenrie make out with an older kid named Josh. The long pair of tunnels were faced end to end, making a fifteen-foot cylinder large enough for the smaller elementary school kids to crawl through effortlessly, but giving anyone in the upper grades a chore. Some of the larger kids were known to have gotten caught or panicked and not been able to get out. The culverts had been donated by the Sewer and Drainage Department of the city when new pipes came through in the seventies. Despite the problems, nobody had seen fit to get rid of them, likely due to their weight. Aaron hadn't crawled through one in the five years he'd been at the school. He was small enough, even in grade four, but he just didn't think it very wise. There was no trusting the other kids, regardless of whether they liked him or not, to behave once he was inside. And fifteen feet seemed a lot of tunnel to travel through.

Carrie and Josh were on the grass behind the tunnels. Carrie wasn't very popular in grade four and her sister, a year older, was even less so. This was a great way to get attention. Josh would never have participated, but he was pinned to the ground by three guys. Occasionally he'd squirm and wrestle which only encouraged Carrie more.

Though Aaron felt it was wrong, though it was one of the school-time things he could never tell his father, he couldn't stop himself from watching. What Carrie was doing was compelling, the boys holding Josh more so. And then there was Josh himself, who made everyone there thankful to be on the other side of it.

Fletcher was the biggest of the boys involved. Aaron wondered why he never washed his hands, or face, or tucked his shirt in. He'd seen Fletcher sneak up as close as he could to seagulls in the playground and shoot rocks at them. Trisha once told him that Fletcher had tied two cats together by their tails and had watched them claw each other in panic.

Two boys held Josh's left hand. Fletcher alone held the right.

Aaron was just telling himself he should leave — he still felt embarassed by that morning — when Fletcher looked up and caught his eye. There was a second where they were looking at each other, Aaron about to move, but unsure if he dared while Fletcher was watching, unsure if he should even look away, though he might be accused of staring. Fletcher gave a small smile. Instinctively, Aaron looked at the ground and began walking towards the school.

Not giving Josh a second thought, Fletcher released his arm and stood up, moving quickly to intercept Aaron. Everyone watched him move to see what was coming next.

"Where are you going?" Fletcher asked.

"To the bathroom."

"I don't think so," Fletcher said, then he grinned, revealing his chipped front tooth.

The other kids faced Aaron with bated breath. Josh sat up and pushed Carrie off his neck so he too could watch. Aaron seized up inside with panic. Would anybody help him? Now he really did feel like he had to pee.

With a left-handed deek, making Aaron dodge to the right, Fletcher used the other hand to snatch Aaron's ballcap off his head. Aaron made a reflex grab but the cap was long gone.

"This is nice," Fletcher said, looking it over.

Aaron stood still, unsure whether to follow as the kid sauntered to the mouth of the tunnel and threw the cap inside. Like a tennis crowd, the group of kids looked from Fletcher to Aaron to Fletcher, anticipating a move. Aaron felt the swell of tears in his eyes, and saw blurry little pools start in the corners, when the bell rang, thank God, and the class, with but a second's hesitation, ran for the front of the yard to line up at the school doors. Fletcher was the last to make a move, but he did, jogging past Aaron close enough to make him flinch.

Aaron raced to the tunnel and looked inside to see the hat thrown well into the hollow of the concrete belly. There was nothing for him to do but crawl in and get it. He was going to be late and he couldn't leave the cap behind.

Even with just his head inside, Aaron could sense the air was different. The tunnel was small, making his breathing echo off the cool walls. Dirt, twigs and gum wrappers pressed into his hands and knees. People had either scratched their initials into the old concrete or written them in liquid paper and nail polish. Once he'd grabbed his cap and had crawled forward, bringing him only three feet from the end, the light suddenly shifted and grew dim. A set of legs blocked the entrance. Aaron stopped still, holding his breath. He was stuck. Again his stomach gave out and his heart beat hard against his chest.

What should he do? Go ahead, or back?

He squished his head around to look over his shoulder. Nobody. The other kids were surely all lined up by now. If he called out he couldn't trust his voice to be steady. What had he been thinking? Of course Fletcher was going to block him in.

Trying to move as fast as he could while making as little

noise as possible, Aaron wiggled backwards towards the end where he'd entered. Fletcher's legs stayed where they were, facing the exit, until Aaron reached just that side of the first tunnel. Then the legs dashed from the opening. Aaron heard the pound of feet passing on the other side before the pants turned up at the south end of the tunnel. It was definite. He was trapped.

Racing as fast as he could, he crawled forward, only to have the same footsteps pound past him and Fletcher appear in front again well before he reached the end.

"Screw off," he called, regretting the tinny sound to his voice. Aaron thought he heard a giggle. Then Fletcher pounded on the concrete and howled like a dog.

There were two options. Crawl back to the other end and try kicking his way out, or stay put in the middle, trying not to pee, which had grown into a major concern, and hope Fletcher would give up on him. There was no saving face if he didn't make an effort. This guy was looking for a confrontation and the odds on Aaron getting out without satisfying that, one way or another, were slim. He was forced into deciding whether or not to fight. His father would tell him no, to satisfy what his mother would have expected, but Aaron knew his dad would have fought. Only he was big. And Aaron wasn't, not compared to this kid. Why had Fletcher picked him?

Aaron was hot and sweaty. His clammy palms picked up all the dirt and dust. He wanted to stand. His body itched to stand right up through the concrete that closed him in. *If only I could stand*, he thought, *then I could win*. Aaron pictured himself punching Fletcher in the face and making him bleed. He imagined he could do it if he could only fight face to face. Fletcher would be surprised to get hit, and he'd crumble with shock. Given the chance, Aaron would pound him, only he was stuck crawling backwards through the concrete readying himself to kick the guy in the knees.

"Screw off!" he shouted one more time, pulling his leg back ready to kick.

Fletcher took a step away and squatted down looking at him all squished up in the tunnel. Aaron half-wanted to release his foot now and smash him in the face, but Fletcher was smiling.

"I was just fooling with ya. Aren't you coming out?"

"You're in the way."

"Here," he said, all manners, "I'll get out of the way."

Though it might have been smarter to kick Fletcher in the face when he had the chance, Aaron, bladder aching, his throat scratchy with a lump in it, crawled out into fresher air. Standing, he was in considerable pain now. He didn't think he could stop himself from peeing. Bully be damned, Aaron faced the fence and unzipped his pants.

"What are you doing?" Fletcher asked, incredulous.

The hot piss streamed from his body in a great rush of relief. Aaron felt a million times better. His face was cool with sweat. When Fletcher took a step towards him and shouted again, "What the hell are you doing?" the shame of the thing, the embarrassment of his naked dink peeing, made him angry. Still going strong, he faced Fletcher and aimed his yellow stream right at him. "Come after me again and I'll piss all over you!" Aaron yelled.

Urine splashed on Fletcher's shoe before he could jump out of the way. He stood farther back, but still didn't retreat to the front of the yard like Aaron had spontaneously hoped. Both boys watched the arc of pee shrink, then dribble, then stop. *Now I'm dead*, Aaron thought. As he tucked and zipped up, he waited for the first hit.

"Woah," Fletcher exhaled, with a shake of his head. He smiled. "We're late for class. We better get going," he said, slapping Aaron on the back and jogging towards the school entrance.

As they crossed the yard, Aaron was sure to keep behind him. He still expected Fletcher to trip him, or to beat the crap out of him. Why would he have let him off after doing something like that? Was he waiting to get him back later? Was he going to tell on him instead? And what would his teacher say, or the principal, or his father, when they heard?

Mrs. Tessier looked them both over, then cleared her throat. "Is there a reason you were late getting back?"

Fletcher piped up, "I didn't hear the bell."

"You didn't."

"I was playing."

"Did you not hear the bell either, Aaron?"

Aaron was about to answer when Fletcher threw his arm around his shoulder. He gave a big grin. "He was with me. We were just fooling around. We didn't hear the bell."

He was so bold. Aaron couldn't believe how easily he could lie. Or the guile. Fletcher's smile was instant charm, pure reckless charm, daring her to doubt him.

Aaron wanted to hate him, but the teacher sent them to their seats with only a warning. And for the rest of the day Fletcher was nice. He asked to see Aaron's answer to a question on the board and then gave him gum in exchange. He passed him the joke going around the class.

Aaron couldn't forget the feel of Fletcher's arm around his shoulder and the safety in that, and the pride — however small and risky.

$\backsim$

"How long is he staying?" Amanda asked. She was making a tomato and cucumber sandwich.

"Well," Bea hesitated, realizing she hadn't been clear. "He's moving in for good, I guess."

Amanda screwed the lid on the mayo. "Oh," she said. She didn't know why Bea was striking up with someone. Men weren't good for much but taking girls out and getting them pregnant when they were ready. What was it about Bea and her mother that they felt they had to live with them? Who the hell wanted to do their chores and all the rest of it? She said as much in a class at school one day when the teacher said Shakespeare's comedies ended in marriage because that was a happy ending. "That is no happy ending," she piped up. Bo Terris in the back of the class asked her, "You aren't going feminist on us, are ya?" and she told him, "You don't have to be a damn feminist to know that."

She opened the fridge door and quickly put everything away. "When does all this start?"

Bea rubbed the palms of her hands together. "He said he could move in this weekend, but we can wait a week or so if you've got plans or something."

Amanda was about to give her a look to say *This weekend, are you crazy?* but the expression on Bea's face stopped her dead. The woman looked so damn hopeful — and, what was it, scared? — that she couldn't let herself be bitchy. Bea had taken her in at the last minute too when she'd needed a place. Amanda had called the number out of the paper and she was here that same day.

"No, I haven't got any plans," she said. Picking up the knife, she cut her sandwich in half. "Does this mean you want me to move out? Do you have to make room or something?" She licked the extra mayo off the edge of the knife.

"You're welcome to stay. I don't know if this'll make you uncomfortable. You like Ernest, don't you?"

"Sure."

"So that's good. We should do well here. I think there's enough room, but if you have a problem with this, just let me know. I'll understand."

Though she wasn't thrilled with the idea, she didn't want to seem ungrateful. Really, if she had to move, where would she go? Amanda tried to sound cheerier. "No, Bea. That's fine," she said, taking a bite of her half-sandwich. "If Alphie weren't such an asshole, I might have moved in with him too."

"He called here again last night."

"You're kidding. So did you tell him I was out?"

"I didn't say where. That boy doesn't stop."

Amanda gave a long sigh, saying, "He's in love with me, I guess."

"Well, about Ernest," Bea said, bringing the subject back, "we'll see how it goes?"

"Sure."

"So it's fine if he comes this weekend? He'll be here for Sunday dinner."

"Why wouldn't it be?" Amanda took the other half of her sandwich and extended it to Bea.

"No thanks," she said.

Amanda shrugged and walked by her, passing into the living room, making Bea follow. Amanda asked, trying to sound nice about it, "Where are you going to put all his stuff? Things are pretty full here."

"I don't think he's bringing much with him."

"No?"

"I don't think so. He didn't give me that impression."

"You didn't talk about that?" It didn't sound like Bea had thought this through. There was a brief pause until Amanda spoke again. "Well, what did he say?"

"He's gonna pack up and come over on the weekend."

"But did he mention selling his stuff? Or renting a van?"

"No."

Amanda took the second half of her sandwich off the plate. "You should clear that up."

"I guess so," Bea said. She leaned against the wall with a finger to her lips, looking around the room.

"You talked to him about my staying here still? He knows you want me to?"

Amanda could see Bea thinking how she'd broach the subject of his things with him. "Mm-hmm," she said.

"So he didn't assume I'd be moving out?"

"No. I never said you would."

"Well, I just thought if he was paying rent he might assume you didn't need me here anymore. But I guess he's out of work, so it helps to split the rent three ways."

"Right," Bea said.

"How much stuff does he have?"

"It's a small one-bedroom. Not a lot. I don't think the fridge and stove are his. We could fit anything extra in storage. Oh, shit." Bea put her coffee cup down.

"What?"

"I forgot. He's got that cat too."

Amanda gave a frown of concern. "And you're allergic, aren't you?"

"A little . . . It's not that bad. Sometimes I'm okay. Different cats affect me differently."

"But you're not sure. Have you been around it to know for sure before he moves in?"

"Not a lot. I'm sure it's okay."

"Yeah," she tried hard to sound reassuring.

"We can try it with the cat."

"Would he want to get rid of it?"

"No."

"Well . . ." Amanda eyed the last bite of her sandwich.

"I don't know. Maybe if he kept it there. Just for the first couple months."

"It wouldn't be such a bad idea to have a way out," Amanda said soothingly.

"Three months."

"Yeah." She popped the last bite in and gave a little tilt to her head. "It's a good idea."

"I guess so," Bea answered.

Amanda slapped the crumbs from her hands and took a drink of her water. "That's yummy," she said. "You should have one of those yourself, Bea." And she sauntered into the kitchen with her plate.

At 3:30, school out, Fletcher ran up beside Aaron as he crossed the road for home. "Where ya goin'?" he asked, keeping abreast of him.

Aaron sniffed. He couldn't stop himself from trying to detect the smell of pee. "Home," he answered.

"Me too. I'm goin' the same way."

Aaron knew that. He shrank at the prospect of what was to

come, some dumb violence, some dare, but Fletcher just talked. He asked what comics Aaron liked and Aaron told him he read books. Fletcher said they should trade with each other, not for keeps, only for a while. He liked books too, though Aaron didn't believe that. Everyone knew he had failed because of his reading skills. He was still in remedial.

The whole way home, past the farmer's market and the Beer Store, past the new and old Canadian Tire buildings, the video store and the block of houses, Fletcher kept up the conversation. Aaron tried to sound friendly and interested, but he was careful with what he said. He felt he had secrets to keep, as though there was something about him that Fletcher was bound to take the wrong way.

When they reached the spot where Aaron had to cross to get to his place in the newer block of houses beside the Barn Apartments, Fletcher asked if he wanted to come over. Aaron liked being asked, but didn't know how to say yes. He hesitated just long enough to give Fletcher the chance to say, "Come on," and head off to the left down Amelia St. Aaron followed, although, having dallied from walking with someone else, he was already later than usual.

They stopped in front of a two-storey apartment building with a green link fence around it. Either the front door was unpainted or it was so old the paint had peeled completely off. Aaron couldn't tell which it was.

"We can play in the garage," Fletcher said. "I've got a fort."

Aaron squinted. "I'm gonna be late for supper."

Fletcher pushed back the gate saying, "Come on, it'll be fun." Just then, a window in the upstairs made a racket as it opened. Aaron looked up to see fingers holding a tube of toothpaste resting against the sill.

A woman with long brown hair in disarray hung her head out the window. "Where the hell have you been? Get in the house!" she yelled.

Fletcher shouted back, "In a minute."

"I said get in the house!"

Nonchalantly, Fletcher turned to Aaron and said, "I gotta go in. Maybe I'll pick you up for school tomorrow. What time do you leave?"

"Before eight-thirty," Aaron answered. He wondered if the woman was still in the window watching them, but didn't dare look up again.

Fletcher walked to the door and opened it, revealing a hallway with a staircase to the upper apartment. "See ya tomorrow," he said as the door at the top of the stairs squeaked open. The woman's voice shouted down, "Mike, what are you doing down there? When I say get in the goddamn house, you move!"

Though the front door swung shut as Aaron took a few paces down the block, he could still hear her yelling as he went. Was that a step-mother? Maybe it was his baby-sitter. Aaron couldn't imagine anyone's mother being like that, not even Fletcher's.

Standing on the corner at Johnson, where they'd just been, Aaron felt happy and an ugly sort of regret. By not speaking up when he had the chance earlier that afternoon, after getting back late for class, he'd locked himself into being nice. Fletcher had recognized that. There were those few seconds when Fletcher's arm was around him that Aaron could have told the truth, but Aaron had left his arm there. He'd liked it. He'd liked feeling important. Fletcher, the biggest boy in school, wanted to be his friend.

As Aaron walked the three blocks to his home, he imagined,

if he could do the day over again, what he would do. He'd punch the guy, or tell Tessier the truth. He wouldn't pee on Fletcher's shoe; he'd pee before he went for lunch like he should have. Aaron climbed the steps to his front porch and held a hand to the doorknob before stepping in, imagining the next morning when Fletcher would be standing right there, likely smiling with his dirty face and chipped tooth when he answered the door.

～

"Ernest it's all shit nowadays," Figgy said, sitting down with a fresh bottle. At the next table, an old guy pushing eighty looked over, curious, so Ernest nodded hello and Figgy lowered his voice. "I can't stick around here any longer, the wife's right. I just got off the welfare a few years ago. How the hell am I going to get a job? Huh? You know what the guy at the Miramon plant said when I went in for the interview the other day? *It's a bit late for ya, eh?* Not that I was late for the appointment," Figgy said, then whispered even more, "meaning I was too old."

"That's just one place, Fig. It won't be so bad."

"A year's not too fucking long a time anymore."

"You got that right," Ernest piped in, but Figgy barely stopped to listen. He was wound up.

"I won't find something here. I'll be out on the welfare in no time and I can't live off that. They get you to fill out these forms and have them signed by whatever business saying you went in and asked for a job. That ain't no good. What fucking good is that going to do, eh? Anybody could sign those forms. If I got enough different pens me and my buddies could sit around and sign the names and numbers for the mills or stores or whatever, it only takes a phone call to find out who runs a place, if I didn't already know, and how would they know if I'd really been there or not? How would they know how I presented myself? They have no idea what it's like. I'm almost sixty, Ernest. How the hell do they expect me to get another job? I'm a good worker, I pull my fucking weight, and no stupid form is going to show otherwise."

It was clear to Ernest he wasn't getting a word in edgewise. Figgy just needed to vent. He told Ernest that the guy in the interview didn't give two shits about the work Figgy had done, the jobs he'd had, the things he'd learned. Figgy knew a few things. He knew a man doesn't drink on the job and if he does he doesn't last since no one'll cover his ass for very long because it ain't worth it if a man can't keep it separate from the job. He knew how many tonnes a forklift can hold before it tips, how long an engine can run on the press before it'll start burning itself out and what the signs are that it's started. He knew how to calm a man down when he'd sliced his fingers off and what it meant to stop the blood, he'd learned that the hard way, a couple times, and no young guy on the floor was going to be of any help when that happened. No young guy was going to reach his hands down into the machine after and hope he took hold of the guy's fingers intact so they could go to the hospital with their owner.

Problem was, a company saw men like Ernest and him as dangerous. They had all learned the best way to file a grievance and get it heard. They knew what the laws were on safety and what you didn't have the right to get a man to do for ten-fifty an hour. Men like them did things cleanly, efficiently, and safely, only sometimes that meant more money, and sometimes that meant less. Trouble was, it was dependent on them how it got done because of what they knew and they weren't worth the gamble for the mill because it was the mill that wanted to call the shots. If there were mistakes to be made, it had to be the worker who was going to be making them. If there were problems to be had, the mill-hand was to be the one to blame, or the steward, or the welder, or even the foreman. It wasn't the company. It wasn't the management. So it was better to hire men who didn't know so much, and could be blamed for more. The company was fucking themselves in the end, but they looked good while doing it, and that's all that counted with them.

When Figgy finished he took a long draught on his beer. This was the break Ernest needed to tell him, if was ever going to. He took a deep breath and said it. "I'm moving in, Fig."

Figgy stopped gulping with the bottle held to his lips. He lowered the bottle, swallowed, and cocked his head. "You are, are ya? Where to?" He was being coy.

Ernest looked around the bar. Sue was running her feet off, Bea was at home. "Oh, just up the block and around the corner."

"Does she know about this?"

"Well, yeeess," Ernest replied, meaning *Don't be ridiculous.*

"Congratulations. You sly fucker. You sure this is the right idea? I wouldn't put myself in your shoes, I'll tell ya. You only known her a few weeks now —"

"Over a year, Figgy. I've known her a year yet."

"You know what I mean, Ernest. Sure, you seen her around the bar, but how long you *known* her? A few weeks, a month? I wouldn't be putting myself in your shoes."

"You don't think it wise."

Figgy shrugged. "What do I know? Really. I been married too long. Good luck, buddy. Want me to buy ya a beer?"

"Could do."

"Yeahhh, sure." He stood. "Hell, why not?" he said, referring to Bea and not the beer. He slapped Ernest on the shoulder.

"Good luck, eh? That's all there is to say, I guess. She's a good lookin' woman, anyhow. You can't go wrong with that, can you?"

The door opened, making Figgy look over and grin. Ernest braced himself as Nick walked in.

"Whadda ya say, Nick?" Ernest asked, smiling.

"Not much," Nick said, standing beside the table and glancing at the bar to get Hank's attention.

Figgy, still standing, adjusted his cap. "Ernest's got news about a woman," he said right away.

Nick looked at Figgy with a grin for what might be coming. "Oh?"

"Seems like Ernie's got himself wrapped up in a nice situation here, eh, Ernest?"

Now Nick gave a full-on smile, enjoying the joke. "And what's that?"

"Ernest's getting married."

"Woah," Nick jumped back from the table as if it was on fire. He approached Ernest carefully. "That true? You getting a conjugal bed, Ernest?"

"Ah," Ernest waved a hand, "I'm just moving."

Nick asked, "Where to?" as Figgy said, "Moving and shaking," with a crude gesture.

For a second, Ernest's temper flared. He swallowed to stay calm. "Are you getting me a beer or not?" he asked Figgy, who then went to the bar.

Nick repeated, "Where you moving to, Ernest?" He sounded more reasonable now that Figgy was gone.

Ernest couldn't look him in the eye. He pretended to be interested in what Figgy was ordering at the bar. "I'm moving in with Bea."

"Seriously?" Nick sounded shocked.

Now Ernest could look him in the face. "Why would I fuck around about that? Yes. I'm moving in."

"When?"

"Next weekend."

"That's pretty quick, isn't it?" Nick didn't say more, but sat back in his seat and blew out his cheeks. Ernest wished he'd just drop it for now. He didn't want to be confronted on this. He didn't want to have to defend his decision.

When Figgy headed back their way, Nick asked, "You got a truck?"

"No."

Figgy sat down, setting a beer in front of Ernest. "There you go. Drink up."

"You want help moving?" Nick asked. Ernest caught him shooting Figgy a look to quiet him.

"Sure, I could use a little help."

"Right-o. What day are you moving?"

"I don't know. I'll have to get back to ya."

"Just let me know. The kid and I have supper at my sister-in-law's on Sunday, but we can squeeze you in somewhere."

Figgy and Ernest both took pulls on their bottles. He couldn't think of something decent to say to switch the subject. There was an uncomfortable pause that left a bad taste in Ernest's mouth. He took another swig.

"Well," Nick stepped in. "Looks like a good idea if you ask me." He was smiling. Ernest relaxed a little. "She's treating you well enough, that's for sure," he said, stretching out his arm and nearly touching the mark on Ernest's neck.

৯

"It's not a hell of a lot of stuff, Bea."

She looked around the room. Ernest had opened all the cupboards in his kitchen for her to see inside. "No, not really," she said.

"What do you need? You need anything? You need kitchen stuff? I got pots and pans, but my dishes are shit. None of them match. We could save this stuff for camping. I'd love to get a trailer some day."

"Sure. I've got the large closet in the hall there. Some of this will fit."

"I'll go through it and throw out what's shit. The rest I'll sell. Shouldn't be too hard."

"Um," Bea was trying to think of the best way to put it. "Maybe we should hold off on that."

Ernest's eyes snapped up to meet hers.

"I've been thinking, Sweetie. This is a pretty big thing we're doing, and neither of us have much experience at it. Twice I lived with a guy when I was younger, and they didn't last more than a couple months. We don't want to put all our eggs in one basket." Ernest wasn't saying anything to help her out. She added, "I don't want you be stuck anywhere you don't want to be, Ernest. If we're a flop . . . Maybe I'm wrong."

"No, Bea. You got a point. Yeah. Well . . . You got a point, there, Bea. Maybe we should hold off a while." Ernest picked up Brutus and began scratching her behind the ear. "You still want me to move in?"

Bea felt embarrassed and small. She took Brutus out of his hands and set her down, then wrapped each of his arms around her waist. "Yes, I do," she said, rubbing her cheek against his chest. She waited to say more until he hugged her back, of his own volition. When he grabbed her up and gave her a nice smooth squeeze between his arms, she added, "We just don't want to wreck it going too fast."

"Yeah, I guess you're right." He leaned his neck back to look her in the face. "So what are we going to do?"

"You still move your stuff in, your clothes and whatnot, but we leave the rest here a while. Just in case. You never know, you may want to move back. You don't know what an old maid I am at home."

Ernest laughed and kissed her. "Okay," he said.

"And I've got another little secret."

"What's that?"

"I may be allergic to Brutus. We'll try her out, but we might have to talk about that if it's a real problem."

"Sure. Sure, Bea."

"Well, that's settled." She took a breath, feeling her shoulders relax. "You got any secrets of your own I should know about?" she laughed, giving him another squeeze for good measure.

"It isn't like he's going to be needing it."

"I don't know," Missy said slowly. "I don't think it's right." She bunched up her nose with distaste, which was one of her expressions Amanda hated.

Missy didn't understand the situation. Amanda was poor, she worked hard for the money she had and it was never enough. She and her mother had gone without for a long time. Amanda never had nice things when she was growing up: her skirts too long or short, the wrong colours for the time of year, bangs that hung too low in her face or cut unevenly by her mother for the first twelve years of her life. Nick worked full-time at a good job with only a kid to support. He had a car, a house, a full lawn that was more than she ever had in the rinky-dink apartments she'd always lived in. There was no reason that he needed those dresses and no reason to hang onto them. But since Amanda couldn't afford new clothes, and knew where there was a great dress just lying around going to waste, she thought it only fair that she could borrow it. Why would it be a perfect fit if she weren't meant to wear it?

"He isn't going to be *using* it, is he?" she asked rhetorically. "No. And it's not like he'd even notice it missing. It was just *sitting* there." Amanda gave a slow turn in the mirror. "How's my ass?" she asked.

"Fine."

"It doesn't look fat?"

Missy barely looked. "No," she said.

"I don't want it to look like yours in that prom dress. That was a horrible dress."

"Then why don't you buy yourself a new one?"

"Du-uh, I work for a living? I can't afford a new dress. *I* pay *rent*." Missy sat in silence. "I'm not spoiled enough to be still living at home and I haven't got a father who makes millions in the Mafia."

"My father isn't in the Mafia."

"Well then, I haven't got a father who's a drug-runner."

"He doesn't run the drugs either."

"Listen to the hydroponics queen over here get defensive."

"Shut up, Amanda. I can't tell you anything without you using it —"

"— I'm sorry," Amanda interrupted. She twisted an invisible key to her lips. "Mum's the word," she promised, then looked like she was sad to have upset her. Switching the subject, she lit up with a fresh idea. "I got it." She took a drag on her cigarette and held the smoke, feigning thought. Amanda hoped to make Missy impatient, but she wasn't responding. Amanda teased her interest more. "Just *feel* the material. I think it's silk."

Missy rubbed the hem between her fingers. "Probably."

"It's got to be. It's like wearing water on your skin. It's like a baby's bottom."

"Gross," Missy spit out, snapping her hand back.

"I mean it's that soft. It's as soft as a baby's bottom."

"Why would you want a dress made from baby skin?"

Amanda rolled her eyes. "You are criminally stupid sometimes. It's an expression."

"I *know that*."

Amanda was impatient. "Do you want to hear my idea or not?"

"Yessss. I do."

"I go to the concert with Alphie, because I said I would — and I have the dress already anyway so I might as well put it to good use — and then I dump him."

"That night?"

"*Yah*."

"I think you should wait till the next day. That's cruel."

"That's why it's going to work this time. Do you want him calling you every day? Do you want to get calls at eight in the morning when you've been on your feet at Giorgio's all night?"

"No," Missy said, pouting.

"Well, neither do I. He takes me to the concert and bam, I tell him to fuck off. He's heart-broken, I'm selfish, he leaves me alone. I'm doing him a *favour*, Missy." Amanda flopped on the bed and leaned back against the headboard. She made her voice go flat and bored. "He's only wasting his life pining for me. I'm giving him his life back. And when it's all over, I dry-clean the dress and put it back."

"What if he notices it gone?"

"Why would he? It's been sitting there for a year, at least, untouched. It's not like I'm going to wreck it or anything."

In the small garage out back of the duplex, Fletcher had built a hide-out. His mother used the garage for storage. There were jars of pears and stewed tomatoes, broken bikes, licence plates, buckets filled with black greasy car parts of various sizes and shapes, paint cans, and a garden hose. The beams in the roof ran kitty-corner instead of in straight lines with the wall. Fletcher had cleared a space in a corner and hung a tarp from the lower rafters, cutting off the space in a triangle, making a sort of tent. This is where he hid his hooter magazine, behind a loose plank in the chipped wall, and where he went to get away from his mother. He wasn't to play in the house.

Fletcher offered the dirty magazine to Aaron. "Here, you want to read it this time?"

Aaron shook his head no. After a few days of hanging out with Fletcher, Aaron still wasn't comfortable around him. Fletcher seemed too desperate to be friends, which made him pushy and careless. He seemed restless, and greedy, the way he smiled at Aaron as if he always wanted something.

"Come on," Fletcher coaxed, "I had my turn. You read better than me."

Aaron shrugged. "I just don't feel like it."

"But you gotta. It's your turn. Just half a page."

Reluctantly, Aaron took hold of the glossy paper. The spine was whitened from wear and all the corners were dog-eared. Fletcher or someone before him had leafed through this a lot.

"What if your mother comes?" Aaron asked. He was terrified of Fletcher's mother, but he'd decided it was better to risk seeing her than to have Fletcher back at his place. The less his father saw of him, the better.

"My mom likes you. She don't trust me with the Sneiders or my cousins, but she likes you. Besides, she don't come out here. It's our rule. She don't come out when I'm here and I don't come in when Shithead is around."

Had Fletcher not been so crude and bad-mannered, Aaron would have had him over to his place, but he knew his father wouldn't approve of half the things Fletcher said. Truth was, Aaron liked that Fletcher was so rough. It wasn't as if Aaron had a lot of friends at school. With Fletcher, he felt smart. And important. Fletcher walked him home from school, shared things he stole from the corner store, and came by with a jar for catching crickets in the field behind Aaron's house.

Aaron flipped to a particularly graphic page in the magazine and tried not to make a face. He was shocked by what people looked like naked and what they did to each other. He was especially surprised by their body hair. It looked so weird.

"Read a story," Fletcher said.

Aaron screwed up his nose. "I don't want to."

"Come on," he coaxed. "Just half of it."

Aaron set the magazine down on the end of the outdoor lounge chair that Fletcher called his bed. "Let's go to the store," he said, hoping to find something else to do.

"I don't have any money."

"I've got money."

Fletcher picked up the magazine. "I don't want anything," he sulked.

"We can climb the tree."

"I already did that today." Fletcher flipped through the pages, mouthing words to himself.

Aaron felt antsy. His stomach tingled; he didn't want to be sitting around anymore. "I'm bored. I don't *want* to read. Let's just go to the store."

"What for? You got any money?"

"I got seventy-five cents."

"That's not even enough for a chocolate bar." Fletcher went back to the pictures. He rubbed a finger on part, scratching the paper with his nail.

Aaron knew he could go home, but Fletcher was bound to call later anyhow and Aaron didn't really want to leave, he just wanted to do something else. Reading the magazine made him feel queasy in his stomach. His body got all anxious and busy. Pulling out his quarters to make the offer more enticing, he said, "We could each get a Freezie. Or split a popsicle."

Fletcher shrugged. "I'm not hungry."

When Aaron didn't suggest anything else, they sat in silence, with Fletcher leafing through the pages. They sat like that for a good five minutes. Aaron kept wondering when he'd stop reading and talk to him, but Fletcher made a deliberate point of ignoring him. Aaron knew he couldn't be the one to say something next or Fletcher would win. Finally, when it was obvious that Fletcher wasn't giving in, Aaron said he had to go and pulled back the tarp to the cabin without causing Fletcher to so much as blink in response.

Amanda wore white shoes with a sheer white scarf tied around her neck. Her hair was pulled back on either side by barrettes covered in tiny fake pearls. She curled the ends to bob just above her shoulder and sprayed the whole thing with hair spray to hold it like that all night. The only drawback to the outfit was that she didn't have a purse to match. She refused to bring her brown one because it didn't go, so she tucked her fake ID into the band of her thigh-highs in case they went for drinks and she got carded. She wouldn't need money, she reasoned, because Alphie would want to buy her drinks and the tickets were already paid for. Maybe she should have bought a new purse, but fuck it, it was too late. Anyhow, she looked damn good. When she came out of her bedroom, Bea was there waiting for the call to pick Ernest up with his stuff.

"How do I look?"

Bea closed her magazine. "Very good. That's a beautiful dress."

"Thank you," she said, smiling. She couldn't resist adding, "It's silk."

"Silk? Where'd you get it?"

"The Sally Ann."

"It looks good on you. It's a bit fancy for a rock concert, isn't it?"

"They aren't rock, Bea. They're New Country."

"All the same."

Amanda walked back down the hall and stepped into the bathroom. "I want to look extra-good tonight."

"How come?"

She was checking out her make-up, to see if she'd missed any zit-spots with the foundation. "Oh," she said lazily, "just because. I figure it would be nice for a change. I don't always have to look like a piece of shit, do I?"

"I don't know if Alphie's going to notice the effort as much as you or I would."

Amanda looked around the corner at her. "I'm not doing this for Alphie," she said impatiently. "I'm doing this for *me*."

Bea nodded her head in an *Oh, I see* — which Amanda took to be patronizing — then went back to reading.

"So Ernest is coming tonight?"

"M-hmm. Don't be scared when you see him in the morning."

"You think he could have moved in the daytime when it was easier to see."

Bea didn't look up from her magazine. "He's not bringing much stuff. It'll be fine."

"And how's he getting here? Cab?"

"I'm just waiting to pick him up. I'm working at eight."

"Eight?" Amanda said, surprised.

"Oh, just to cover Sue. She's going up the road to a wedding reception for a couple hours and Theresa couldn't do it, so I said I would. I'm picking Ernest up on the way. He's only bringing his clothes and a few personal effects, like we talked about, so we'll see how it goes, right? No rushing into things."

Amanda softened her voice. "I think that's the best, Bea. I mean, you don't want to get burned. There's no reason not to wait." She didn't answer to that so Amanda checked her teeth in the mirror and left, sounding as cheery as she could saying goodbye. It was good solid advice. Bea was likely just stressed about the whole thing. She would be too, if she had a man moving in with her. Alphie? That'd be a joke. Ernest didn't seem like a prize either. At least Alphie had a job, and a waistline. But that wasn't fair. She wasn't being fair to Ernest. He seemed good enough. Bea was happy, so why begrudge her a boyfriend? If things were too crowded there after a month, she could always move. There wasn't anything keeping her in the apartment, other than it was cheap enough, but she could get that elsewhere.

With a pop and a flash, the overhead light blew out. Ernest was just shutting the door behind him, suitcase in hand, when it all went black on the stairs.

Bea rolled down her window on the car. "You need help, Ernest?"

"Nah."

"You don't want to change that?"

He walked round the front of the car and opened the side door before answering. "I won't be needing it, will I? No, why bother," he said, dropping into the seat beside her. Everything he would need or want was all packed up and placed in her trunk, except Brutus who was meowing under the seat. Ernest took a last look at the place. With the lights off, his curtains looked lame and limp hanging in the windows. Having always left a light and the stereo on, he'd rarely seen the room completely dark. Ernest felt he'd accomplished something grand, small, but grand, in having all the lights off. He wouldn't be coming back here. He was entering a whole new chapter. An entirely different turn of events. *He who laughs last*, he thought to himself, though he didn't know exactly why it felt so fitting. Good-bye, good riddance.

Everything about him felt lighter. Bea was beautiful beside him, with her fingers riding on top of the steering wheel, and her rings reflecting the light. Every store and corner they passed, Ernest felt it was the last time he'd see them. He took a close look at everything, as if he was leaving for good. Never again would he see these places in the same mindset. He'd be a different person once they got home, to his new home, through the door and into a better life. He reached a hand out on the top of the seat, and Bea glanced over, giving him a smile. She placed her right hand in his left, wrapping her slender fingers around his thick and work-battered ones, and together they gave a squeeze.

∽

"Why have you been such a jerk all night?" Amanda asked. The concert was fun, but Alphie insisted on leaving before the encore.

"I saw you with that guy."

"What guy? Who? Where?"

"That fucking old guy," Alphie spit out. Amanda could tell he was frustrated. *Oh, come on*, he was saying.

"I don't know what the hell you're talking about. What old guy?"

"The guy with his fucking Range Rover."

Just then, a waitress came to take their order. They were in a booth at The Colossus, in the Promenade shopping district — a big idea in the seventies for a strip of stores that never took off. In the east end, The Colossus was an institution. They'd been around since before Amanda was born and were still the only place outside of Mr. Submarine to get food after one, which meant the clientele were young kids coming from the bar, old lonely seniors, mostly veterans, with nowhere else to be, or drunks trying to sober up before they drove home.

Amanda ordered a milkshake and Alphie got a bacon burger and coke. As soon as the waitress left, Amanda leaned far over the table. She spoke very slowly, trying to sound threatening. "Are you following me?"

"Nooo," he answered sarcastically. "I came to see you yesterday and the fucking truck pulled out right in front of me, with you in it."

"It's not a truck," she corrected. "It's an all-terrain vehicle."
Alphie's bottom lip hung loose, giving him a blank look of
disbelief. "What are you talking about?"

"The Range Rover. It's not a truck."

"I'm not talking about the fucking Range Rover. I'm asking
you why you're hanging out with that old guy."

Amanda pulled down her dress, smoothing it over her knee.
"He's only thirty-six," she said calmly.

"Thirty-six? *Thirty*-six?!"

"Maybe he's thirty-five, I don't know. He's not that old. It's
not like he's forty."

"He could be your father."

"My dad wasn't nineteen when he had me, nimrod."

"But he's old enough —"

"— And his kid's only eight," she interrupted. That worked.
That floored him. That shut him up good.

When the waitress returned with their drinks, Alphie didn't
so much as blink at her. His mouth had dropped even lower,
ready to cough up a golf ball. He was so damn obvious. When
the waitress left, he pretended to have nothing else to do with
her. He leaned way back and set an arm on top of the seat.
"You're fucking stupid." He tipped his ball cap back, looking
around at the other customers.

She didn't want him to be the one to pick the fight that ended
it for good. *I'm not going to give him the satisfaction*, Amanda
thought. She sipped slowly on her shake, stirring it with her
straw, then lifted a strawberry out with her spoon. "Yum," she
said aloud to prove she was ignoring him. She could have stood
for a glass of water, she was dehydrated after the concert, but
the shake was nice and cold. The metal glass they served them
in was the best part. It was all sweaty with condensation.

"You know that?" Alphie asked. "You're *fucking stupid*."

"Hmm?" she said, like she hadn't been paying attention.

"Oh, fuck off. Fuck you," he said, raising his voice and pointing at her. "Fuck you, Amanda. You hear me? Fuck *you*."

The waitress glanced over, then tucked her pen behind her ear and checked her nail polish like she'd seen it all too many times, but the other customers were staring. Alphie was promising to be the last show of the night. *Well, let him go right ahead*. Amanda could care less.

"Sometimes I think you're just a fucking whore. You playing me for an idiot?"

"Well, aren't you?" she asked casually. Alphie didn't know when to quit. He was no match for her. She knew his limits and how to work them. He was bound to get hurt at the end of this, he always did, so she couldn't get why he'd want to provoke a fight. That's what she wanted, of course, but why he'd be starting it was beyond her.

"I'm not going to sit here and take this. You can find your own fucking way home," he said as he stood up.

"Alphie, sit down."

"No, I'm not sitting down."

Amanda saw the waitress glance over again, then scoot into the back. "You're gonna get us kicked out."

"I can't get kicked out, I'm leaving. Hey!" he called to the full restaurant, "Anybody want a good hand job, take this bitch home," then he turned and stormed out the door. Just then the waitress came from the back with a big guy in a blue apron. Amanda felt a gulp grow in her throat. She hadn't any cash on her, of course.

She stood and jogged to the door. "Just a second," she said to the waitress, trying to sound exasperated, like he'd done this before and she had the whole thing under control.

She ran out onto the street. The air hit her cool and refreshing, making her feel like things would be fine.

Alphie was at his car door already, unlocking it, half a block down. "Alphie!" she called. "*Alphie*, wait!" He opened the door and looked up. She considered what kind of picture they must make, she in her dress running to him in the middle of the night. "We haven't paid yet," she said, trying to sound sweet. "We can't leave until we pay."

"I bought the tickets. You pay."

Amanda was at the car. "But I didn't bring a purse. I haven't any money."

"That's your problem. Call your boyfriend," he sneered, and jumped in his seat. He slammed the door and turned the ignition.

"Alphie, *wait!*" She tried the handle on the passenger door. Locked. "Wait," she pleaded. "Wait." But he revved the engine and pulled out, squealing the Chevy's tires.

Amanda was standing on the road, just off the curb, watching him speed away. She expected him to turn in at the movie theatre and come back, but he didn't. The car raced around the bend in the road and was out of sight. The sickly realization that she was definitely stranded sunk into her belly and legs. She didn't have any money on her, nor any way of getting some. She was a half-hour walk from home and had a bill to pay in the restaurant behind her. What was she going to do now? Wash dishes? Could she get off that easily? Maybe they'd trust her to cab it home and come back. Or she could call Bea. What time did she say she'd be getting off work? She might be home by now and would be dead to the world after work. *Oh, fuck, Ernest*. Ernest moved in today. There was no way in hell Amanda could call now. This was no way to start off his first night. Eventually they'd ask her to leave; this would be their first excuse. Amanda took a deep breath, stifling tears.

"You comin' back in, or you gonna high-tail it out of here too, though I should warn you, I'm not gonna get stiffed without a good run after ya."

Amanda turned to face the waitress. "No, I'm coming back in," she said, as belligerent as she could muster. When she got to the entrance, the waitress held the door open for her. "Get off my back," Amanda snapped defensively. "I don't need any more shit tonight."

"Don't be mouthy with me, honey. I didn't screw you over." The woman's voice sounded as if she was trying to be decent. "I have to make a living, that's all. And I can't afford to pay for every Tom, Dick and Harry that pulls through here."

Amanda turned in the doorframe to face her. She was right. "I'm sorry," she said.

The waitress shrugged to say it made no difference to her. "That's fine," she said.

"Um," Amanda breathed out a huge sigh, bracing herself. "I haven't any money. Can I do dishes?"

"That isn't gonna help me much; I don't get paid for doing dishes. Don't you got someone you can call?"

Amanda bit her bottom lip and took a peek at her dress. She straightened her back. "Where's your telephone?" she asked.

He was back. Ernest fell asleep as soon as he got home, but he began the dreams again.

This time he was cruising in the park. Everything was in shades of grey — the trees, and water, the lawn, the people —

and though it was night-time, the sun was out, large and orange, casting shadows more purple than black. The grass was wet with dew, the maples and weeping willows were full, but the pines were barren. Summer was at its peak. A few men stood along the laneway, others passed by, glancing at one another, none of them pairing up. As Ernest approached, in white shorts and T-shirt, twenty years younger, his gut smaller, his skin smooth except for the calluses on his hands, the men all turned to him, one by one as he passed. Everyone had the same thought; they wanted him. He was the lucky guy, he was the guy who could take any of them away and make them happy. But each looked too greedy. One had needy eyes, another licked his lips. A man he passed turned immediately around and called something to him, though Ernest wasn't paying attention. He'd found someone. A guy at the end of the laneway sat on a bench with his back to Ernest.

That's the one he wanted. That's the man.

Ernest picked up his step. He looked to the dull haze of the orange sun without needing to squint. It was a beautiful night. As he came round the far side of the bench, Ernest made a point not to look over right away. He kept the guy in his peripheral vision. Ernest felt shaky with nerves. His heart raced. When a black seagull landed with a clickety-clack on the back of the bench, Ernest took a look at it. Then he glanced at the man.

He'd been mistaken. There he was, a small boy. Nick's boy, Ernest knew, Aaron, though he had yet to meet him. The kid raised a hand and fed the bird from his palm. Ernest felt a drop on his collar. His white shirt. Blood smudged across his white shirt. How did that get there? He looked to the sky to see if it was raining. With his head back, he felt dizzy. His heart threw itself against his chest, wanting out. *Bang. Bang.* Ernest woke with a start, sweaty in the sheets.

Jesus, he was back in his dreams.

Climbing out of bed, he dragged himself into the kitchen to wait up for Bea. There was no sleeping now. Brutus stirred on the couch when she saw him. He poured himself one last beer and spent the two hours until she got home sitting at the kitchen table listening to the teapot clock on the wall behind him tick. She came in a little after 1:30. Hank did the last hour alone, but she had a half-hour cleanup before she could go. Ernest heard the downstairs front entrance open and close, but she was in sneakers so he couldn't hear her feet on the stairs. The top door opened, then her key was in the slot. Ernest didn't know what he expected. He just wanted to see the look on her face when she got home. He had to see what she knew. His first night here and already something to deal with. Things were supposed to be easier.

When she came around the corner, she looked surprised to see him. "You're still up? I thought you were going to bed."

"I am. I thought I'd wait up for you," he said, smiling nicely. "That's the thing to do, ain't it?"

Bea smiled and put her arms around his neck. She kissed his forehead. "Let's go to bed."

"I wanted to tell ya something, Bea. Can you sit down a minute? I don't want to make it a big deal or nuthin', but I should have said something a week ago, before I moved my stuff over here and all."

"Sure, let me take my shoes off," she said, walking to the hall. Ernest heard the shoes drop to the floor. She came back in and sat down at the table beside him.

Ernest wasn't sure what he was going to say, but felt he had to tell her something, to be fair. "I don't know, Bea. I don't want to make this a big deal, but there's a lot about me you don't know. I've got a lot of secrets, Bea. I'm a good person, I don't try to cross anyone, but there's things I don't talk about. There's things I won't *ever* talk about. I won't ever get married again. I can't marry you, Bea —"

"— Are you going to cheat on me?" she interrupted.

"No."

"Are you going to stay with me?" Ernest could tell she was concerned and trying to put it delicately. "Or is this short term?" she asked.

"I don't know what's going to happen, but yeah, I think so, I think I'll stay. That's the best I can do."

"Good enough, Ernest." She put her hand over his.

They sat quiet for a few seconds while Ernest tried to collect his thoughts. He was getting choked up, but felt he had more to say and hadn't managed to get it across, which only made him angry. He knew she didn't want anything else from him, she was satisfied with that, but he wasn't. He felt he could barely stop himself from talking. He could tell it all if he wanted to, right now. Bea was the first person in a long time that Ernest felt he trusted. She wouldn't hurt a fly. Bea was pure fucking gold.

With each word he got out, he struggled to restrain himself and say less. "I've had a big life. It hasn't all been good. There's things I could tell you that would make you sick. I had a bad time growing up. Things have happened to me . . ." Where was he going with this? She wasn't debating him. Ernest could feel himself getting angry at something. Maybe himself, he couldn't tell. His words came out forced. "Things have happened to me like you wouldn't believe. My wife left me. I can't ever tell you why," he said, with the feeling in him getting to be too much. "There's lots of things happened I can't talk about." Surprising both of them, he slammed a hand down on the table. Bea jumped. "So don't ask, 'cos I can't talk about 'em," he said through his teeth, holding himself together. "Don't even ask."

The cab travelled down Johnson Street towards Nick's place. Missy was camping. Amanda hadn't known who else to call. Nick's house was close enough to Bea's that she could walk home later; it was half the distance from the restaurant anyway. They'd arranged for the cab to return to his place so he could collect the change when it arrived. Nick had sent the man with a fifty to cover her bill. Amanda was supposed to walk home after that. She smoothed a hand down her dress. She was a bit cold. Tonight wasn't as warm as she'd expected. What would Nick say when he saw her in the dress? She'd take it off and hand it back to him, and wear something else home, something of his maybe. Or she'd offer to get it dry-cleaned and wear it home. She didn't think it would be a big deal, but then the closer they got to his block, the more she reconsidered her judgment. Her heart sank at what was likely to face her when she got there. What was she thinking?

As the cab pulled onto his street, she could feel herself wanting to cry. Nick came out onto the front steps when he saw the car pull up. He came over and paid the driver. Before he could get a good look at her, she climbed out and entered the house right away.

She turned the lamp off in the living room so the place was dark, except for the light spilling in off the front step. Amanda stood beside the table waiting for him. He walked up the steps and opened the screen door.

"Amanda? You turned the light off."

"I don't want you to see me," she said. Her voice was cracking. She couldn't stop herself from crying.

Nick came over to her and took her by the elbow. "Why? What's wrong? Did he hit you?" With a finger under her chin, he lifted her face up to look at him.

"No," she peeped.

"Then what is it? Is it because you're crying? I've seen girls cry before, you know. I'm not proud to admit I've even made a few do it myself."

Amanda laughed a little out of surprise. "I'm gonna put the light on here, okay?" he asked, making her cry even harder. He reached around her and clicked the switch, flooding the room with light. Amanda bent over, covering her eyes with a hand.

Nick pulled her into his chest in a hug, stroking his hand down the back of her neck. She cried on his shoulder, wishing it would just end, wishing she could just get it over with and go home, but not wanting to start it while he held her like this, until Nick got the wrong impression as to why she was crying. "He's just an idiot, kiddo. Don't give him a second thought. You don't want to have anything to do with a guy like that. He's just a stupid kid. Grown men don't skip out on their bill. You'll find yourself someone more mature next time, eh? Tomorrow you call him up and tell him to go fuck himself."

Amanda's voice came out despairing, "That's not it."

"What then? Hm?" He took a step back and lifted her chin again.

Amanda tried to gulp a deep breath in, but she couldn't get enough air. It was coming too shallow. She closed her eyes a second and took a couple steps back from him. He looked at her like he didn't understand. Her eyes welled up again as she rubbed a hand over the dress along her thigh. Nick's eyes looked at the hand, and then the dress, and the recognition crawled across his face.

"I'm really sorry," Amanda said through her tears.

Within a second, Nick's face was white and drawn. He opened his mouth to say something, but didn't. His mouth hung open, useless. He sat down on the couch, facing straight ahead for a long time. Amanda stood where she was, crying, and feeling stupid. She wanted him to say something. She wanted him to tell her to leave so she could get out of there, or to sit down at least, or to take the dress off. There were a dozen ways to feel about this, and a hundred different things to ask of her, and she didn't know what to say to make it better, or what to do, so she just stood, hoping Nick would do something to get her out of the situation.

She must have waited five minutes or more until he asked her, "How long have you had it?"

"Just since yesterday."

"When you were sitting." That didn't sound like a question so she didn't respond. "Did Aaron know you had it?"

"No." She walked to the chair across from him to sit down.

"Not there," he said. "Not where I can see you."

That stung. She had to stifle a sob at the sound of it.

"Sit on the other end of the couch," he said more gently. She came around the coffee table and sat on the couch, carefully, so they were both staring at the closed sheers of the picture window.

"I was just borrowing it," she ventured. "I wasn't stealing it. I don't know why I looked for it. I saw the picture there and she looked so pretty . . ."

Nick took a big loud breath and let it out. "That's our wedding photo."

"I know."

"That's her wedding dress." Nick paused. She could see him remembering all sorts of things, with his eyes distant but racing. "She wanted yellow so she could wear it again. We got married at Niagara Falls. It wasn't a church wedding or anything so it didn't really matter to her. But that was the only time she wore it. She never found a better occasion, she said."

"I'm so sorry," Amanda whispered hoarsely, trying not to cry. It seemed cheap when he was the one who was hurt.

"That's why I still have it. Lue wanted us to bury her in it, but I couldn't. Not knowing she'd said that. *I haven't found a be* —" Nick broke down in tears. They burst out of him for a second, then he pulled himself back up. He sniffed and dried his eyes. "Well. I shouldn't have been keeping that stuff anyway. You want the dress, you can have it. I'll call you a cab, okay?"

Amanda didn't know how to respond. "I can walk," she said timidly.

"I'll call you a cab. It's getting colder. It's fine, you know. It was a stupid thing to do, but I'm trusting you, Amanda."

"I'm sorry. I'm so sorry." She hated herself that she couldn't get her voice to sound as sincere as she meant.

"I was seventeen once too. You learn from your best mistakes, right?"

She shook her head.

"Just do me a favour. If you don't want it, give it away. I don't want it back."

"Okay."

"And I don't want to see you in it . . ." Nick paused again. "You look a lot alike. That sort of scares me."

Amanda didn't know why, but he made her smile. She couldn't help herself. It had to mean something: she may have been fully responsible for herself, in another fight with her stupid boyfriend, but here she was in a grown man's living room and he was frightened by how he felt about her. She had to like that.

అ

She came to Aaron in his dreams, of course. She felt like a small release in his chest, like a muscle relaxing in his heart when he first saw her, but the comfort wouldn't last. Every time, she appeared differently. Once it was a hairpin he'd never seen her wear, sometimes she was holding a baseball bat, and another time a small hammer. The objects would look like they belonged to her, she looked perfectly natural, as if there were a side to her he'd never known and only after her death was he allowed a peek into this world of hers, a world without him. Occasionally there would be a stranger talking animatedly with his mother, which upset him. Or music. A few weeks after her burial, he'd heard a sort of piano tinkling outdoors as his mind watched his mother bend in the garden taking up the weeds. Always, there was this pull between his being comfortable in his skin from seeing her, and then anxiety that she wasn't as he'd remembered.

Aaron woke in the middle of the night with the room cool on his face. He'd been dreaming of her again, this time she was swimming in an in-ground pool. Sitting on a plastic lounge chair a few feet away from the edge, he didn't like how she looked underwater. A phone rang briefly inside the house, but still he didn't want to take his eyes from her. He couldn't fix a hold on her body, slithering and distorted in the water. That's how she seemed to him, distant and unpredictable. When she rose out of the water, she looked right at him. She'd swum from one end of the pool to the other and had him in her sights the minute she pushed her head above the surface. She'd known exactly where he was the whole time. It felt good. And it unnerved him. Though he couldn't say what about it was scary, Aaron's skin crawled.

Under the covers, he was in a damp sweat, too warm. He had to pee. His dad had let him have a second glass of juice before bed and now he regretted it. Was his father in bed? What time was it? His head wasn't clear. His eyes were caked with sleep and his abdomen was really sore with the need for a toilet. Throwing back the covers, he climbed out of bed. 2:01 in the morning on the clock radio. His dad must be in bed by now. The air was so cold compared to the bedcovers. Trundling to the door, he held his arms around his chest to keep warm.

The window in the hall was open, that's why it was cold. He would shut it after he went pee. He walked to the bathroom, peed too carelessly over the edge, then came back down the hall feeling more alert. He thought he heard his father's voice. Was he calling him? Spooked and feeling vulnerable in the hall, Aaron knocked on his father's door. No answer. But he could hear voices. That was his father's voice, he knew it was, though it sounded far away. He knocked again, then turned the handle and peeked in, thinking maybe he could crawl into bed with his dad.

The bed was unmade, but he wasn't in it. Where'd he go? Aaron had a sinking feeling he was alone in the house. There were no lights coming from the living room, so maybe he was in the basement. Maybe his father's voice had drifted up from there. Then he heard again the low sound of him talking. The window was open a crack in there too, so he crossed the room and looked out onto the front yard. There they were, his parents, standing in the driveway. His mother was wearing her wedding dress for some reason.

With a rush of excitement he opened his mouth to shout to her, then, in a beat, his heart dropped. His mother. That wasn't her. She was dead, he was in his father's room, and he was awake. He'd made a mistake. The woman in his driveway laughed and Aaron recognized her as Amanda. She was wearing a yellow dress, talking to his father in the driveway. He felt a mean small feeling in the bottom of his throat. Why was she here in the middle of the night?

A cab turned the corner of his block making the two of them look. Amanda touched the neck of the dress and said something that made his dad smile and nod. When the cab crawled to a stop at the foot of the driveway, she jumped forward and kissed his father on the cheek. But she didn't pull back right away. It was like she was whispering in his ear. Or smelling him. Aaron felt as though he'd been slapped.

Amanda ran for the cab. When she'd climbed inside, his father waved. The car pulled away around the next corner before he turned towards the house and came up the drive. Aaron rushed for his room before his father could hear him out of bed. His face felt hot. He pushed into the cold pillow, though it didn't seem to help. He should have stayed in bed, even if he peed there.

৻৶

Bea cradled Ernest most of the night. He had nightmares. Something was haunting him enough to keep him sweating for hours. She thought of waking him, but hoped if she held him long enough, he'd quiet down. He just needed to be loved. She ran a hand across his forehead wishing it all away. Did he suffer from these often? The possibility that Ernest could have had countless nightmares with no one to comfort him made Bea's heart rush into her throat. She wanted to love him. Hadn't she been wanting all this time for someone to pour herself into?

She felt her breasts pressed against his back. They were warm. Her nipples felt like hot coins. The grey hairs on the back of his neck tickled her chin. That quickly, she was wet. Maybe if she woke him up, they'd hold each other. He'd slide himself inside her. She wanted to feel herself surround him. That was it. That was the same sort of comfort. She wanted to take him inside her and protect him. She wanted to hold his whole body at once.

～

The next morning, Aaron couldn't look his father in the face. He barely stopped to eat breakfast before heading out the door to Fletcher's. He left without saying good-bye. Aaron knew he was early, but didn't care.

Fletcher asked if he wanted to hang out in the fort before they went to school because they had so much time, but the minute he drew the material across the beam, closing them in, Fletcher started bugging him about the magazine, which Aaron refused to read.

"I like it when you read," Fletcher said. "You read better than me. It makes my dink hard."

Aaron laughed, surprised, then stopped himself. Fletcher grinned, showing his chipped tooth, holding the magazine out to him.

"Please," he said. "Just the parts under the pictures."

Aaron shrugged. He took the magazine and opened it up to a bent page. A woman in a tiger print bikini was sitting on a couch with a long gold feather in her hand. She had a green jewel in her belly button. "I don't like the stories."

"You like the pictures?"

"They look funny," Aaron said, setting the magazine beside him.

"Let me see," Fletcher asked, holding his hand out.

Aaron picked the magazine up and put it behind his back. "I don't want to read it."

"You don't have to, I will."

Aaron kept the magazine in his hand behind him. "No, let's do something."

"Give it to me," Fletcher ordered, and Aaron shook his head no.

When Fletcher repeated, "Give it to me," Aaron laid back on the carpet, squashing the magazine underneath him.

Immediately, Fletcher pounced on him, straddling his chest, which made Aaron giggle with nervousness. Aaron's wrists were pinned beneath his legs as Fletcher tickled him. "Get off-ff," he giggled out, choking with laughter. "Don't," he moaned. He could barely catch his breath, making his voice come low and deep out of his throat. He couldn't stop himself from laughing.

Taking a break so Aaron could recuperate a second, Fletcher rested his hands in his lap. "That better?" he asked.

"No. Get off me."

"Are you going to hand it over?"

Aaron shook his head no.

"If you're not gonna hand it over, I'll just keep tickling you." Fletcher wiggled fingers in Aaron's armpits, making him squirm. He tried hard not to laugh, but he was too ticklish. Fletcher's fingers made the feeling bubble up under his skin and spill out of his mouth. His stomach hurt from laughing, with Fletcher on top of him and all the muscles stretched sore. There was an anxious buzz in his belly, being trapped under Fletcher. *That's it*, he thought. Taking as deep a breath as he could muster, he closed his eyes and bit down on his tongue. He wouldn't give in. Fletcher's fingers jiggled away on and around his arms, but he held tight to his breath, keeping the giggling down where it couldn't get out. The fingers felt like worms on his skin. Or little octopus arms tasting him.

When Aaron had to let out his breath, he took another one right after. The fingers wiggled under his chin, then a set on each side crawled around his ears. Then they stopped. He waited to see if it was over. Fletcher was still on top of him. Aaron wouldn't open his eyes until he let him go. If he didn't respond, Fletcher would get bored and climb off.

The band of Aaron's Adidas pants stretched. His stomach seized up and shrank. Two fingers tickled him at his waist. Another finger slipped in briefly, then the whole hand slid down the outside of his leg. Fletcher's fingers tapped against Aaron's thigh one after the other, brushing the tips across his skin. Aaron's eyes burned, he squeezed them so tight.

When the fingers crawled around under the back of his leg and brushed his bum, there wasn't any calling out, there wasn't any chance of that. He was trapped under Fletcher with his heart slapping against his ribcage, making the blood bounce up into his throat in a tough ball. The tingling of his skin made him flush all over. He couldn't help himself. As scared as he was, he didn't want Fletcher to stop. Deep in the middle of his anxiety was something lighter. He was excited. He didn't know what was happening. His body had prickles rising from right down deep inside him and sparkling out through his skin.

This wouldn't be happening if his pants didn't have an elastic band. Aaron lay there long enough, unmoving, to consider that maybe Fletcher was doing this to tell the kids at school later in the day. He could see in his head the boys huddled around Fletcher, laughing with each other about it, or the girls curling up their lips, crying, *That's gross*.

Then, like the day at the tunnels, Fletcher backed off for no apparent reason. He climbed off Aaron and picked up the magazine as though nothing had happened. They were still friends.

"I have to go. We'll be late for school," Aaron said, but couldn't bring himself to look Fletcher in the eyes.

"Sure," Fletcher shrugged, but didn't move.

Aaron walked out of the dark garage, busting into the sunlight where it was safe. His body took a huge breath and let it out slow.

He shook, cold, the whole walk to school, worried that Fletcher might catch up to him. But he didn't. Once Aaron reached the fence for the grounds, he turned around to see if Fletcher was anywhere behind him. He wasn't. Aaron's stomach was a squirming knot of nerves. Maybe Fletcher wouldn't go to school at all today, which meant Aaron would be playing in the school yard alone, and that didn't seem any better.

LATE JUNE

Without a car, Ernest had no way of getting there. Every year, on the anniversary, he went by taxi even though it was twenty bucks or more. And every year the cost went up. The horrible thing was that he knew he couldn't afford it, and he gauged that by how much a two-four cost. The ride was sure to be more this year. So how was he going to get there, except by asking Bea?

He'd spent weeks agonizing over how he'd put it to her, how he'd explain the situation. How to avoid revealing anything at all. If he could, he'd just borrow the car and not say where he was going, though somehow that felt like cheating. Would he lie if she asked? The best solution seemed to be to prepare to tell the truth regardless because he wouldn't want to find himself having to make something up if she did happen to ask. But how would he put it? What could he say that would prompt her to ask fewer questions? Or did he even want her to? Of course he did. He in no way wanted to talk about it. There was nothing he could say that hadn't already been said to Claire. And likewise Bea couldn't offer any advice or support that Claire hadn't already given him, without much success.

Ernest spent the whole day worrying how to approach Bea, until it was the evening and he had no choice but to say something. Making tea, he invited Bea to sit down at the table with him so he could ask her something. He tried not to notice her look of concern as she sat there watching him. He poured them each a cup from the white pot on the table. The cups and saucers were pale blue from a different set; Bea said they were prettier. Coming back to the table, Ernest sat down gingerly. He took a sip of the tea, though it was steaming hot.

There was no simple way to ease into this. He held a breath and let it out slow before beginning. "I want to visit my son."

"Your son?" Bea asked.

"It's his anniversary."

"Your son, Ernest? Who?"

"I need fifty bucks to do it. Maybe more. I'd like to borrow fifty dollars." His voice was shaky and he couldn't get the waver out of it.

"Sure, Ernest," Bea said quickly. "Sure, I'll give it to you." She took his hand and squeezed it between her two palms, which made him notice how wet and thick it was, too heavy for only one hand. "You have to take a bus, do you?" she asked.

Ernest tried clearing his throat. "A taxi."

"Is he in the city, Ernest? I'll drive you. Or you can take the car. Where's he live?"

"Out along the Number Two."

"Well take the car."

"I don't think so, Bea."

She lifted the teacup but didn't take a sip. "What do you mean? Why not?"

Ernest could feel his lip begin to wobble. He didn't want to break down. He took another sip of the tea. It burnt his tongue. "I don't trust myself to go if I have to drive. If I get in the cab, I'll go. I can't do it if I drive." As tears welled in his eyes, Ernest put his free hand to his face. It covered him like a small thick pillow as he cried.

Bea stroked the hand she held. "Don't worry, Ernest. I'll drive you. I'll drive you there. Shh," she said. "Just let me know when, okay?"

This was exactly what he didn't want. He didn't want to break down, he didn't want to make anything seem out of the ordinary. If he could have just let it seem like the most natural thing in the world, and either avoid or refuse to answer questions, then, sure, she'd be curious, but nothing would seem suspect.

"When's his anniversary? When do you have to visit?"

"Tomorrow."

"Sure. We can go tomorrow. I'm not even working tomorrow. I've got the whole day free."

Ernest breathed a huge sigh of relief, trying to show he'd calmed down. At least he was going. If it weren't for Bea, he didn't know where he'd get the money. Pulling himself together as best he could, he nodded. "Thanks, Bea. I'm fine now."

"You sure?" she asked.

Slapping his hands together, he said buoyantly, "Sure. What'll we have for breakfast?"

∽

There was something wrong with a man who didn't want to have sex. Or wouldn't. Wouldn't was more like it. Amanda could maybe understand if he flat-out wasn't interested, but Nick was, she knew he was. He had to be. She was still baby-sitting, which was part of the problem. But it was a sign he wanted her around.

Amanda was doing her toes with nail polish, alternating between dark blue and purple, mulling over what to do. It seemed all so complicated when really it should be simple. He should be asking her over for supper, or to dine out, with Aaron coming along too. Then they'd take a walk in the park where Aaron would run around entertaining himself, maybe a swing on the swingsets, and they'd eventually put the kid to bed and fool around on the living room couch until he'd pick her up and carry her into the bedroom. But there's that damn wedding photo looming on the bedside table, and the whole dress incident weighing on his mind, and hers too. She couldn't stand to see the picture sitting there anymore when she baby-sat and she wished he'd just get rid of it. Why leave out a picture of your happy but dead wife if it's only going to keep you from moving on with your life?

If only he'd see her as more than a baby-sitter, more than a waitress at a crappy restaurant. Amanda pictured herself coming down the aisle in the yellow wedding dress, but that was a bit sick, wasn't it? She imagined them getting engaged, and she'd introduce Nick to Georgie. They'd play pool in the basement, or check out Georgie's weights. They'd drink beer together from his fancy glasses. Her own father would have been a nightmare, but for this, Georgie would come in handy. That's what selling real estate does, it teaches how to impress people.

It wasn't really regret she was feeling, she didn't want to be living in that house under ridiculous new rules. She didn't want to be someone's daughter anymore, but the appeal of that comfort, the look of the lifestyle, the nice house and car, the patio, the dining room set, the large bedroom and the quiet street, she could live with that. Why did she get cheated out of it? It looked so good for her mother, but Amanda couldn't pull it off. So she lost it, which wasn't any big deal considering she never expected to get that sort of money in the first place, though she'd thought of it. Besides, she wouldn't have met Nick had she stayed.

Maybe she should just tell Nick what was going on. If she said she didn't want to look after Aaron anymore, he'd see her as more than a baby-sitter. And if he wanted to see her again, he'd have to call, which would make his intentions clear. That seemed like the smartest answer. If he couldn't bring himself to act on his emotions, then she would have to help him into it.

The telephone rang. Bea and Ernest were still in bed. Amanda was in the living room so the walk to the kitchen table would have been nothing, except she was busy. She wasn't going to hobble over there and risk a smudge to her toenails. After two rings, Ernest ran out of his room without a shirt on and grabbed the phone.

He spotted her sitting on the couch. His face made a curious look, as if he thought she was crazy for not answering it. Well, she didn't want to answer it, and she didn't have to. The machine could pick it up just as easily.

"Hello," he said, rubbing a hand over his belly. "Yeah, this is the right number. Yes, she is." He held out the receiver. "It's for you," he said.

Amanda made a sour face, screwing the lid on the purple polish. She only had a pinkie toe left in blue, having already painted the other ones purple. "Just set it there," she told him as she stood. "You don't have to hold it up." With the spongy comb between her toes to keep them separated, she walked on the heels of her feet to the telephone. "Hell-o?" she sang into the receiver to prevent her voice from sounding frustrated.

"Hi, Amanda," the voice on the other end answered.

For a second she didn't know what to say. All she thought was *Son of a bitch*. Then, finally, her tongue loosened. "Where'd you get this phone number, Estelle?"

"From your work. Janice saw you there last week, but you mustn't have seen her. You didn't say hello."

"I saw her."

Her mother hesitated. "Should I not have called?"

"Depends. What do you want?" she asked coldly.

"It's been a while, so we thought . . . we'd have you over for supper."

"Why?" she asked. When her mother didn't have an answer, she added, "You planning on poisoning me?"

"Oh, come on, Honey. Don't start off on that foot. We're inviting you for supper."

"I'm not hungry."

Her mother let that one go. "Not today. This weekend. We thought you could have Missy too, if that would make you more comfortable. Or Alphie . . ." She was nervous, her voice gave her away when she said his name. "We'd like to get to know him better."

"Then it's too bad I dumped him."

"Oh. You broke up? I-I'm sorry to hear that."

"I bet you are, Estelle. I bet you're crying your heart out."

Her mom gave a quiet, tired sigh. "Listen, Amanda, I don't want to fight. I didn't call for that. I'm inviting you over for supper. Georgie and I both. We're both inviting you. You don't have to answer right away. You can call us up the day before if you want to leave it that long. Just let me know. We'll throw some steaks on the barbecue. I've got them in the freezer already. So just let me know."

Amanda tried, but couldn't bring herself to say no. She wanted to say no or hang up, but couldn't carry through with either.

"So," her mother ventured, "you're doing well?"

"Yeah, I'm peachy, Estelle. Thanks for asking. But I gotta go right now. I got nail polish on my toes."

"What colour?"

"Blue. Blue and purple."

"That sounds cute."

"Thanks. I'll see ya."

"So call me before Sunday," she said quickly.

"Right." There was a pause while Amanda waited for her mother to say the customary *I love you*, but she didn't. "Bye, Estelle," she said.

"Bye bye —"

Then Amanda clicked the connection closed with her finger, just in case. Ernest was in the kitchen behind her, making coffee. As she set the phone in its cradle, he asked, "Problems?"

"Not really. That was my mother."

"You two don't get along."

Amanda was irritated with the obviousness of that, and with the intrusion, but she tried being nice. "You noticed?"

she said jokingly.

His cat came walking through the kitchen, with its tail up, rubbing against everything.

"Hey, Brutus," Ernest said. He measured two scoops of coffee into the filter and held another heaping scoop over the top. "You want some?"

She shook her head.

"She can't be all that bad, you know."

"Well, she is."

"I'm sure she loves you a lot. You have to give your parents credit for that." Ernest turned the tap on hard to fill the pot.

Amanda spoke over top of the noise from the water. "What's that supposed to mean?"

"Anyone who cares is worth the effort. Ain't that right? Otherwise you're putting yourself in the hands of strangers and they don't necessarily give a shit."

"And what would you know about that Ernest? You're not married. I don't see you with any kids."

She waited for a response as he poured the water into the top of the coffee maker and set the lid down, then placed the pot in its holder and clicked the timer switch on.

"I didn't come from no orphanage, for one thing. And I don't know what your situation was like," he said, and his voice grew firmer, "but if they didn't beat you, or molest you, and they didn't lock you in your room every night, then you're doing a lot better than half the kids I grew up with. You gotta be grateful for what you got, and if they love you, well then . . ."

Amanda wanted him to finish his sentence. "What?" she asked, knowing she sounded mouthy.

"If they love you, you're just being selfish asking for more."

Amanda felt awkward at the accusation. He might be right,

but who cares? She didn't want him to have the upper hand, so she giggled as if the idea was funny and he was only being cute.

⌇

The windshield was covered in the grey-green smear of bugs. Bea pressed the button to get the window cleaner to spray, but there was only a dull moan from the motor sucking air. Nothing came out. Then the wipers made three passes, streaking the guts into curved lines.

Bea grimaced and mumbled, "Shit." She looked at Ernest sitting next to her, but he didn't seem to notice. He was looking out the right-hand window instead of watching the road in front. Perhaps he hadn't noticed the wipers start up.

Bea cleared her throat. "Do you mind if we stop up here at the service station? I want to clean these bugs off if I can. It'll just take a minute."

"What?" Ernest snapped alert, but sounded lazy. "Sure, Bea. I'm in no rush." Then he muttered, ". . . not going anywhere."

Bea pulled the car over into the Macmillan's. They were at the parkway in Long Sault, at the intersection. She pulled up to the pumps saying she might as well fill up while she was here.

When the car stopped, Ernest got out.

"It's full service, Ernest," she called after him, but the door closed. A young guy came out of the hutch wiping his hands on his overalls. He nodded at Ernest and continued around the pumps to Bea. In the short time it took for her to roll down her window and tell him to fill it up, Ernest had already picked something up at the store and was paying for it at the cash. The girl in the window smiled at him and spoke, but Bea couldn't see him say anything in response.

A son. So he had a son. Why the hell couldn't he have

mentioned that before? What's the big deal? They mustn't have been on speaking terms or he'd surely have been calling in the last couple months. When Ernest walked out of the door with a bundle of blue carnations in hand, that decided it. They'd been fighting and Ernest was going over to make up.

The gas pump clicked off, the boy put the cap back on and came for the money as Ernest climbed back into the car. Bea could smell the carnations' perfume right away. She paid the guy his twenty bucks, started the car and pulled out onto the highway with Ernest silent the whole time. She figured she should try to comfort him. What could she say unless he told her what was going on? If she assumed the wrong thing, she'd only piss him off with her prying.

She scratched the back of her head with her finger nail, trying not to mess her hair. "Does he like flowers, Ernest?"

"Who?"

"Your son. Did you buy those for him?"

"Yeah. Yeah, I bought them for him." His voice sounded angry, impatient with her, though Bea couldn't think what she'd done to upset him. Maybe he didn't want her to come. Maybe he felt she'd insinuated herself into meeting this son of his he'd kept secret. She wanted to know what this was all about, of course. But if he'd been wanting to keep him a secret, she'd have understood. What could make a son an embarrassment? Why would Ernest insist on visiting him on his anniversary anyway if he didn't seem to have anything to do with him the rest of the year?

They drove the long thin stretch of highway at ninety, ten kilometres above the speed limit. That was both as fast as Bea would speed and as slow as she'd go. They passed the large white farm houses of seventy or more years ago, bought by retired doctors or lawyers, and kept up by them, but with the barns nearly caved in behind them or the land all gone. And they passed the new brick bungalows built by the businessmen in Ottawa, on property sold when the farms went under. Out front on the yards, little ceramic gnomes dug in the garden, the arms of miniature windmills spun or a dark silhouette of a cowboy leaned against a tree with only a bright red bandanna tied about the neck to give him colour.

She passed the Antique Barn where she sometimes went to look at crafts, but still Ernest gave no indication where they were going. When the turn-off for Newington came up, Ernest said to slow down.

"It's up here."

"I have to turn here, Ernest?"

"Yeah," he said curtly. "It's just up here."

Bea signalled right, for the turn-off with the ice cream shop and flea market on the corner.

"Left," Ernest barked.

"The cemetery?" Bea's heart sank. The River Gardens Cemetery entrance began at the other side of the road, where Highway Five ended. It ran along the waterfront, with a painted black iron gate bordering it. In something of a small panic, Bea went right, pulling into the parking lot for the market. She wasn't sure if Ernest meant left or not, if she really was to pull into the cemetery. The car stopped in front of the sign of a large strawberry ice cream cone.

"Left. I said left. Left."

"The cemetery?" Bea asked again. Her eye twitched and fluttered involuntarily for a moment. She felt stupid.

"*Left*, Bea."

"Okay, okay, Sweetie," she said. The car inched out of the

parking lot and onto Highway Five so they faced the iron entrance. Its gates open, the cemetery gave a clear view of the river at the end of the laneway. Bea drove the car across Highway Two and under the ivy metalwork arc at the entrance. Twenty or so feet in, she pulled over to the side and turned off the ignition, leaving the engine to tick for a few minutes from the heat of driving.

Ernest was quiet, his lips puckered out, considering something.

Bea was too self-conscious to move her hands from the steering wheel. She looked at the carnations in Ernest's lap. Some of the outside petals were a very light brown already. They weren't all that fresh. Water had been dripping from the stem bottoms onto his pants without him noticing. There was a wet spot the size of two loonies on his left thigh below the pocket.

"Well," Ernest finally said, opening his car door. "Let's go see the boy."

Fuck, Bea thought. *God-almighty, please let the kid be working here.*

～

Often Aaron would walk down the street on his way home from school and look up at the sky, wondering if he'd see the doors of heaven. Maybe they'd leave them open, just once, forgetting to close them. He still wanted his mother back. He still missed her. How long would he have to wait before he saw her again?

Never seemed impossible. He couldn't get his mind around *never. I'll never see her again.* That didn't seem possible.

The nights he missed her most and cried with the pain of the year before — the last hospital visit, the wake where she looked so plastic — those were the nights she wouldn't show up in his dreams. When he wanted to see her most, when he felt he couldn't stand it anymore, she wouldn't come. Sometimes he lay in bed imagining himself falling out of his bedroom window, or running across the street and getting hit by a car, and his mother would pick him up and take him to her new home.

That was all his own doing. He imagined that. But when he wasn't thinking about her, when he'd had a good day and had gone to bed like he used to and didn't cry himself to sleep or lie awake waiting, she'd slip inside his mind. If he didn't expect her, there she'd be. It made Aaron think that ghosts lived in his dreams. Or that, in dreaming, he went to where ghosts were. He could see them in his sleep. Maybe that's what dreaming was, a world of ghosts.

It occurred to Aaron that maybe he was dying. A new feeling had crept inside his torso and sat there. An extra small organ had hooked on somewhere, another heart. A dark plum pumping in time with his regular beat, spilling out pain instead of health. Could a body grow another organ? Did he have cancer like his mother? She had it spreading inside her without knowing, until it was too late. Aaron had the fear that perhaps his game with Fletcher had caused him to make a cancer. Couldn't that happen? What had made his mother sick? When he thought of the things he and Fletcher had done together, the ache inside him was worse. He felt the small organ grow heavier and give way, pulling down on his heart as it sank.

His whole body responded differently when Fletcher was around. Even alone, when he least expected it, Aaron could taste him on his tongue. He worried that his hands smelled like Fletcher; he walked with them buried deep in his pockets. School was out for the summer and Aaron didn't have other friends in the neighbourhood. The twins in the townhouse across the park behind his house wouldn't bother with him when they were all at the swingsets. It was hard being ignored by the two of them. And that only left the slow kid in the Barn apartments who picked at his butt and let snot run down his face. Fletcher was the only kid from school he could see; Aaron was allowed no more than five blocks from home. If only Fletcher would move away, Aaron wouldn't be at his place, in the cabin, playing their hooter game.

They were lying together in the fort, both of them with their clothes off, with Fletcher's toes placed on Aaron's lips. To play the hooter game, they each took turns making up poses similar to the ones they saw in the magazine. They weren't allowed to refuse a pose, but Aaron had quickly learned that if he was asked to do something unpleasant, Fletcher could be made to do the same thing right after. Because it was Fletcher's game, he always chose first.

Though he thought they couldn't be very clean, Aaron opened his mouth and drew Fletcher's toes inside. His tongue rolled wet under the middle ones. They were candies, salty tasting. *One . . . two.* Aaron counted. They were going to ten. The toes felt spongy in his mouth. Aaron had the urge to chew on them, to bite them and make Fletcher yell. *Three . . . four.* He squinted his eyes open, in slits, to see if Fletcher was leaving his shut, which he was. *Five, six, seven.* With saliva pooling in his mouth, he counted quicker to get to the end. *Eight, nine, ten.*

Aaron took his mouth from around Fletcher's toes and scraped his tongue with his fingers. Fletcher grinned.

"Taste good?" he asked.

Aaron scowled. "My turn to pick," he announced. He knew what pose he wanted to do next.

Holding his heel in his palm, Fletcher grabbed his socks and put one on. "Let's go to the mall," he said.

"I can't go that far," Aaron answered.

"You can if you're with me."

"No, I can't."

"My mom will take us."

Frustrated, Aaron rested a hand on a two-by-four of the wall. He tapped his fingers. "I don't feel like it. Your mother never says yes when you ask."

"Then we'll go alone. Come on."

"My dad won't let me, I know it."

"So don't ask."

Aaron crossed one leg over the other, with his hands in his lap, as he leaned against the plastic camping cooler behind him. "Which mall?"

"Doesn't matter."

"I don't want to cross Westside."

"Then we'll go to the Square." Fletcher looked whiney, as though he hadn't eaten supper and was asking for dessert already.

"Well . . ." Aaron said, hating how Fletcher always cheated on the rules, "I still didn't get my turn. I'll go after that."

"What, then?" Fletcher asked.

Aaron leaned over and looked inside his belly button, pretending there was something he was interested in there. "Mouth on dink," he said, not looking up.

There was a pause. Fletcher picked up a green Bic lighter, thinking it over. "Whose?" he asked.

"Your mouth."

Aaron tried to look bored as Fletcher flicked the lighter on, then turned the knob to lengthen the flame. He placed a sliver of wood in the inch of fire. It curled back on itself, burning up. "I don't really want to go to the mall," Fletcher said.

Aaron shrugged. "Me neither. But it's still my turn."

Setting the Bic down, Fletcher patted his pockets. "You got the pen?" When Aaron handed it over, Fletcher wrote on the wall in thick lines: Mike is cool. He tossed the pen to Aaron, saying, "Thanks."

As Aaron put it back in his pocket, Fletcher added, "You gotta go home now. I've got chores."

Aaron knew Fletcher didn't have to go in. "It's my turn first next time," he said, provoking him, but Fletcher only shrugged. "You have to do what I say, that's the rules. I'm going to pick that first next time."

"So?"

"So, you'll have to do it." Aaron knew Fletcher was thinking it over because he wasn't putting his clothes on. He waited him out.

After stretching his arms, Fletcher said, "Fine. But I can pick that too, you know."

That didn't bother Aaron. This could be the last of it, the last time he and Fletcher would play the game. Aaron wouldn't have to give him a turn again, ever. If he *was* giving himself cancer, Aaron thought, he could make it stop. "Okay," he answered.

"Lay down," Fletcher said. "And you have to close your eyes. And count out loud."

Stretching himself across the carpet, Aaron closed his eyes and waited. Fletcher bent over him; Aaron could feel him there. He could hear Fletcher's breathing, and then his mouth closed around him.

"One . . . two," Aaron counted aloud. The sound of his own

voice in the small cabin was embarrassing. Aaron could feel his whole body at once: the carpet against his skin, the scratching bits from wood or dirt poking into his back, and Fletcher's breath warm on his stomach, his mouth warmer.

"Three," he continued, unsure if he could really make them stop. He knew what Fletcher was like. He wouldn't quit that easy. If Aaron could hurt him, maybe he'd give up. Maybe Aaron could scare him into stopping. But what could he do to a boy a whole grade bigger than him?

If he pissed, Aaron thought, in Fletcher's mouth, that would get rid of him for good. Maybe it would poison him. It would be the end of the game anyhow. Though scared at the idea, with everything he had in him, Aaron tried to pee. He bore down and tried to push the pee out. He thought of the toilet flushing, and of water running in the sink, but couldn't get his bladder to give way. If only he'd drank more juice before he came. *Pee*, he urged himself on the count of seven, *come onnn.*

No go. He hit nine, then ten, and Fletcher got off him. It was over. Too late.

"You next," Fletcher said.

"No," Aaron retorted, "that was the last turn today. You said."

"One more."

Aaron shook his head, grabbing his underwear and putting it on. "I gotta go."

Fletcher didn't say anything in response, but after Aaron got his pants and shirt on, Fletcher held up Aaron's socks.

"Give them."

Fletcher looked very pleased with himself. He knew Aaron could try to wrestle them away, but wouldn't win.

"I'll leave without them."

"What will your dad say?"

"He won't notice."

"Yes, he will. You left with socks on."

Aaron grew mouthier with impatience. "Then I'll tell him I took them off."

"But why would you do that?"

"Because I wanted to."

"One more turn," he said.

"You started so I go last. If you go again, I get to too."

Fletcher shrugged. "Sure."

Aaron put his hands out to get the socks back and Fletcher handed them over. Once Aaron had them on, he jumped up, saying, "I don't want another turn. I'm late."

"You just promised," Fletcher complained.

"No, I didn't."

"You just said we'd have another turn."

Aaron scowled to say Fletcher was really stupid. "*No*. I said I'd have another one if you did, but I don't want one. So you can't either."

Fletcher offered to steal pens for him from the drug store in the mall, then threatened not to come by, which Aaron didn't blink at, and which set Fletcher more out of sorts. He was still naked in the fort, holding his underwear as if he couldn't believe Aaron was actually leaving, until he almost sounded sad saying he didn't want him to go yet and Aaron answered, "Tough shit," and took off.

༺༽

The sun beamed down, glaring off the water, making the air dry with dust from the highway. The exposed skin on Bea's lower arms prickled. The top of her head heated up too. And with the lilacs in full bloom, things smelled sweet. Hot, sticky and sweet.

Bea could feel herself perspiring inside her blouse.

Ernest led the way down the path that headed to the river. The grass was a light green, different from the lawns in the city. When Ernest turned right, cutting between gravestones, Bea followed, reluctant to step across the rectangles of land where the bodies were buried. She obeyed the grid system, and left Ernest to speed along ahead, stepping across the other graves.

They walked a fair piece, about forty or so gravestones from the path, to where the ground was neither as flat nor the grass as nice and full. There was more clover, and the occasional dandelion.

Ernest stopped at a small grey tombstone and stood staring. When Bea came up to the plot, she stood a pace behind him, not really wanting to look, but she had to know for sure. Below the image of a small lamb read: *Kelly Mackey, 1966-1972. Gone too soon. Much loved.*

Ernest ran a hand along the top of the stone. "Hey there, buddy," he half-whispered. The back of his shirt was wrinkled from the drive. Two flies landed just below his shoulder blade. Bea got close enough to wave them off, but one only landed elsewhere on Ernest and the other settled on her forehead for a second. She really didn't feel well. Her stomach was turning. She blinked, looking at the river with sunlight playing off its waves.

With Ernest not saying anything, she waited as long as she could. "I'll be over in the shade, okay?"

Without looking at her, he nodded.

As she walked to the edge of the lawn, Bea's head pounded with the heat. Luckily the other side of the fence was lined with trees so Bea could stand in the shade of a large pine.

There was no breeze to speak of, making the air cry with the high buzzing of the cicadas. The trees were electric, humming like power lines. Bea felt as though the buzzing was inside her head. Squatting, she put one hand to her forehead and another to her mouth. "Oh, fuck," she mumbled. How could she be sick here, and why now? Her stomach gave a turn, but she held it down. As cool perspiration beaded on her brow, her blood moved in warm waves through her body. One more rise in her belly came up too high for her to hold it. With a hand on the fence to steady herself, she vomited into the grass.

Though it made her cough, she felt better immediately. Her body was cooler, her stomach tight but more settled.

Relaxing her shoulders and leaning against the fence post, she saw Ernest walking towards her. Opening her purse, she quickly dug for a Kleenex to wipe her mouth before he got there. She pulled out a tissue and a stick of gum, stood, took a few paces without looking back, trying to seem as if nothing had happened. He must have seen, but Bea thought if he didn't address it, she could pretend everything was normal.

When Ernest took her arm, she felt how sweaty she'd become. She wiped her free hand on her skirt.

"You get sun stroke, Bea?" He looked concerned, partly from the drawn expression of his own crying.

She nodded. "Oh, I'm fine. The heat was just a bit too much and it caught up to me."

"I'll take you home." He held his hands out for the keys. Bea placed them in his palm, saying, "Thanks, Ernest," noticing how burnt her throat felt, and the roughness that lent to her voice.

They were silent the drive back. It seemed Ernest wanted to be left to his own thoughts just as much as Bea, though she was curious to ask him questions and didn't know how. When he pulled into the parking lot of the apartment, he offered to buy her Pepto Bismal at the pharmacy. Bea thanked him and opened the car door. She was reluctant to kiss him given the state of her breath, so opted for a kiss on the cheek and a squeeze of his hand. Some contact seemed necessary.

Walking up the steps, with the car pulling onto the road, she felt a great relief to be alone. She took a deep breath. Her stomach was nothing but acid and gas. It was only eleven o'clock in the morning and she already felt exhausted from the day. She planned to brush her teeth and hair, then take a nap after Ernest got back if he didn't look like he wanted to talk, though she hoped he would. Things were getting complicated and she felt too overcome to do much about them.

All evening, Ernest felt he wanted to break everything in the house. He wanted to smash things, slam a fist into the wall until the wood gave or his bones broke. The small black feeling climbed up out of the ditch in the back of his mind and rooted in his heart. He struggled to breathe. Ernest wanted to kill someone for the injustices. He wanted to kill someone to quit the feeling of being useless.

He would go to the park and get blown by the men he found there. He would have sex with the men he couldn't be, step out of his weak untruth, and embrace the ridiculous feeling he buried. He would admit his failures, face his hopelessness, embrace the weakness he needed and couldn't seem to live without. And for however long it lasted and some hours later, he would care less.

Living was brief, but sweet, when he faced himself.

To hell with his responsibility to Bea. They weren't married.

He *had* a wife, and she left him. He had a kid who was dead. Ernest felt a responsibility only for people who weren't in his life anymore, so he had none to speak of. Bea didn't love him. She needed someone. Any man could give her what she wanted. She needed to be useful and sometimes appreciated. Ernest was lonelier than that. Ernest had a darker life hunting him down these last thirty years. What did Bea know about his suffering? What did she know about being needed? What did she know about love?

Ernest looked around the bedroom. *What the fuck am I doing here?* he asked himself. *Why the fuck am I bothering?* Tonight, he had nothing left in the world. His sisters hadn't spoken to him in years and his own parents were long dead. There wasn't a soul in the world to love him. Nick and Figgy were the closest thing he had to people who cared about him, but they had their own families. And Figgy wasn't even part of the picture; he was in Brockville now. If Ernest didn't show in the bar for a few weeks, Nick would find someone else to sit in his spot. He'd forget about him after a few months. Would anyone even come looking if he never went back to the bar again?

In the hall, he grabbed up his jacket and the car keys from Bea's coat pocket. "I'm going for a drive," he said. Bea looked up from her book. She looked very tired.

"Sure," she said. "I'll probably be in bed when you get back."

Ernest could only bring himself to nod. It wasn't smart to be so curt, but he couldn't help himself. *Tough shit*, he thought. *Tough fucking shit.* He charged down the hall, leaving the apartment door to swing shut behind him.

৩

Aaron heard a stone hit the side of the house before a second hit the window and it was clear what was happening. He padded across the cool floorboards. He couldn't see anything at first through the window — nothing down in the yard, a car pulling into the Anderson's across the street — but then a bobbing head below caught his eye. Fletcher was shimmying up the ironwork of the front porch. Aaron hoped no one saw him. What if Mr. Anderson looked over and came to the house? Or what if he called the police? Fletcher's hands gripped the windowsill. His forehead was sweaty but he was grinning. When Aaron didn't make a move, Fletcher bugged out his eyes with impatience and motioned to open the window. Aaron looked to the closed door of his room. Amanda was still downstairs watching a movie. Unhitching the latch, he slid the window open, letting the heavy smell of the lilac bushes into the room.

"The screen, the screen too," Fletcher said.

"I don't know how to open it."

"Just slide it back."

The screen stuck at first, but with Fletcher giving it an extra push from his side, the frame let go and banged open. Aaron's heart jumped at the thump. "Wait," he hissed, but Fletcher was eager to get inside. He threw an arm around the window and kicked his outer leg over the sill, pulling himself in. Aaron backed up and suddenly realized he was in his pjs and felt awkward with Fletcher in pants and a sweatshirt. It was cool out now that the sun had gone down. The breeze from the window was cool wrapping around his ankles and climbing up his legs. Fletcher slid the screen closed but left the window open. He looked at Aaron, proud of himself.

"What are you doing here?"

Fletcher shrugged. "Visiting."

"My baby-sitter's here. I'm gonna get in trouble."

"She won't find out."

"Maybe she heard."

"If she comes up, I'll hide. She won't find me."

Aaron didn't know how to get out of this. He was all hyped up and nervous, but trying not to let Fletcher know. "What are we supposed to do? We can't play cards. I can't turn a light on."

"We'll play *our* game."

"What?" he said, as if he didn't understand.

"You know." Fletcher walked over to the bed and sat down. The messed up sheets made Aaron embarrassed. He wished they were all made neatly like in the morning. He couldn't make out the features of Fletcher's face in the dark, which helped.

"We can't," he said.

"Sure we can."

"But," Aaron's voice wasn't as confident as he wanted it to be, "we're not in the fort. We have to be in the fort to play."

"No, we don't."

"That's the rules."

Fletcher grinned in the dark, briefly, making the whites of his teeth flash. "Who said that rule? We never made that rule."

But that wasn't true. It *was* a rule. They'd never done anything outside of the fort, never even mentioned it. "You've got to leave."

"Uh-uh." Fletcher shook his head. "Can't, unless I go out the front door."

"No!" Aaron said, a little louder than he should have.

"Can't leave until we play. I can't climb down the porch if we don't. That's a rule too. No climbing."

"Well . . ." Aaron said, stalling. He didn't know how to

answer that. "Well . . . we're going to wait a long time then," and he sat down on the floor.

Fletcher didn't respond right away, maybe he was thinking it over, or maybe he just didn't care to answer, but then he stretched himself out on the bed saying, "Okay," and lay down. Aaron wished he'd take his shoes off, he didn't like the gritty feel of dirt in the sheets. It was late. When would his dad come home? What if he came back and saw Fletcher as he was crawling out the window? Maybe he'd have to wait until his dad came home to get him out, just in case, though he didn't want Fletcher still in the house either.

The cancer-feeling in Aaron's chest pulled downwards, as if it might tumble into his belly. "You'll leave right after?" he asked.

"Yup."

Aaron got up, standing beside the bed. "Swear?"

"Swear," said Fletcher, already pulling his sweatshirt over his head.

As soon as the door shut, Bea rested the book in her lap. She set her head back on the arm of the couch and closed her eyes. There was too much tension in the apartment. She was glad he was gone. There had to be something she could say or do to make him feel better, but she couldn't bring herself to figure it out. If she didn't feel so damn worried herself, she'd know what needed to be done. Bea was exhausted. She still felt queasy. She needed time to think.

There was a lot she could live with. She had the sort of practical mind that knew enough to avoid a whole lot of shit, and how to do that, or to be able to recognize and deal with the set of problems she got herself into. And because she was practical this way, she more or less chose her problems. There wasn't much that snuck up on her.

Ernest she loved because he was the lesser of two evils. Once over forty, she'd come to think it was better to be with a man who made her feel pretty and wanted, who may not be *in* love with her, but who loved her because he needed to, whose hands were more gentle in private than he'd ever care to admit in public, who talked less and thought more, who listened, than to sit in front of a television with the lights turned down, reading a book at commercials to keep herself from noticing how quiet the room was.

She wasn't cold to the situation. She loved Ernest, the longer she was with him, but having been burnt often enough, she learned to ask herself a few questions. Bea had kept herself afloat by figuring stuff out. She had had her troubles with men and learned to ask, *Am I really better off in this relationship than going it on my own? Why am I doing this? Is it good? Is it better than last time?*

After so many years alone, where she figured things out enough to know what her basic options were and at what cost, Bea knew she found it easier to struggle with caring for someone than to cope with having no one at all. Ernest had done well by her in the past few months, and having weighed the pluses against his minuses, she had come to the solid conclusion she was happy with him. Nearly two months he'd been living with her, and it had been two good months.

A week ago, she had had no reason for questioning further where it was going, or how well, or to what purpose, because she was content. She'd wanted something and she'd gotten it at a cost she was aware of from the start. Yes, she knew he drank too much, that he was older by a decade, and that he was unemployed. She knew he had a failed marriage and no contact to speak of with his sisters and their families.

Bea let out a huge sigh. But this kid. There was no way she could ignore a gravestone.

This afternoon, he came back from the store and didn't say a word about it. It was clear the way he carried himself that he wanted to be left alone with this. He was bright and cheery when he came in. Bea asked if he was all right and he looked surprised, said he was great, like anything other was unthinkable.

It was like the day never happened: they hadn't climbed in the car and driven to a graveyard, for God's sake. He hadn't revealed a son he never talked about and he hadn't stood over the grave.

Sure, he might not have wanted to talk about it, but he owed her something of an explanation, didn't he? He'd brought her there. She knew now. The old woman at the bar some months back must have known too, and that's what she'd been talking about. *If you're sleeping with Ernest Mackey, I hope to God you don't have kids.* Maybe Bea could ask her, if she came in again. But no, not really, that wouldn't be fair. Except Ernest wasn't being fair either.

Dammit, she didn't need this, not now, not feeling the way she was, not with her own worries.

༄

There wasn't much on TV. Amanda was sick of the bad movies where everyone cries and hugs each other at the end and she didn't want to watch the rerun sitcoms. Even Much Music had some lame sixties show replay with a stupid plot and bad hair. Maybe Missy was home. She called her and thank God Missy picked up.

"What are you doing?" she asked.

"Nothing."

"Come over."

"Nnnn, I don't feel like it," Missy said, sounding tired.

"I'm baby-sitting, Missy. I'm bored."

"But it's so far for me. And it's already past ten o'clock." Her voice was whiney, which drove Amanda nuts.

"I'd go see you if you called me."

"No you wouldn't. You can't drive."

"But if I could, I would. You know that."

"No, Amanda, I don't want to go out. I'm tired. I'm going to get up tomorrow and go to the flea market in Pointe Claire. I gotta be up early."

"So stay at my house tonight and leave from there. I'll go with you."

"I'm going with my mother and my aunt."

Amanda turned the television off with a click of the remote. "Well, do you want to spend a Saturday night on the shithole island? Or in the city?"

"As if there's much difference."

"Sometimes you really piss —" Amanda stopped. There was a noise upstairs. Like someone in shoes.

"What?" Missy asked. "What were you going to say?"

"Shh," Amanda hissed into the phone. "Someone's here."

"Who's th —"

"— Shh."

The footsteps stopped. She could hear a few cars up and down Johnson Street, the clock ticking from the back room, and Missy sighing through the receiver, but nothing upstairs. "I think someone's in the house," she whispered.

"Who?"

"I don't know."

"Maybe Nick's home."

"No, it's upstairs, idiot."

"Well how was I supposed to know? You're always bitching at me for things I can't do nothing about."

"Shut up," she hissed. "I gotta listen."

There was another long pause while Amanda strained to hear the faintest sound, then she heard a *thunk* — a clear *thunk* — unmistakable. "Oh, fuck. Someone's in the house. Get over here. *Right now.*"

"You sure it isn't just the kid?"

"He's asleep. He's always out like a light."

"Call the police."

"Well if it isn't someone I'm going to look pretty stupid, aren't I?"

"You'll look pretty stupid chopped into pieces too. Call the police."

"Maybe it's Aaron. I'm going to look. Stay on the phone. If you hear me scream, hang up and call 911, okay?"

"Amanda, I'm going to call them right now."

"No!" she said as emphatically as she could while keeping her voice down. "Stay on the phone. Don't leave me alone. Okay? I'm putting the receiver down. If you're not there when I'm being killed I'll never forgive you. Okay? I'm putting the receiver down."

"Okay. But be careful. Bring a knife."

Amanda set the phone down and tiptoed into the kitchen. Taking a long knife from the drying rack, she held her breath and moved to the stairs. Thank God they left a light on in the hall. Maybe it *was* Aaron, though that seemed unlikely. What shoes would he have on? His runners were by the front door. Jesus, don't let anything bad happen to the kid.

At the top of the stairs, she expected anything to happen. The doors were closed to all the bedrooms. Only the bathroom door was open. She peeked in there. Shower curtain pulled back already so that was one nightmare avoided. Was Missy still on the line? Would she even hear if Amanda did scream from the second level? It seemed so far away.

And then voices from Aaron's room. The knife was sweaty in her grip. She snuck down the hall, following as close to the wall as possible to avoid creaking the floorboards. There was definitely talking coming from behind the door, and it sounded like kids. Just in case, Amanda held her arm at her side, with the knife behind her leg. She didn't want to scare Aaron if it was only him talking to himself, but she could use the element of surprise if it was some pervert or thief.

With her hand at the door handle, she took a deep breath to steady herself. Then twisted, and swung the door open.

The lights were off in the room, but the hall light threw enough inside to make out Aaron and some other kid on the bed, both stripped naked, their arms and legs all tangled together.

"What the hell are you doing?" Amanda asked, flicking on the overhead bulb.

Aaron's face had frozen up with fear, clearly terrified, whereas the other kid got busy climbing into his clothes. It was a boy. A voice clicked on in her head not to overreact. Really she wanted to scream at the kid to get the hell out, get the fuck out of the house. She could have smacked him the whole way there and thrown him out the window for fun. It took everything in her to hold back. *What would Oprah do?* That was the only thing keeping her cool, was wondering how Oprah would handle it, for Aaron's sake, she didn't want to cause any more damage. How did the kid get inside? The window?

She asked him, "What's your name?" but the kid didn't answer. "What's his name?" she asked again, turning to Aaron.

"Fletcher," Aaron said. She could see in his face he was terrified.

"Fletcher, put your clothes on and go out the front door," she ordered, pointing down the hall with the knife. Oh, fuck, she still had the knife. She put her arm down and tried to hide it again behind her.

"We weren't doing nuthin' wrong," Fletcher said belligerently, like he'd been judged unfairly. "We were just going to sleep. We weren't doing *nuthin'*."

"Good for you. Now get out. It's the middle of the night. It's late. You're not allowed here at *midnight*, genius, so don't tell me you weren't doing something wrong."

The kid pulled his sweatshirt over his head and reached for his shoes off the floor. He either didn't have socks or was leaving them, because he put the shoes on and stood.

"Now get out," she said.

"You have to move."

She was in the doorway, with the knife. It was no wonder she was intimidating. She stepped into the room and cleared a path for him to pass. Aaron was still in the bed, under the covers, looking pretty blank and pale. "You stay there," she said to him. "Put your pjs on."

Fletcher took his sweet time going down the hall and then the stairs. Amanda felt like kicking him in the ass, but tried hard to keep her cool. When he reached the bottom of the staircase, he sauntered into the living room and looked around.

"The door," she said firmly. "There's the door. Use it."

"I'm just looking," he said, mouthy.

"You won't be looking long if I pull the eyeballs out of your head, now move."

Finally, he went to the door and stepped out onto the front porch. When the outside door closed, he turned to face her. "You're not the boss of me," he said. Then he spit a big gob on the glass and grinned. Amanda slammed the inside door shut and locked it. She was a little spooked, as much by her own hardness as the kid's. She could feel her arms and legs shaking. Immediately she thought, What was she going to do about Aaron? Tell Nick? What would he do? Or should she have a talk with him herself?

In a flash it occurred to her that she'd done as much with boys when she was growing up. Her mother caught her once and they'd had an ugly fight. How old was she then? Ten? Something like that. Now with the shoe on the other foot, Amanda got an insight into what her mother must have gone through with her. What did she do? She grounded her for a few days. And had a talk. But that was all very different. She couldn't ground Aaron. And she didn't know how she'd tell Nick. And this was two boys, which made it a whole other story. Maybe Missy would know what to do.

Missy. She'd forgotten about the phone. She raced to the receiver and called, "Miss?"

"Where the hell were you? I was just about to hang up."

"Yeah, I gotta go."

"Are you okay?"

"I'm fine."

"What the hell —"

"— I'm fine, I'm fine, I'm fine," she said hurriedly. "But I gotta go."

"Well, call me back."

"Right. I'll call you later."

"There isn't someone holding a knife to your throat?"

Amanda looked at the kitchen knife still in her hand and set it on the coffee table. "No. Okay?"

"Okay," Missy said, sounding exasperated. The line went click. Amanda took a deep breath and thought, *Who the fuck knows what to do*, but headed up to Aaron's room all the same. She had to try something, didn't she?

∽

This time he had the car.

Two months he'd stayed away from the park, two easy simple months of sex with Bea. But tonight he couldn't stand the thought of climbing under the covers with her and having everything seem normal. He'd gone to the cemetery and faced again everything he'd lost; he'd done so each and every year since they'd buried Kelly. He was a hopeless man, he felt it in his blood, everything running through him was cold and thin, in his arms and his joints, his bones and eyes. He itched, sitting or standing, to escape himself, to tear out of his skin and be something better. He was and would be forever a hopeless man. What else could he find as a distraction from the great aching loss of the life he ruined? His boy was dead. Twenty-eight years he was dead and Ernest still waited for redemption, for an understanding of what it was that had happened to him.

Though each year it lasted for a shorter time, and was more tolerable because he recognized it and could see it coming and knew it would eventually pass again and leave him dumb and in some kind of peace, there was a panic that seized Ernest. He once dreamt a long black spider crawled inside his chest through his belly button and wrapped its hairy legs tightly around his heart. He had woken with a start, sweating, nauseous, and profoundly restless. That was the panic, made tangible. That was what he faced every year, regardless of the precautions he took, his resolve, his dread, and his drinking. Twice he had made calculated trips out of town as the day approached only to rush back early on the anniversary to visit him. The anniversary was unavoidable. When a psychiatrist, on Ernest's first visit, suggested he would have to move on with his life, Ernest had jumped across the desk, grabbed the man by the throat and threatened him. He wouldn't forget, he said, and the psychiatrist couldn't make him forget. No man had the right to ask him to do that. And though really he knew the therapist hadn't suggested any such thing, just the hint of it had set Ernest off. Therapy wasn't for him. What could someone tell him that he didn't already know? What could they say that would change what had happened? Could they bring him back his son? Or his wife? The thought of needing help sickened Ernest. His feelings about the past didn't need fixing. His past did.

The closer he got to the park, the more he relaxed. He wanted sex again, with a man. Of all the bodies he'd seen parading past him in the park under the dim light of the moon, only two had ever taken their shirts off, as if the others were modest, despite having their cocks in hand and their testicles hanging wrinkled below them. So much attention was paid to their genitals, Ernest forgot the touch of a hand on his skin. This is how Bea surprised him, what made sex with her so good. He didn't just have to enter her for pleasure; he could be touched. Her fingers were so simple. His back would light up at the long lines of her digits. Between each warm finger, the space was cooler than air. He might not have wanted her so much had he any sort of intimacy from the men. With Bea there was a great deal of affection — a generosity in her skin — which affirmed Ernest, which made him recognize he was whole and real.

The closer he got to the river, the more he settled into being eager. He was closer to something true, closer to the loss and pain of being a man who's made himself hungry by his own undoing. His life with Bea wasn't so bad, he reasoned, but he needed this too. There was something here he couldn't figure out, but when he did, he'd be satisfied and stop altogether.

The spotlight on the old RCAF plane was burnt out, making the propped-up shell look even more like a ghost ship in the night. One half was lit a milky silver and the other was but a dark empty shadow, with the cockpit a glowing bubble of glass. Ernest drove further, turning at the entrance to the marina. There were no cars in the lot on the left, or ahead of him, but when he passed the arena, he could see a four-door Sunfire parked in the far corner. A figure sat in the driver's seat, the car backed in to face the river.

Signaling, Ernest turned right, the click of the blinker light making him feel ridiculous. He edged the car towards the Sunfire and pulled up along its driver's side. Though it was nighttime, and light came only from the half-moon somewhere behind the clouds, the man in the car opposite held open a magazine at the steering wheel.

Ernest waited what must have been a minute. The man didn't look up, didn't take his eyes from the magazine, nor turn a page.

He was somewhere around forty. He could have been younger and looking mature for his age, but something about the way he carried himself made Ernest think he was likely older than he seemed. He had salt-and-pepper hair, still more black than grey, and a trim beard. Ernest's mouth felt very dry. He was restless in the seat with his hands held slippery at the bottom of the steering wheel. His cock was half-hard, pressed down the side of his leg, and his heart raced and throbbed in an exaggerated way.

He was sober. This was the first time he had sat in the park with his full faculties. He was feeling a wreck, but excited, and getting more so all the time.

Finally, the man folded his magazine. He gave a small practiced stretch and looked Ernest's way. With a slight smile, he nodded, looked away, then looked back again. Ernest hadn't moved a muscle, but his hand gave a sudden twitch, so he grabbed the handle for the window to give it something to do.

He waited as his breath pooled against the window and disappeared. Ernest wanted the guy to roll his window down first, but the man set the magazine on the dash, placed his hand on the steering wheel and clicked his keys in the ignition. Ernest's heart dropped, thinking he was leaving, but the engine didn't turn over. The window slid down. Electric. Quickly Ernest wiped his hands dry on his jeans and rolled his window down too, faster than he'd intended.

"Nice night," the man said, leaning out the window slightly, which allowed light to fall across his face. Ernest couldn't help thinking that the man, though greyer, looked like Nick.

Ernest hoped his voice was steady as he answered, "Yeah." He cleared his throat. For a long time they sat there, Ernest occasionally glancing up from the damp grey pavement to catch the other man's eyes. The guy seemed much more comfortable with the silence than Ernest did.

"I don't do this very much," Ernest said.

The man raised his eyebrows in surprise. "No?" he asked.

"No."

"I could have sworn I saw you before, but you don't normally drive."

"Oh, well, I've been here before, but not often."

The man looked at his hand on the steering wheel, taking a second to consider, then faced him directly. "You don't have to be embarrassed. Everyone who comes down here a few times gets known. I've got a reputation as much as you."

"What do you mean?"

"You don't like to talk. You don't go home with anyone. You like to drink or you only come when you have. And you don't kiss."

Ernest's head swam. How could a stranger know this about him? Maybe the guy and he had done it before; Ernest tried to provoke him into saying as much. "I don't know anyone here. None of these guys knows who I am."

"But you've been here before, right? You can't come down here every other night and not get to recognizing the people."

Ernest knew that for himself. Every guy has his pattern, the man said. Some just watch. Some only do stuff in groups, some won't at all. There's a big guy who only walks by once or twice before heading home so he learned to catch him on the first pass because he wouldn't be back. And he remembered who did what, which saved a lot of time if he was looking for something in particular. More important, if there was something he wanted to avoid.

"Does that make you nervous?" the guy asked.

"What?" Ernest countered, trying to keep his cool and sound aloof.

"That I've seen you before. I don't kiss and tell, if that's what you're afraid of. A man has a right to his privacy. I got family too, you know. I don't want anyone knowing my business either. Okay?"

Ernest took a breath. "Right." He was squeezing his cock, precum wet against his leg.

The guy sniffed. "I was beginning to lose hope tonight with the selection down here. There's only the real regulars, and the worst of them at that." He leaned a little further out his window and lowered his voice. "Me, I don't like to fuck. That's why I was glad to see you. This Dave character, he was chatting me up earlier, he's still down there, I guess," he pointed towards the marina, "but I got sick of him pressuring me to bend over. 'Good riddance,' I said. And I counted on someone else coming along and here you are. What's your name?"

In a brief, nervous panic, Ernest blurted out, "Nick."

"Nick," the man echoed, "pleased to meet you. I'm Todd." He stretched a thick full arm out the window and shook with a tight grip. Ernest hoped his palm wasn't still sweaty; he forgot to wipe it first. The guy held on a second longer than Ernest, smiling out the window of his car. His hand was warm. A silver ring on the first finger. *Yes*, Ernest thought to himself, *I'll do this*.

What Bea needed most right now was time to herself. Or time away from Ernest. She briefly considered confiding in Amanda but reasoned that it wasn't smart to tell anyone right now until she was sure what was going on. If only the horrible feeling would go away. Maybe fresh air would help. It wasn't so late that she couldn't step out for a walk. The nights were plenty warm enough lately. The air would do her good.

Bea grabbed a light coat out of the closet. She wrote a quick note on the message board on the fridge, *Gone out*, then wiped it off. It would be obvious that she wasn't home, and since she didn't know where to say she'd gone, there was no point leaving anything.

The minute she stepped outside, her lungs took in a deep breath and her whole body relaxed some. She walked towards the river, down Augustus Street, until she hit her favourite house with the large stone walls and the big round porch that swept mid-way in the front to right around its side. She didn't know how old the place was, but imagined it had to be a hundred years or more. Often she drove by and wondered who lived in the house, but she'd never seen anyone out front. There was a light on in the upper window on the left. Someone was in their bedroom. Reading, probably. That's what Bea would be doing if she had a place like that. She'd read every romance in the library and never work again.

Turning the corner, a car caught her in its headlights. Bea carried on, walking up the road, so that she wouldn't look suspicious. Briefly, she considered going to the park by the river to watch the moon on the water like she used to with boys when she was a teenager, but alone, at her age, that only seemed depressing. She turned east up Second Street to get away from the smell of the papermill and walked for the better part of an hour, rolling over in her head what she was going to do.

When she arrived at the Zeller's mall in the east end, it occurred to her that she was nearly parallel with her work, four blocks north. She could feel the fatigue in her legs. Maybe Ernest was in the bar and they could drive home together. After the day they'd had today, he may have had one too many. He'd need her to drive. It seemed obvious to Bea, suddenly, that Ernest would be at the bar. Where else would he go to unwind?

Bea walked across the parking lot to the pay phone in the small lobby of the Tim Horton's. Dropping a quarter in the machine, she dialed Malouf's, then pushed the volume control up, holding the receiver out from her ear. Hank answered.

"Hi, Hank."

"Bea? Hey, cutie, how are ya? Why are you calling?"

"I thought maybe Ernest was there."

"Nope, haven't seen him," Hank said. "You guys have a fight?"

"No no, I'm just out for a walk and I got tired. He's not home yet," she said, realizing that she should have called the apartment first, "so I thought I'd try him there."

"Nick's here, if you want to talk to him. Maybe he'll give you a lift."

"Nick?" she said. "Hm. Tell him I'm on my way. I'm just around the corner."

Heading towards the bar, with the moon sliced into a bright thin line over the town, Bea felt more relaxed. She was tired enough to unwind. Everything would work itself out.

She came into the bar, blew Hank a kiss, waved to Theresa, and sat down with Nick who was in the front window, oddly, instead of in his usual place at the bar. He wasn't drunk, but Bea could see it in his face that he was morose. He looked drained, with more lines on his face than usual.

"Hey Bea, you're not who I was expecting."

"You got a hot date, Nick?" she teased, hoping to perk him up.

"I thought Ernest might be here, but whatever. Where'd he get to?"

"Not sure," Bea said. She didn't know how much she should tell him. "He's going through a rough time this week."

"Being out of work pretty much sucks the life out of you."

"He'll figure something out," Bea said, thankful Nick made up his own reason. "I need to keep him busier, I guess, to get his mind off things."

"I hear ya," Nick said. "I need to get out of the house for a while too. I was thinking of taking a couple days off work and bringing the kid for a long weekend."

That explains the look in his face, Bea thought. He's missing his wife. Why didn't he sell the house and get out of there?

"Hey, Bea," Nick said, leaning a little over the table. "Do you and Ernest like camping? That'd keep you guys busy. Why don't you come with us?"

What would be better, Bea thought, *than to get Ernest away for a couple of days?*

Nick continued, trying to sell the idea. "I got three weeks of holidays. I was going to take a couple days of it and spend them at Mille Roches. Woodlands is too full of kids and I don't like the beach on the others."

"Sounds great," Bea said. "Ernest could use some time out in the fresh air, to get away for a while. He's not looking for work. I don't think he's even filled out his EI cards yet. He's been pretty down in the dumps."

"When do you want to go?"

"Just a sec," Bea said. She got up from the table and went to the calendar behind the bar, knowing full well that she was working three out of four of the days Nick would be gone. Theresa had pre-booked to recuperate from having her wisdom teeth pulled, which left only her and Sue to trade off between days and nights. Hank came over and asked what she was doing. She told him she was just double-checking the schedule. The music was loud enough that Nick wouldn't be able to hear, so when she'd sat back down with him, she said, "I can't get the time off, actually. Theresa's getting teeth pulled. But there's nothing stopping you and Ernest from going."

"Well that's a bummer," Nick said, but Bea assured him she could take advantage of the time. She had lots to keep her busy while Ernest was away.

Aaron couldn't believe what had happened. He couldn't believe he'd been caught. That he was naked with another boy and someone saw him. He was naked. Fletcher was naked. The look on Amanda's face when the light came on. What was he doing? He pictured the scene all over again, but this time when the door opened, Aaron pulled out a long knife and stuck it through Fletcher's stomach. He screamed, *Get off me*. Blood ran over his torso, soaking him. Or he'd slam Fletcher's head against the wall and rush into Amanda's arms, crying. But he'd have to kill Fletcher, accidentally, so he couldn't talk. Maybe cut his tongue out. Maybe Fletcher would bite his tongue off when he slammed into the wall. Aaron had to be the only one to tell the story.

What would they be saying downstairs? Would Amanda ask him questions? And what would Fletcher say? Would he blame it all on him? Aaron would have to know what things Fletcher said in order to lie properly. He couldn't tell the truth. There was no way to admit to what they'd been doing. He hadn't wanted to play that game. He didn't even want to hang out with Fletcher in the first place, but the kid wouldn't leave him alone. He'd been bugging him for months. *I hate him, I hate him like shit*, Aaron whispered to himself.

The front door opened. Aaron could hear the screen squeak and click shut. He quickly scrambled into his pajamas before Amanda came upstairs. Then the inside door was pushed tight and the lock clicked. He thought he could hear that. Was she coming upstairs? What would she say? Aaron wanted to know how to lie to her so that she wouldn't tell his dad. Fletcher had forced him to do it, but promised it would only be once? Or maybe Aaron was dreaming and he didn't know what happened until she woke him up when she came in. And now he wouldn't see Fletcher again so she didn't have to say anything to anyone about it.

She was on the stairs, definitely. The fourth board from the top creaked. Aaron pulled the covers over him and shut his eyes. The light was still on, but he closed his eyes and pretended to be asleep.

The sound of her footsteps shuffled down the hall carpet and stopped at his doorway. She was standing there waiting to see if he was sleeping. *Turn the light off*, he begged. His whole body ached to have the light off.

"I guess this is how he came in," she said, making Aaron's heart jump. Her voice came from the window. He didn't hear her walk over there. She slid it shut and clicked closed the lock. "You know, you could catch pneumonia with the window open at night."

Aaron tried hard not to open his eyes, but every time she spoke he jumped, not expecting her. The sound of her voice was large in the room. The house seemed very quiet, everything had suddenly grown full and empty. Amanda was a stranger in his bedroom. She was over-size. And the house was echoing.

This time, he heard her come to the side of the bed. "Did he hurt you?" she asked. Aaron breathed in and out in a slow rhythm, pretending to be deep in sleep. "Eh, kiddo?"

She put a hand on his foot under the covers.

Just leave. Let me go and leave, he chanted. Everything in him tried to get her to go away. He wanted her to leave so badly he thought maybe he could wish it strong enough for it to happen. He'd have died to make the situation come to an end.

"You don't want to talk?"

What would he say? Aaron was racing in his mind for an explanation that she'd believe. What if he promised never to do it again? Would that be enough?

"I'll tell you what," she said, "I won't say anything for a while, I'm not going to tell your dad or anything for a week, but you'll have to talk to me before that. If you don't, then I'll be worried and I'll *have* to talk to Nick."

She gave his foot an extra squeeze and let go. "Okay, Sweetie? I'm going downstairs now, if you don't want to talk."

In a few seconds, the light was out, his door was pulled to, and she was downstairs again. Aaron felt sick to his stomach. He didn't dare get up to go to the bathroom in case she heard. He'd have to lie there and get over it. At least he had a week. He had a week to come up with something believable.

"So you wanna go somewhere, Nick?"

Ernest glanced down the dark trail behind them. "Sure," he answered, shrugging.

"Not down there. I mean away. I got a place I could take us to. It's comfortable." Todd gestured to the seat beside him. "Get in."

Ernest was briefly confused. He hesitated, looking from the seat to Todd, to his own steering wheel and back again. He knew there was always his own apartment, which sat unused still, but he couldn't imagine going back there.

"I'll bring you to your car, don't worry. There's no sense both of us driving out there. It's a ways away." Todd looked him in the eyes, smiling. "You got enough time?"

"I guess," Ernest answered. He tried shifting his cock in his pants so it wouldn't show when he stood up, but it was trapped too awkwardly down his leg by his briefs. As he stepped out of the car, he heard the click of the electric doors unlocking next to him. He walked around the front of Todd's car slowly, as though he had a cramp somewhere, hoping his erection would-n't spring up, suddenly unsnagged.

When he sat down in the passenger seat, Todd said, "Nice," and gave him a shit-eating grin. Ernest was too nervous to ask, but figured he knew anyhow.

As they drove along the narrow Number Two highway out of town, they passed cottages from thirty years ago, with one or two rooms, small windows, and old curtains always drawn. When he was younger, Ernest often wondered what it was like to have the river as your front yard and a highway as the back. He never saw any kids come from inside those cottages but he pictured them out running, bounding across the water the way bugs skim the surface, or he imagined men mowing the weeds like grass. That kind of living always seemed unreal. Ernest shifted his weight on the vinyl seat next to Todd, making a squeaking noise. It was a new car. When was the last time he'd driven in a new car? Everything about this made him anxious. He didn't know what he was doing, but he was doing something.

He was still aroused. He felt like a hand was already grab-bing his balls — there was a steady pressure pulling on them, right down inside his skin. "Where do you work?" Ernest asked, to distract himself.

The man gave a wry grin. "For the government. I'm a civil servant."

"That's steady work."

"Yes, it sure is. I guess I'm the stereotype."

Ernest didn't know what he meant. "What's that?"

"The gay civil servant," he said.

Ernest shrugged. "I don't know nothing about that."

The guy only nodded. He put the blinker light on and pulled into a long slim laneway lined with cedar bushes. "Here we are," he said. The lane came out onto a large point in the land with half a dozen cottages on it and tall pines dividing up the property. They pulled into the second cottage, a small war-time house with white siding. "This is my hideaway."

"You live here?"

"No. The wife and I come out most weekends. But I entertain sometimes during the week."

Ernest didn't respond. He felt the silence in his hands, numb in his lap, as he half-hoped they wouldn't get out of the car.

"We're thinking of winterizing," Todd added, his voice a bit strained, "but it costs a fortune, so we only use it half the year, or less, which is great for me, but it's awfully cold in the winter."

Ernest nodded, wondering what came next.

"Shall we?" Todd asked, opening his car door and stepping out.

Amanda was feeling a little fried by the time Nick pulled into the driveway. He wasn't late, but she'd been stressed for an hour wondering what the hell she was supposed to do. Things had finally sorted themselves out between them after the dress incident, so that Nick came to trusting her again. They'd come to some silent understanding that encouraged Amanda. Nick liked her, obviously, or she wouldn't still be here. In some way, the dress fiasco had brought them closer. She wasn't going to spoil that with another mistake.

When he stepped into the living room, a rush of nerves sprang from her belly. She closed the *Jane* magazine she hadn't been reading and took a deep breath.

He said first-thing, "How'd it go tonight? Was he good?"

"Yeah," she answered. What else was she going to say? *No, he had some naked kid in his room.*

He sat down on the couch with a sigh. "Ohh, it was a rough night."

"How come?"

Staring out the picture window, Nick pouted out a lip and shrugged. "No reason. I sat at the bar next to Larry who was trying to pick up this Via Rail girl. I think she was from Halifax and got stuck here or something. I tried not to listen. When I couldn't stand it anymore, I went to the window seats, then Bea showed up. I just drove her home, but I should have got you first and saved me the trip."

Amanda was briefly curious about Bea being out without Ernest, or the car, but she was feeling so stressed she could only think to nod.

Nick turned his head and looked at her. "You're quiet. You okay?"

"Yeah, sure," she said, knowing she didn't sound convincing. There was a pause while she tried to think of how best to get on the subject, but nothing was coming. She'd fucked up, for one. And Nick wasn't going to want to hear bad news about his kid.

He was crazy about Aaron.

"We're going camping this weekend."

"Who's 'we'?" Amanda asked, thankful to have something to talk about.

"Aaron and I. I think we're going to take Ernest too."

"Is Bea going?" Amanda asked too quickly.

"She was going to, but she can't get the time off work. So I guess it's just the boys."

Amanda nodded. She wasn't impressed at being overlooked and didn't hide it very well, not tonight.

"I was going to ask you, but with Bea not going, it likely wouldn't be much fun. Just the guys and all. And Aaron's been strange the last little while. I thought it might do him some good to get outdoors and away from that Fletcher kid."

Amanda shivered. "I don't like him — Fletcher. At all," she said.

"Oh, you've met."

"Yeah," Amanda said cautiously. "And I didn't like him."

"Well, what can you do? Aaron's never had friends in the neighbourhood. Bobby Trang moved away six months before Aaron's mother died and he hasn't gone out much since then. Not until Fletcher showed up. A kid needs friends."

"I don't think friends like Fletcher will do any good."

"Well, he likes you. That's one good influence. I'm glad to see how well you get along."

"Not so much. Not lately."

"Yeah, well, we've been having some problems. It's just a phase. He's trying out his independence."

It was a perfect lead-in, but Amanda couldn't bring herself to say it. She only nodded, again, stupidly, which more or less ended the conversation. Any other night she stayed as long as she could, keeping Nick talking, until he yawned himself into oblivion and said he had to go to bed. Tonight she was glad to get out. On top of the mess she didn't want to get into, the camping trip pissed her off. She'd have liked the chance to turn it down herself, which she wouldn't have done. If Bea was invited, the least Nick could have done was to not let her know she'd been skipped. As with Nick, what she didn't know couldn't hurt her.

✄

In a matter of seconds, they were in the back bedroom. Todd had his clothes off. A slim trail of thick curly hair ran down this torso, spreading out across his pubes in the same general pattern as the hair on his chest, making a barbell shape. He had a nice chest, but a looser stomach than what had appeared in jeans. In the light, he looked to be about Nick's age after all.

Standing in the doorframe, watching, Ernest felt lost as to what to do with himself. His hands were dumb at his side. Was he supposed to strip naked and just jump into bed? Todd's dick was stubby and flaccid in his pubic hair, more obscene to Ernest than the erect ones he saw in the park.

"You cold?" Todd asked.

"No," Ernest answered with a cracking sound in his voice. It showed how nervous he was.

"Aren't you going to take your clothes off?" He was pulling on his dick hard enough that it looked like rubber stretching.

Ernest looked at the bed. "I'm not sure about this."

"Why not? What's the problem?" he asked.

Ernest was searching for the right words to answer, hoping he wouldn't have to.

"We're not going to fuck," Todd said. "We can just jerk each other off if you want. You don't even have to blow me." He sat down on the bed. "Here," he said, "sit down. Sit here beside me."

Ernest's heart was racing in his chest. He could feel the adrenaline in his blood giving him a rush. He was glad to sit. If he could calm himself down. He was hard, as much as he didn't want to be. His cock was jumping in his pants.

"Just relax." The guy rubbed his left hand along Ernest's back, with his right still pulling on his cock. He ran his fingers up in the small hairs of Ernest's neck, pulling on them a little. "I like your grey. You look good."

"I'm not getting any younger," Ernest said.

"But you're still hot, aren't you? You look good." He set his hand on the back of Ernest's neck and left it there, his fingers rubbing back and forth a little.

Ernest really wanted to see the guy's cock. He was staring at the yellow wall, with its small cracks in the paint, wishing he could bring his eyes to look at the guy's other hand working himself. He could just see the motion from the corner of his eye.

"I like sitting on the bed with you while I touch myself," Todd said. "You ever blown someone?"

Ernest shook his head no.

"Never? All the times you've been down there? You are shy. Ever had a guy blow you?"

He nodded at that. "A few times."

"How many?"

"A dozen maybe."

"Or more."

"Maybe."

Ernest darted his eyes over to the guy's dick. It was longer now, filling out. He was rubbing his finger over the head.

"You never tasted cum before then?"

Ernest shook his head and said, "No."

"Not even your own."

"Well . . ."

"In someone else's mouth?"

"No, not like that."

"Here," Todd said. "Taste this." He set a finger at Ernest's lips.

Ernest opened his mouth a little and Todd slid the finger in, wiggling it slowly against the tip of his tongue. "That's precum," he said. His other hand rubbed lightly up and down the base of Ernest's neck.

Ernest closed his lips around the finger. It felt good in his mouth. Innocent, and easy.

He couldn't taste much, but there was something there. It was salty, but that might have been just the skin.

"Suck on it a little," Todd said lightly. "Is that nice? It feels really good." Todd slowly pulled his finger out, then applied pressure to the back of Ernest's neck. He was guiding him to bend over in his lap.

Ernest's tongue touched it first. The cock felt warmer than skin. Fleshy and firm in his mouth in a way he didn't expect. There was no give. His groin smelled of clean soap, and then behind that, hair, and sweat. Everywhere Todd touched him, he felt hot. When he'd put himself in other men's mouths, he'd felt in control of himself, in a dark act he didn't want to admit, but which made him more whole, for a time, more worthwhile, despite what ugliness people would think.

Here, on the other end of things, it wasn't what he'd thought. Ernest was a man with his dick in his hand, hard, working it. He was hot and aggressive with a man over top of him who was married and did this all the time. Todd had a family of his own, and Ernest just had Bea, who he wasn't married to, who he'd never had children with, so what was the harm?

He played with himself, both of them getting close, Ernest could tell by the breathing, a few minutes and already they were going to come until Ernest started and came in his jeans, surely staining them. He came as Todd heaved over him, releasing, bent double and noisy with gasping. Ernest waited, motionless, swallowing so as not to choke, until he removed his lips and, as quickly as that, felt empty again. His mouth was wet.

Todd rubbed him on the shoulder. "Thanks," he said. "I wouldn't have known this was your first time. You swallowed. You're a bigger man than I am, Nick."

With the bitter taste in his mouth, Ernest could feel his eyes burning at the sound of those words. Now that it was all over, he considered telling him his real name, then thought better of it. He was still the same man, real name or not, before and after. *What had changed*, he thought, *what's the harm*, and wiped the saliva from his lips.

The next morning at home, Amanda heard him in the living room watching TV and went out to see him. It wasn't even eight o'clock yet; Bea was still in bed.

"Hey, Ernest?" she asked, leaning against the doorframe. She didn't want to go the whole way into the room. Better to play being shy and unsure.

He looked over from the television and raised his eyebrows.

"I was wondering if I could talk to you a minute."

"Sure," he said, so she stepped into the room. "What's your problem?"

She sat on the other wing of the sectional. "It's not my problem, actually."

He wrinkled a brow like he was trying to understand. "Okay," he said patiently.

"It's Aaron."

"Oh. Wait a minute, let me turn this off," Ernest said, clicking the television remote. The screen snapped closed, ending the game show. Though Amanda caught the slight, she knew it wasn't intentional. So he'd turn the TV off for Aaron, but not for her. Big deal.

"What's the problem?"

"It's that little bully Fletcher that he hangs around with."

"I don't know who that is."

"You haven't met him?"

"I haven't met Aaron either, really."

"You haven't?"

"No, I haven't."

"Oh," Amanda said. That was surprising. "I thought I'd ask you for advice because I thought you'd met him. You and Nick are such good friends and stuff."

"Well, we're buddies, sure, but I don't hang out over there. I only see him at Malouf's, you know. I've only known him a little over a year."

"But he's been to your place on Sumac."

"He doesn't bring the boy with him. Nick stops in when he's got free time. When someone's babysitting and stuff. When you're there, or Aaron's at his aunt's. I'm not much fun for a kid. Bea's met him."

Amanda couldn't hide being disappointed. She'd hoped Ernest would be more of a help.

Ernest sounded reassuring. "I still got advice though. I know a thing or two about bullies. *Inside* knowledge, I guess. We weren't the best of kids growing up."

"Well, I don't think you had much experience with this."

"What?"

"Well . . ." She took a deep breath to relax herself. "I was baby-sitting last night and I heard a noise upstairs. Voices, people talking. It was freaking spooky at first; I didn't know where it was coming from."

"But it was Aaron?"

She nodded. "And this Fletcher kid." Amanda could feel herself start to chicken out. Ernest was sitting right there and she was feeling embarrassed. This was stupid, really. She should just tell Nick and get it over with, though that didn't seem more possible, or any easier.

"So you sent the kid home? That's not so bad. We used to sneak into other people's houses when they *weren't* there. Kids like to stay up late if they can — you must remember that — especially with baby-sitters in the place."

"No, no, that's not it. I can handle *that*."

"What then?" Ernest furrowed his brow. All the lines of his forehead were turned to rolls of skin, like speed bumps.

"They were doing things. Naked."

"Oh," he said, leaning back.

Amanda waited for a reaction, but Ernest just looked at her and sort of shrugged. He didn't know what to say. Then she felt completely stupid, until she saw his cheeks blushing, and the red around the back of his ears. He was embarrassed by it too.

"Shouldn't I do something about it? Talk to him or something? Or tell his dad? Someone should tell Aaron about the birds and the bees."

"I wouldn't tell his father," Ernest said, whispering now.

Amanda didn't know if it was because Bea was in bed, or he was uncomfortable.

"No?"

"What good would that do? Kids are kids. It's normal. This happens."

"Yeah, but . . . shouldn't someone set him right? I mean, it was another boy."

"I don't know. Does it have to *mean* something? I mean, they're kids, right?"

"Yeah."

"So, it's normal then, ain't it?"

Amanda didn't know what he was getting at. "But that was with a boy."

"Does he have any girl friends around?"

"No."

"So he's curious. Kids don't care who it is when the feeling comes along. You never heard any child psychology? He'll grow out of it. Everyone grows out of it."

"Unless he's gay."

"I don't know, he —" Ernest raked a hand through his hair, thinking. "Put it this way, what's telling his dad going to do? Is that gonna prove anything? If he's not being hurt, there's no harm done. They're just doing things. They don't know why they're doing them."

"So should I get him a book or something?"

"What did you say when you caught them?"

"I told the Fletcher kid to get out of the house. He scared me shitless. I didn't know who was walking around upstairs."

"Well, that probably put the fear of God into Aaron too."

"I was carrying a knife."

Ernest made a sour face, but he laughed to brush it off.

Amanda felt bad. She'd tried not to overreact in the situation, but then she *was* carrying a knife. She hadn't really thought what that would look like from Aaron's perspective. He must have been scared half to death too.

"I think it's better left alone. He's likely turned off that sort of stuff now, anyhow. Kids are only curious so long. He'll move on to girls soon enough and you won't stop him after that."

"So I shouldn't do anything about it?"

"Nahhh. Just act normal with him. You don't want to give him a complex."

"No," Amanda said. "No, I don't." She wasn't sure if Ernest was right, but she felt relieved at the prospect of staying out of it.

Bea finished up the dishes and dried her hands. She felt her stomach turn over, making the acid slosh and burn. She felt sick again, and each time her stomach rolled over with gas, she thought of Ernest's son. She came around the corner to see the television on the news channel with the sound off. Ernest sat on the couch, still in jean shorts, with his shirt only half done up and the cat curled into his lap. It was already nearly afternoon and he hadn't made any move to get out there and look for work. For one thing, Bea wouldn't have him sitting around feeling sorry for himself, and though she didn't want to mention the camping trip — Nick could do that, it would go over better — she had to get him out of the house, for both their sakes. Her stomach was a wreck and she thought she should make a phone call.

"Are you not going to Manpower this morning?"

Ernest glanced at her, then went back to the TV. "I don't think so," he said. He switched to another station with wrestling replays.

"Why not?"

"What do you mean?"

"Well, how come? Shouldn't you check out the board?"

"I just went the other day. You don't need to go more than once a week. When is there anything new?" Ernest put down the remote and petted the cat with both hands.

Pushing, she said, "Maybe there is today."

"I'm not walking down there again today."

"Well, take the bus."

"I can't take the bus," Ernest said.

"Why not?"

He screwed up his face. "I don't know how to do that."

"What do you mean? You just get on." Bea cocked an eyebrow, puzzled, wondering if he was serious or not.

"How am I supposed to know where it goes? I'll end up in Long Sault or something."

"Ernest, the buses don't go to Long Sault."

"Well I don't know that." He sounded mildly exasperated with her.

Bea tried another tactic. There was no way she was going to make the call from a pay phone. "You think you could run some errands for me if I give you the car? That way you can check at Manpower and I won't have to go out."

"Sure," Ernest said, brightening up. He picked up Brutus and set her on the couch beside him. She turned around twice before lying down.

"I want to clean up while you're gone. We'll pool our resources."

"Well, I can do some cleaning, Bea."

"I'm not gonna make you do it."

"It's not like I've never done it before. I cleaned at my place, you know. If you want to run errands, I'll stay home and wash or whatever. What are you looking to get done?"

"Nothing, Ernest." It came out snappy and impatient before Bea could stop to think. She just wanted him gone, she didn't want to stand here debating this.

Ernest grinned, "Well that shouldn't take too long."

"No, I just have lots to do, just the usual stuff, but it would be better for me if you weren't in the way."

"Oh, sure, Bea."

Ernest gave her a look to see what she meant by that, but she couldn't bring herself to soften her face, and she knew she'd give him the wrong idea. She wasn't mad, but it was easier to let him think that she was than to make her expression any nicer.

"I'll just get my shoes. You got a list?"

"It's on the fridge. Here, I'll get it for you," she said and headed to the kitchen. When she had the piece of paper in her hand, she took a breath and tried to sigh quietly, to relax herself. She didn't want to be mean to Ernest, nor to get him alarmed and have him asking her questions. Better to make an effort to seem like nothing was the matter.

Ernest was tying up a shoelace in a double knot when she came back in. "That the list?" he asked.

"Mm-hmm. It's all there. Just get what you can. And don't worry about me here. I like cleaning."

Ernest gave a chuckle that made Bea smile back. "Okie-doke," he said, tying up the second lace.

Bea took a step back as he approached the closet so he could get in the door. "You need any money?"

He took a brief glance at the list and kissed her. "Nope." He just looked at her, smiling uncomfortably, and for a second she wondered if he guessed something was up.

"What?" she asked.

"Car keys."

"Oh! Here," she said, diving into the closet herself now and digging them out of her coat pocket.

He took them from her, tossed them once in the air, and headed out the door saying, "See ya."

When it shut tight, Bea locked it and stood there for a few seconds listening to the sound of his footfalls descending the stairs. Not until she was sure he was gone did she lift the chain latch and fix it in its hold, quietly, just in case. She wasn't going to feel good about this until everything was known for sure.

⁓

Ernest didn't want to think about the other night because, in his mind, there was nothing to think about. He and Bea were together. He liked her a whole hell of a lot. And though he would have liked to still have a job and a better place for him and Bea to live — without feeling like he was living off a woman, and without a young girl cramping them in an apartment too small for two already — he wasn't about to complain about what he had. The little talk with Amanda had set him on edge slightly, and then Bea wanted him out of the house. What could he make of that? Nothing. Not until someone said something, anyhow. Hoping to keep himself busy, Ernest drove around instead of checking out the employment office, and, inevitably, he ended up at the bar.

He didn't know why, but he hadn't expected to see Nick, who was sitting in the window when Ernest pulled up out front. Ernest didn't want to be around him. Not today, not so soon after the other night. He walked in and said hello and before

Ernest knew it, Nick had it in his head to spend the coming weekend together, camping. The first time Nick asked him, Ernest gave a nice 'no thank you', and Nick ribbed him. Ernest didn't want to see him with his boy, especially not now.

Later, when Nick asked again, Ernest said he was busy and then they'd laughed it off because they both knew he wasn't. Then Nick asked to be driven home, leaving his truck in the parking lot, saying he'd drank too much, though it was only two o'clock.

As Ernest drove along Water Street, Nick pressed the point. He told Ernest he wanted him to go for his own good, to get some fresh air and give him a little space, a change of scenery. "Just think of the beach, and the campfires," Nick said, though Ernest knew what camping was like, he'd done it enough with his own father when he was young.

"I'm just trying to get through this rough spot, you know. Keep myself busy. Aaron and I could use a little time away, I think. A little time away from that house." He was persistent, Ernest could say that much for him.

They rode along Montreal Road a few blocks and hit the lights at MacDonell. Nick didn't say anything else. Waiting for the light, he squinted sideways across the street, looking for something.

"So, are you up for it, Ernest?" Nick asked finally.

"I don't know," Ernest said with a slowness in his voice. He was trying to sound like he was thinking it over but he already knew he still didn't want to go. He could stand to get away from Bea for a while, for a breather, to relax, only Nick felt like the other half of the bind he was in.

"It's just the weekend. We'll get a couple of sites between us. Bea won't mind. Waddaya say? You don't have plans, do you?"

"No," he admitted. "I haven't got any plans."

"There you go then." Nick gave Ernest a smile. He took two cigarettes out of his pack and tapped them on the cardboard.

"Want one?" he offered.

Ernest gave him a sidelong look, then grinned to brighten the moment. "Hell, I guess it won't kill me, will it."

✑

Amanda wasn't too impressed, to say the least. "I don't get why I'm not invited. I like camping. So I'm not good enough?"

She and Bea were cooking supper together, which they rarely did. Amanda was in charge of chopping the vegetables while Bea kept an eye on the stove and did the spices. It was only spaghetti. Amanda saw enough of that at work, but she didn't complain. Bea was offering supper to be nice.

"I guess it's mostly my fault," Bea said. "I can't get the time off work after all so they're making it a man's weekend. You wouldn't want to be the only woman there anyway, would you? What would you do?"

"Hang out. Camping stuff. I like roasting marshmallows and going to the beach. I baby-sit Aaron all the time —"

"— Well, there you go," Bea interrupted. "You don't need to do more of that. It gives you a break."

"Yeah, but this would have been different." It was a perfect chance to spend time with Nick *and* the kid, so he'd see how good she was with him. Yes, it was something of a mess right now with that Fletcher incident on her mind, but Aaron would relax with her if they could spend some fun time together.

"It seems kinda cheap —" she began, but then the phone rang.

To prove she was pissed off, Amanda didn't make a move to

answer it. After the second ring, Bea set the spoon in the pot and picked the receiver up off the table. It was Missy.

Amanda took the call in her bedroom. Bea could finish getting the sauce ready.

"Hey," she said, flopping down on her bed. She waited for the click of the receiver in the other room, then continued, "What are you doing this weekend?"

"Nothing," Missy answered. "Why?"

"Want to go to the campsites?"

"Can you get us a case of twelve?"

"Sure. Why can't your brother do it?"

"I broke the CD player. He's a bit pissed at me."

"Hel-lo, Earth to Missy. Isn't that *your* stereo?"

"Yeah."

"So why would he be mad at you?"

"Well, he uses it all the time, doesn't he? Now he can't play it."

"Well, I'll get us the booze. Maybe I can go shopping at work. We got cases in the back. Or should I get us a whole keg instead?"

"Yeah!" Missy squeaked.

"I was kidding. I can't carry a keg. And how would I get it out of there without anyone noticing? Under my shirt?"

"Roll it out the back."

Amanda laughed at that, though she knew it wasn't very funny. "I'll see what I can do."

"You know, Alphie might be there."

"Numb-nuts? I don't care. It's a big place."

"I'm just saying . . ."

"Well it's not like we can't handle it. I don't have to hang out with him or anything. There'll be lots of people to see. I got friends of my own going."

"Who?"

"Oh, nobody. Nick."

"Nick's going to the *campsites*?"

"Not at Woodlands. One of the others. He's camping, Missy. With his kid. That's what parents do."

"Will I get to meet him?"

"I doubt we'll run into him. But maybe. You never know."

"I'm pretty freaking curious."

"Well, don't be. You act like an idiot and embarrass me, I'll kill you. We likely won't run into him anyway. It's a big place. What are we going to do? Scope him out? I don't think so."

The park was empty after supper except for a women's ball game in the very back of the field. Aaron was swinging on the monkey bars upside down as Fletcher stood over him, banging on the metal of the pipes, trying to bug him. Aaron wouldn't pay him any attention, imagining what the world would be like if he walked on his hands, or if the clouds were the ground. He could imagine the sky was a big blue glass bowl that he could walk across and the clouds were pillows. He hadn't seen Fletcher since earlier in the week — with Amanda — and had hoped to never see him again either. Fletcher had called, but Aaron didn't answer the phone and he said he was busy each time his dad came to get him.

"Aaron Aaron Aaron," Fletcher chanted. "Hey, Aaron Aaron Aaron Aaron. Hey, Aaron, hey, Aaron." He banged the piping of the monkey bars in time with his rhythm, but still Aaron ignored him.

There were ants on the ground crawling through the grass just a foot below his head. He liked how they climbed over everything, upside down too, and wouldn't stop when they came across something big. If he banged on the ground beside them, they crawled all over each other to get away. Aaron was about to pull himself back up, his face was hot with the blood running into it, and his knees sore from the weight of hanging there, when Fletcher grabbed him by the ankles.

"Don't!" Aaron shouted, but Fletcher didn't let go. "Stop it!"

"Say, 'Uncle'. Say, 'Sorry Uncle Mikey.'"

"Screw off, Fletcher."

"I'm not Fletcher, I'm Uncle Mikey. Say it and I'll let you go."

Aaron tried pulling himself up with his straining stomach muscles, but Fletcher used a palm to his forehead to push him back. It made him swing, forcing more pressure on the backs of his knees. His feet were tingling, falling asleep.

"Say it. I'll let ya go when ya've said it."

"Screw off, Fletcher, or I'll yell. You'll be in deep trouble."

"Who's gonna come running? You gonna get the *ladies* after me? The *ladies* playing *baseball*?"

"I'll tell my dad."

Fletcher let him go then, but said, "We're just playing, ain't we? We're just having fun. I can tell him myself. That don't matter. If he ain't said nothing about the other night, then I can do anything I want."

Aaron stood up, feeling the pins and needles spreading into his feet as the blood came rushing back into them. "He doesn't know. I could tell him and he'd kick your butt."

"Go ahead and tell. Come on," he said, grabbing Aaron by the arm. "Let's go tell him."

"No!" Aaron squealed, pulling his arm back, instantly regretting the sound of his voice. He stood there a second, breathing heavily, his heart racing so hard he was dizzy. Fletcher turned to him with a flushed face. They stood staring at each other a minute. Fletcher hadn't really been wanting to tell, had he? He wouldn't have. He wouldn't dare. But Aaron thought that maybe Fletcher really didn't care who knew.

"You ain't answering when I call," he said.

Aaron shrugged like he couldn't care less.

"We're still friends, eh? You and me are still friends. We don't gotta play that game any more, but we're still gonna be friends. Right?" he said. "Your babysitter don't know where I live, does she? You don't tell her where I live and we'll stay friends."

కు

As Ernest showered first thing in the morning, Bea made him a nice big bacon and egg breakfast with fried leftover potatoes. Then she went about packing up the cooler with the food she'd prepared the night before.

She gave him two packages of hot dogs, buns, napkins, a small jar of pickles, little packets of salt, pepper, ketchup, mustard, and relish that she took from work, two salads she made (coleslaw and macaroni), a plastic bag of marshmallows for when they had a fire — more for the boy than for Ernest since he didn't eat sweets really — a few plastic forks and knives she had in the drawer though Ernest insisted Nick was bringing that stuff, his sleeping bag, which she'd aired out over the rail on the balcony the whole day before, a small pillow, her tent, a flashlight, and his case of beer. By ten o'clock, everything was piled on the couch, ready to go. Nick buzzed downstairs, Ernest gave Bea a kiss and away he went.

The minute he was out the door, Bea jumped in the shower herself. She needed to pee, so made the shower a quick one. She couldn't pee until she got back. She spent next to no time on her hair, tying it in a ponytail, which she rarely did, especially not when she was going out of the house.

As Bea headed into her room to get her purse, Amanda hauled herself up out of bed. Damn, Bea thought. The girl stood in the hall leaning on the wall waiting for her. She rubbed sleep out of her eye, with long pillow lines creased across her right cheek.

"You going out?"

Bea didn't want to talk. "Mhmm," she said, giving what she thought was a friendly little nod.

"Where?" she asked innocently. Bea guessed she wanted something.

"I have some errands to run. The mall, I guess."

"I need some tampons. Could you pick me up some?"

"Sure," Bea answered. "You need some this morning? I have a couple pads in the bottom cabinet you can borrow."

"Thank you," she said sweetly, but it made Bea cringe. "Can you get me OBs? Let me get you some money."

"That's fine, Amanda." Bea squeezed passed her. "You can pay me when I get back." She went to the front entrance, got her sneakers, and sat on the couch putting them on.

"Okay, but I might not be here. I'm seeing my mother this afternoon," Amanda said, following her into the living room. She patted her hair down.

"This is news."

"Whatever. I don't think it's such a big deal. Guilt. She's calling out of guilt, I'm sure."

When Bea stood up to go, Amanda looked at her funny. "You're in a rush?"

"I'm late," Bea explained.

"Oh. You have an appointment?"

Bea looked at her. "No. I'm just behind schedule. I have a lot to do today." Bea's physical discomfort was growing. Her bladder wasn't very happy with her, but the pharmacy was just a couple blocks around the corner. Quickly, she slung her purse over her shoulder and grabbed the car keys off the end table. "We'll talk later," she said.

"Okay," Amanda responded. "Thanks again. I'm going in the tub for a while to relax. I feel like shit. I'm seeing my mom in two hours and then Missy and me are doing the campsites tonight. You'll be on your own."

With her hand on the door knob all set to go, Bea's hope sunk. That meant the girl would likely be in the bathroom when she got back; there was no way Bea could wait longer than getting there and back. "Oh, hang on," she said, putting her purse on the couch. "I have to go to the washroom."

The house didn't seem much different. There was a new plant in the living room, a big one by the picture window, which was her mother's idea, for sure. And the breakfast table was moved to the closed-in patio for the summer, right off the kitchen. Georgie didn't need to tan indoors during the summer.

Amanda wanted to see what, if anything, they'd done with her room. When she went to the bathroom, she hoped to get a peek in, but the door was closed. Would they have left it empty? Or would Georgie have made it the weight room again? Her mom had insisted he move the dirty weights to the basement. They didn't belong in a room, they were made for outdoors, or underground, or something. When her mother'd gone on about that, Amanda figured it was mostly for her benefit, so Georgie wouldn't resent giving up his weight room to the daughter he never wanted.

"Things look good here, Estelle," she said.

Her mother was at the counter in the kitchen, washing radishes in the sink. "Thanks," she said. "I still can't get him to tar the driveway properly, but I'm working on him."

"And no pool yet."

"No, no pool. Next year. He promised that much. I don't think he wants to give up any lawn space. It would cut down on his mowing time. He loves to ride that damn thing around. You should see him on it."

Amanda had been here half an hour and hadn't seen Georgie yet. She'd been wondering where he was, but didn't know how to bring him up. He was the sore spot between them. "So," she asked casually, "where is he this afternoon?"

When she didn't look up from the sink, Amanda could tell she was feeling just as sensitive. "Oh, out back or something. He's around."

Which might have meant he was hiding out from her. Estelle may have been lying, maybe he wasn't part of this plan at all, maybe he didn't want her here. But then Georgie came in and he was fine, almost cheery, which was likely because he could turn it on and off — handy when you sold real estate. They sat down to lunch and her mother relaxed a little, which helped. She waited until they were partway into their meal before sliding into what they'd invited her for. Amanda had been waiting for it. She thought maybe they were pregnant, which would have killed her, but that wasn't it, thank God.

"So how is work, really?" her mom asked. She'd eaten all of her garden salad first and now was on the mashed potatoes. She ate everything in sequence. The pork chop came last.

"Fine," Amanda answered. "Good. The tips at lunch still suck, but I'm babysitting too, and that's fun."

"Do you plan on being there long?" She looked at Georgie. "I mean, do you like it enough that you think you might be there a while, or is this just to get by for now, until you find something better?"

"It's fine for now, I guess. I'm not looking for anything else. It pays the bills." Amanda tried not to let that sound snarky, but wasn't sure she was successful. She tried to lighten things up. "How's your work, Georgie? You're not thinking of retiring?"

"I have a few years yet. Not till fifty."

"Five years? That's not so bad."

"And you're not going to stop altogether," her mother half-asked. "He'll still do stuff on the side."

"So long as it doesn't cut into my golf time," Georgie said, laughing. He made that joke a lot. Amanda decided not to let it bother her this time.

"We were wondering if you liked your job?" her mother ventured. She was getting at something all right.

"Um," Amanda swallowed a bite of pork chop. "One of the dishwashers is pretty gross, but the rest of them are fine. And the tips are tips."

"You make enough?"

"No, not really. But it's work. It isn't meant to be a lot of fun." Amanda took a long drink of water for a dramatic pause.

When she set her glass down, her mother tried again. "Well, we were thinking maybe you'd like to finish your high school diploma."

"It's called a secondary school diploma now. OSSD."

"Did you get it?"

"No, Estelle. I'm still illiterate."

"You didn't do that badly, when you applied yourself. You did fine."

"I'm no genius."

Georgie was out-doing himself when he threw in, "I didn't do hot-hell in high school either." Amanda thought maybe she should thank him for the effort. He was trying, at least.

"Well, I don't have the time right now, I guess."

Her mother straightened herself in her seat and set her fork down. "Well," she started, but looked at Georgie and paused a second. He wasn't talking. "Well," she said again, "we were thinking that if you *did* want to get your high — your secondary school diploma, then we'd help out."

"You got to have an education to get somewhere, even in Cumberland," Georgie said. "And if you ever want to get out of this city, you got to have college, at least."

"We thought you might want to take courses at the college, here, too. Maybe nursing. Or computers, if that interested you. Something to get you going."

"Oh," Amanda said. It was all she could come up with. They'd all stopped eating. Amanda looked at the food speared on her fork. She wanted to set the thing down on her plate, but that would be facing the situation head on, and she didn't know what to say. "I'll think about it, I guess." She wondered what the catch was, but asking would kill it. Were they asking her to move back in? She looked to the front door and then back at her mother, who seemed to understand.

"You could keep your job and everything, you know, and we'd help out."

No, they weren't opening the door to her. When she started back eating, her mother picked up her fork too. There was a little silence among the three of them, until Amanda realized she'd forgot something. "Thanks," she said, which wasn't as hard to get out as she expected.

✎

The pharmacy in the mini-mall was reasonably empty, but Bea couldn't help herself feeling nervous. She'd already spent the morning doing a million small chores, delaying. She felt like a schoolgirl buying rubbers. She was standing at the toothpaste, pretending to look at all the brands and the prices, getting up the nerve. After taking ten minutes to casually go up and down the aisles, passing once already the area she wanted, she was sure she didn't know anyone in the store. Getting up the gumption was still hard. If someone saw her, she'd be mortified. Maybe she could pass it off as Amanda's, but that didn't seem fair, and what if it got back to the girl? Bea wished they sold the kits in public washrooms.

She had to do this, she told herself. She couldn't let it go. The sooner she found out, the better off she'd be. Steeling herself, Bea spun on her heel and tried to look as casual as she could going to the aisle, picking up the first box she saw and heading for the cash. Her whole body was hot. She was sure she was blushing, the heat had flushed right up her cheeks and was moistening her eyes. At the end of the aisle by the foot care products, Gloria Martin passed by. Bea had lived in the same building as her a decade ago. Her ex-husband used to come into the bar and flirt with the women before running off with one of Bea's co-workers, the girl that Theresa replaced. *Fuck*, Bea thought, her stomach sinking. She immediately set the box on the shelf by the mole cloth and made a straight line for the door, avoiding Gloria's direction in case she'd bother to say hello.

Once outside, she breathed in the open air. It smelled of

parking lot car exhaust. *Now what?* she thought, heading for the car. Maybe she could go out of town a little. Long Sault again, which wasn't appealing. She couldn't bear being reminded of the cemetery. Lancaster then. Did Lancaster have a pharmacy? It was only twenty minutes on the 401. Or wait, there was a rinky-dink pharmacy just up Second Street, in River Heights. She wouldn't know anyone there.

Bea climbed into the car and revved the engine. The whole drive there, she had to stop herself from flooring it. As it was, she sped a good fifteen clicks over the limit and nearly squealed the tires pulling in. With the ignition off and her car facing the wooden door of the place, she waited a second to relax herself. She should seem perfectly calm and disinterested. God, she was old enough to be buying this for a daughter, so why be nervous? No one would know her here, no one would care. They sold this sort of thing all the time. That's what the pharmacy was for.

Taking her purse from the passenger seat, Bea opened her door, locked it, and gave it a swing shut. The heavy wooden door dingled bells when she walked in. An old white-haired man sat behind the counter and looked up, smiling, giving a small wave. Bea noticed his hands were huge compared to the rest of him, as if he'd shrunk with age.

As she approached the counter, he asked if she needed some help. "Yes," she said, not entirely expecting herself to talk. Away she went, with her heart racing — she couldn't back down now. "Yes, please. I need a pregnancy test."

"Oh, sure," he said. He put on the pair of glasses hanging on a string around his neck and got up from the stool. "Over here," he said. "Watch your step. I was just taking a break from unpacking my boxes. I'm not so bendable nowadays," he said with a light chuckle.

Bea followed him down a small aisle with two open boxes full of toilet paper in the middle of it. The man stopped at the other side of them and cocked his head back to get a better angle out of his lenses. "Now, you've got two choices. These here you hold in your stream, and this one's for collectors."

"Collectors?"

"You collect it in a cup and stick the tester in."

"Oh, the first one."

"Well, you've got two more choices. It can turn blue, or get stripes on it. The blue one's easier. If it's blue, it's blue, right? But some people get mixed up on the stripes. One stripe, two stripes. It's a little fuzzier."

"I'll take the blue one then."

"Well it doesn't start out blue. It turns that way if you're lucky."

Bea couldn't tell if he was still joking or not so she wasn't sure if she was expected to laugh. He handed her the box and she gave him a warm smile instead. "Thanks," she said.

They walked back to the counter and he rang it up. After she paid, he offered her a bag and she thought she sounded too eager answering yes, which embarrassed her, though he didn't let on he noticed. Handing her the bag, he wished her luck. Bea wanted to thank him, but she was tearing up — he'd sounded so sincere, as though he could tell she needed it.

∽

Ernest didn't swim anymore. When he was thirteen, a Pinto drove off the bridge by his house and word went out that the police were looking for divers. All the kids from the neighbourhood would go down and jump off the rocks for the chance at twenty bucks, which was a lot back then. Marty Finley found a car once and bought himself hubcaps for his Chevy with the money. So this Thursday evening the call went out just after supper and Ernest found himself down at the highway, climbing across the rocks in his cut-offs with his sister watching his socks and shoes.

He made about three dives, swimming out a little further each time because when the cars fly through the guardrail and land they still travel underwater, sliding deeper into the river before they come to a stop on the bottom and slowly start to sink in the sand and the water weeds. That's what always made it hard to find a car and why so many people would be called to go out. The momentum of the car, the current carrying its flashing metallic body and setting it into the weeds or valleys of the river bottom, like a small ship, lost.

According to his sister, it was the third dive down that he found them. Ernest broke water in a tear of arms and legs. He must have started screaming underwater and lost his air because he was both gasping for breath when he came up and choking out sounds at the same time. Marianne told him he was bleached white when he scrambled onto the rocks, his shorts falling low on one side of his hip as he ran for the road. He stopped on the other side of it and collapsed on the gravel. Only with the pavement between him and the water did he feel safe enough to rest.

He'd found a woman in the car, a child in her arms. Ernest hadn't found a body before and he wasn't ready for that. He didn't talk about it, he didn't tell anybody what they looked like, or how it was to come upon them, no matter how often they asked or looked at him like they wanted him to tell them something that'd shock them, or make them sick. And eventually people stopped asking and then forgot about it. If he'd wanted to, he could have told them the type of hairpin she wore, the print of her dress and the shoes on the little girl. He'd seen it all in a flash in the darkness down there and it stuck with him with the quality of a dream — all the murky light and subdued colours.

What he did with the money, he can't remember. It was enough to know he couldn't swim again. For years he told people the chlorine in the pools, or cramps, or asthma kept him away. He used whatever he thought someone would believe, which either worked, or made him get angry and walk away. His wife knew better than to ask, but his son didn't, so Ernest had avoided the water at all costs. He had no use for beaches. He stopped swimming and figured he'd never have to again. For that, he was thankful.

So the prospect of packing up a truck full of supplies and spending three straight days at a campsite on the St. Lawrence with Nick and his kid wasn't all that appealing. He'd fish. Ernest didn't mind boats so much. He was known to spend a good deal of time in one in early summer before it got too hot fishing for perch, or pickerel, sometimes mudpout, but ask him to go waist deep in the water and he'd turn tail in a minute.

Of course, it was the kid that was intimidating. If Nick was going to sit around and drink the weekend through, he'd do that, gladly, but a kid, a kid had to be entertained. A kid would want to go to the beach and Nick wouldn't always want to do it, or to go alone, and inevitably Ernest would be expected to come along. Nick wouldn't pressure him into anything, Ernest knew that. But also knowing he would be asked and would have to find the right excuse, the one that would work, that wouldn't seem too foolish or awkward, or force him to seem angry, that's what worried him, and made him drink.

How would he handle seeing Nick with his son? *Could* he handle it? There was a reason Ernest hadn't met the kid yet. And knowing Aaron had this thing going on with some kid, and Nick not aware of it, only made matters worse.

The minute he met the kid, his heart broke for him. Aaron was scared. He was a tough little guy — Ernest could recognize that from himself at his age — but under it all, the boy was scared shitless and didn't even know it.

Within an hour of being there Ernest had drunk two more beer — it was a hot morning, he'd already had one at home — and was feeling no pain. When it came time to put up his tent he was awkward with the poles, trying to keep the ends in their grooves and lift and peg them at the same time.

"You need some help, Ernest?" Nick asked.

"I got it," he said. "I think I've got it."

"Let me give you a hand with that."

"No, I'm fine here."

Ernest didn't want help. The tent embarrassed him. Nick called it a pup tent and Ernest guessed it was. Nick had a real fancy-looking one, igloo-shaped. Ernest had said he didn't need no ugly-looking tent like that, and what good was a round tent, he wasn't round, then he slapped the side of his belly and said well maybe he was, and they all laughed. So Ernest didn't want help. He'd put up tents alone before, and preferred to do it himself, only today he couldn't get the poles to work right.

Aaron came over and stood a few feet away to watch. Ernest tried to pretend he wasn't uncomfortable with the kid staring at him, watching everything he was doing.

Finally, he stared the boy down.

"My dad sent me to help," he said shyly.

"Well, okay then," Ernest said with a shrug. "Just hold this pole up straight. I've got to stretch the rope tight and nail it in like that."

They did the one side first and then the other.

"Now you see these?" Ernest asked. "These ropes stretch the sides out, each corner, and two extra in the middle. How be I do one side and you do the other? Just pull them snug and hammer the pegs in through the loops."

Ernest handed him a small hammer and the boy walked around to a corner on the other side. While he used the palm of his hand to slide the pegs in, he could hear the boy tapping away at the metal. He came around and saw him squatted there, making little progress.

"Having trouble, kiddo?"

The boy looked up with his face crumpled in frustration. "It's stuck."

"I think you likely hit a rock down there or something. Try it on an angle."

The boy tilted the peg and gave a few whacks with the hammer and still the peg wouldn't go into the ground.

"Hang on. Hold it for me like that. We'll fix this bugger."

Ernest took the hammer from him and gave it a smack on the top of the peg. The boy jumped a little when Ernest brought the hammer down. He wasn't holding the peg steady and Ernest was afraid he'd miss if he didn't keep it still.

"Keep it still now. I won't miss this thing. I've been doing this since before you were born."

With a couple more hits, the peg went in. The boy stood and ran over to his own tent, looking for something.

"Where you going?" Ernest asked.

"Oh," he said, turning around.

"We got two more pegs here."

"I forgot," he said, though he didn't make any motion to come over.

"Don't worry about it," Ernest winked, "I got 'em." Then he remembered and shouted over, "Thanks for the help, there, son," but the boy was behind his canvas igloo already and if he heard he didn't come out, so Ernest let it go and finished up alone.

Amanda used to love the campsites. She'd know half the people there and the other half were always changing. Guys in from Quebec, or occasional backpackers from overseas, there was always someone new and exciting. Someone hot that she and Missy would flirt with. The nights camping held the feeling that anything could happen. They were slightly dangerous. She never knew what they might get up to. Drinking till you puked was common, though they always tried to push it up to that point and get away with it. Missy lost the battle most nights. She said she couldn't handle her liquor because she was native. Amanda was the white man poisoning her.

And they'd fight. Someone would. Two men punching at each other was exciting, but never lasted as long and didn't seem as wicked as two girls going at it. And people would pair up. At the beginning of a night you never knew who would fight whom, or who would screw, or when any of it would happen.

She used to like that, the potential, the wait, with its slow drunken climactic build. But everything bugged her this time. Missy got drunk right away, by seven, and was puking in the bushes before it even got dark. And the guys there all seemed stupid and juvenile. Why hadn't she noticed before? They pranced around flexing their muscles like they were hot shit, but their ball caps were on backwards, or hung low over their eyes so you couldn't see their faces, and everyone's hair was either shaved off or gelled. T-shirts and jeans. Or baggy track pants. They all looked plain and stupid.

She spent the night on their lot, keeping a fire going, and trying to avoid the ridiculous passes of whatever geek came round to talk. She'd only had three drinks by the time midnight rolled around. Missy had long since passed out in the tent, clothed, with the flap back so the bugs were bound to be in there by the time Amanda decided to pack it in. At one point, Stefan stopped in, teetering a little because, as he explained, it was dark and the ground was uneven, and he'd drunk his six-pack already and was now left stealing from other coolers.

Though Stefan wasn't half-bad looking — he had a great body and his parents were loaded — he was generally considered square. There was something too nice about him that kept him from being cool. Amanda liked him. He and Missy had done it a few times the summer before, a fact Missy didn't like to be reminded of, though she was still nice to Stefan when he was around.

Amanda was glad to see a friendly face; she'd been getting bored with the whole stinking scene. She tried to keep Stefan happy so he'd stick around. He'd pretty much settled in when she told him she had two vodka coolers left which she didn't want. He was finishing up the first one and all he'd said so far was pretty much two things. How very drunk he was and how much he was going to miss everyone.

"I'm going away, Amanda. Far far away. Bye bye." He waved to no one in particular. "I don't know where yet. Everyone's going to school. Not me. No —" he burped. "I'm fucking off to another continent."

"You're travelling?"

"Me and my backpack."

"Wow," she said, sounding more impressed than she was.

"You wanna go? Hey, why don't you come with me?"

"I can't."

"Ahh, sure you can. I like company. You're a good friend of mine. We'll see the Awful Tower."

Amanda wasn't sure if he mispronounced it to be funny, or was just drunk, so she didn't laugh.

"Yeah, we'll have a blast. Where do you want to go?"

"I *can't* go."

"You're not going to school or nothing, are you?"

"No. I work."

"Well, then, you can come with me. What else are you going to do? You can't stay here."

"I can't get the time off work, Stefan. I have bills to pay."

He waved the problems away. "Bah. Listen, you quit your job, and give up your apartment, then you don't have bills. You spend your money in Europe. Or Australia. I'm leaning towards Australia. Becky's from there — you know Becky? *She's* nice. I'm thinking Australia." He opened the second cooler and threw the cap into the fire. "You want to go to Australia? The men down-under?"

Amanda was starting to feel stupid. She tried to explain without looking like a loser. "Stefan. I can't afford to go away, you know? I have to work. I don't have that kind of money to just take off."

"Get your parents to pay."

This wasn't going anywhere fast. She just wanted him to leave by this point, to save them the embarrassment. "My mother and I aren't really talking. Not really. And they wouldn't dish out for any trip."

"Your folks wouldn't pay?"

"No," she said, relieved to be getting somewhere.

Stefan was looking at her, clearly trying to understand, as he took a long swig on the bottle, tipping it way back though he didn't need to. He wiped his mouth when he was done. "So what are you going to do here?" he asked, looking around like there was something he'd missed.

"I don't know, Stefan," she said wearily. "Who the fuck knows?"

Then out of nowhere, Alphie was standing next to them, smirking. "Hey, get out of the way, Stefan." Alphie gave him a shove off the picnic table seat and sat down in his spot.

"Oh, great," Amanda said. She'd expected him to show sooner or later, but had hoped he wouldn't. "Shit falls from the sky and spoils my picnic. Let him sit down, Alphie."

Stefan stood where he was, wondering what he should do. Amanda felt sorry for him. He looked like a little boy lost.

"He can fuck off, can't you, Stefan? Me and my ex are having a private discussion."

"No, we're not. Stefan, come sit on this side." She moved over, though it made her closer to Alphie, who smelled like rye.

"I'm going to go look for beer," Stefan said, repressing a belch.

She didn't want to be left alone with Alphie. "You got most of that cooler left. If you keep mixing, you'll be sick."

"Yeah, I'm not so hot now."

Alphie piped up. "Go puke in the bushes. And don't come back."

Amanda hit him in the arm.

"What?" he asked innocently. "He's knows I'm just kidding." He turned to Stefan with a soft face. "I think Becky was looking for you. Really. She's in the back of a car or something, calling your name. She sounded to me like she wanted it pretty bad, man."

Humiliated, Stefan trundled off telling Amanda he'd see her around. She called after him not to go, but he didn't bother turning around.

Alphie was snickering.

"You are *such* a loser."

"He'll get over it."

"You can't sit by my fire."

"It's going out," he said, and picked up her last log. Using it as a lever, he shifted some of the burnt pieces over, flipping their bark sides down. The flames licked up immediately. He set the log in his hands at the edge of the circle of flames and let it fall gently on the pile. "A man's touch."

"I was doing it all night, asshole. I *wanted* it to go out. I'm going to bed."

"Sounds good. Let's go." He threw an arm around her, which she fought off.

"You can't stay."

"I don't have to stay, but we should roll around for a bit. I miss you."

"If that was an attempt to be nice, you're stupid."

"What?"

"You're wasting your time, Alphie."

Just then, five guys came charging around the corner, at full speed, running from some prank or other. As they passed their lot, one slid on the gravel and rolled across the grass. He jumped back up and kept going, holding his elbow with his other hand.

Alphie tried to smooth a strand of hair behind her ear, but she batted his hand away. When he tried again, she slapped it harder. "Come on," he said, "I've been lonely without you."

"Haven't you found someone else to fuck by now?"

"No one as good as you."

"Oh, you're just too fucking smooth, aren't you?"

He puffed out his chest, stuck his chin out and said, "Yeah," in a belch.

He really was just a kid. A kid with a hard-on. "I'm going to bed, Alphie."

"Let's go."

She just ignored that. "Put out the fire when you're done," she said and got up from the picnic table. He must have thought she was kidding, or that she'd change her mind, because he sat there quietly. She pushed Missy over, zipped up the flap, and crawled into the sleeping bag, waiting for him to make another scene. She was ready. This one would kill him. She had a dozen lines ready to pull out if he didn't fuck off and leave her alone, but he did. Ten minutes later he mumbled what she thought was, "Good fucking night" and she didn't hear any more from him.

The next day, Ernest woke up boiling in the tent with the sweat and smell of sleep on him. He unzipped the fly and felt the air break in with the morning sun stretched mid-way up the trees. Everything was wet with dew, the grass under his hand wet, and the windshield of Nick's truck clouded over with beads and streaks of water.

A few people five lots down were whispering as they packed up kitchen supplies to wash at the bathroom sinks. Ernest saw them walk down the gravel in flip-flops with towels over their shoulders. The woman's hair was a mess but the man wore a ballcap. Ernest could hear their feet on the gravel and their voices all clear and whispery, and the smacking sound of their feet on the padded soles.

He put his own bare feet into his sneakers and slid jean shorts on and stepped out. It felt good to stretch in the air after the tent. He grabbed his cigarettes, lit a smoke and sat at the picnic table with his arms on his knees, watching the tree leaves blink and change in the sun. Morning was the best part of the day here too. No motorboats out, no engines or cars on the highway over behind the trees, no babies screaming or arguments, none of the drunkenness from the nighttime, only the constant noise of birds and the occasional carp slapping the surface of the water with its tail as it turned towards the riverbottom.

It went like that for a few hours until Nick got up. They started cooking, Nick using a knife to peel potatoes for hash browns, Ernest sorting out the dishes and cleaning the mess of pop cans and bottles from around the empty campfire and then getting the Coleman out of the truck, and lit. They had been silent for a good ten minutes, each going about their business. Ernest loved it. He was very happy to be here, with Nick, and his boy, and feeling close to them. And at the same time it depressed him no end.

"You lonely, Nick?" he asked.

He looked up from frying potatoes, surprised, and nearly laughed. "I guess so," he shrugged. "But I got Aaron. I don't need much more distraction."

Ernest just nodded.

"Well . . . I wouldn't have it any other way, either. You know? I got married once. I loved my wife. You only get one biggie in your lifetime, I figure."

"I don't know if that's true."

"No? I guess not. You got Bea now, don't ya."

"Yeah," Ernest said. "But you're still young, Nick. You might find someone. You never know where you might get lucky."

"But I got my kid to think of too. You can't just bring anybody home. I gotta think of my son, and what he needs. You can't do whatever you feel like when you're a father. Unless you have kids you don't know what it's like, Ernest."

"No," he said. "No, that might be true. That very well might be true, Nick."

In the morning when he woke it was lonely in all the brightness of the day, with his father at the picnic table preparing breakfast on the Coleman stove like he used to, and Ernest now there setting out the plates instead of his mother.

In the last months when his mother was sick in the hospital, she was very far away. Even when she made a great effort to pay attention to Aaron, he couldn't help feel that behind her eyes she was struggling just to see him there. He'd run about the room, crashing things, jumping on the chair, making faces for her, just to get a response. His dad wouldn't stand for it, so he'd only come alive when his father was out of the room. His teacher that year, Mrs. Sullivan, had told him that we all make our own futures. He believed that. His mother hadn't loved him enough; she'd decided Heaven was better than down here with him. Ernest had the same vague look on his face as though he was somewhere far off. At first Aaron felt it was the same sort of thing, and he wondered if the man was sick. But Ernest wasn't relaxed the way his mother was, he wasn't calm and waiting to die like his mom, he was just far away. Aaron felt unimportant with Ernest the way he often did around his mom in the hospital, which frightened him. Nobody cared about him anymore.

He'd come out of the tent on hands and knees and had wiped the dew off on his pajama bottoms. As he approached the table, he said, "Morning," but only his dad answered. Ernest pretended not to hear. His dad tipped the blue tankard of water and told him to wash his hands first, then served up his plate. There was a place setting across from his dad, which put him next to Ernest, but Aaron walked around the table to sit at the end, which meant his dad had to hand the fork and knife over to him. As Ernest watched him for a second now, Aaron pretended not to notice him until Ernest began to eat. After that, Ernest ate breakfast without looking up.

Amanda felt different the next day. It was with her since she got up in the morning, and now into the afternoon. Something felt bigger or smaller, she couldn't tell which, but definitely something had changed. When Missy came back from washing the puke out of her hair — she'd slept in awfully late even though she'd passed out before 11:00 — she had a look of pain on her face.

"What's the matter?" Amanda asked. She was picking up the small boxes of cereal that they'd eaten for breakfast.

"Um, I just talked to Shawna. She told me she saw Alphie with that Australian girl last night."

That hit pretty low, but Amanda didn't want it to seem like any big deal. "So? I'm glad he's getting it."

"You don't care?"

"Why should I?" she asked. "He'll leave me alone now. Big deal. So he screwed another continent. Maybe he'll move back there with her. I'm going to shower."

She gathered up her bathrobe and her bag with shampoo and soap and headed for the washrooms, which looked like cabins, painted brown with gaudy yellow trim. Amanda remembered Alphie teasing Stefan that Becky was in the back seat of the car, wanting it bad. Her stomach turned. When he'd come by to see her, they'd already done it. Would he really have had sex with her too, if she'd agreed?

Not that she'd never been lonely before, but with Alphie gone, with Alphie sleeping with other girls, she felt a little more lost. He'd been something solid, something reliable. Even when they weren't going out, she could still count on him being around, as annoying as the phone calls got, and that was important.

Standing in the shower stall with the curtain not able to close all the way, naked, washing herself, she felt pale and ugly. The hot water ran over her head. There was mould in the corners of the stall. Standing here wasn't going to make her feel any better, but she figured she knew what would.

Amanda rinsed off, turned the hot up for a second, then shut the taps right off and shook herself as dry as she could get. She slipped her sandals on, wrapped the robe around her, packed her stuff in her bag and walked outside. The pay phone was right there, in the spot between the two bathroom doors. She picked up the receiver and dialed the operator, claiming she'd lost her quarter to the machine, which got her a free call. She gave the operator the number for Nick's cell phone and waited for it to ring.

Bea tracked Doctor Cowley down at the clinic, knowing he worked somewhere on the weekends. He was young, younger than Bea, anyway. He didn't wear ties, only v-neck sweaters in the cold and polo shirts in the heat. Under either, he always had a new white T-shirt that Bea thought very sharp. He looked clean-cut in a way that was intimidating. She couldn't imagine him ever getting into trouble.

"Have you been pregnant before, Bea?"

"No," she hesitated, then changed her mind. "Yes."

"Yes?" he asked, raising his eyebrows to ask if she was sure.

"It was a long time ago. I was fifteen, sixteen."

"And what happened to that pregnancy?"

"I got rid of it," she said, then added for clarity, "We didn't know who the father was. I . . . I didn't consent to it." Bea had the urge to bite her lip, but stopped herself in time. She sat more upright on the table, making the paper crinkle.

Cowley wrote stuff in his file. "And are you still smoking?"

"Yes."

"Well, until this test comes in, you might think about stopping, in case you carry through this time. You know who the father is?"

"Definitely."

Cowley smiled a very little and set his pen down, turning to her. "Is this unexpected?"

"Yes. Very."

"Well if you're a few weeks late, it isn't so uncommon that this might be early menopause. Or sometimes the period is just late, that's all, some people skip a month. Have you been under a great deal of stress lately?"

"No," Bea said, then added, "Actually, I took a home test before coming."

"Which kind?"

"I don't remember the name, but it was one of the ones where it turns blue if you're pregnant."

"And it was blue?"

"Very blue."

"Well . . ." he paused, "then you might be very pregnant." The doctor waited for a response, but Bea only nodded. "I'll tell you what, we'll get a blood sample and we'll know for sure." He opened the top drawer in the desk, pulled out a form and began writing on it. "You'll have to go down to the lab. Then in a few days you come back here to see me. We don't like to give those results over the phone, okay?"

"Okay," Bea said, nodding.

"Do you have someone you want to bring with you next time?"

"When?"

"Friday, when you come back for the results."

"Oh, no."

"I didn't mean necessarily the father. You can bring whomever you choose. Sometimes patients like to have a friend with them, just in case. If it's your first time. Or, in your case, if it's unexpected."

"I don't have anyone to bring. I'll be fine," Bea said flatly. She smoothed the palm of her hand around her kneecap.

The doctor cleared his throat. "Okay, Bea. But think about it. Just in case. If you are pregnant — and that's only an *if*, those home tests aren't perfect — then there's lots to discuss. You're over forty, so there *are* more considerations. Okay?"

Bea nodded. "Thanks very much, Dr. Cowley," she said. She thought maybe she should shake his hand or something.

He clapped shut her file. "That's what I'm here for; that's my job," he said as he stood and held open the door. With a light-hearted ring in his voice, he added, "I'll see you soon," and raised his eyebrows with a smile Bea thought was meant to be more encouraging than cheery.

సా

It must have been going on 2:00 when the heat was too much for him and he went for a walk down the roadway running along the river to the beach. Everyone was packed into swim suits or wrapped up in towels, enjoying each other, seemingly unbothered by the temperature. To stay out of the crowds on the sand, and to cool off, Ernest tried wading knee-deep. He walked with his shoes in one hand and the other at his side, occasionally bending to scoop water in his cupped palm and splash it down his back or over his chest. It only seemed hotter seconds later — the hot sun prickling like pins on his skin.

He stopped soon enough and turned his back on the noise at the beach, the splashing and giggling, all the roar of the young people's voices and their ghettoblasters blaring. Ernest wanted some peace and quiet.

When he got back to the campsite the dinghy was out in the middle between the two tents, in the only shade on either lot. Nick and the boy were taking turns blowing it up, the child's cheeks bulging out ridiculously and his eyes wider with each attempt. They were about half-way there — the plastic body was limp and unwrinkling slowly.

"How's it going?" Ernest asked.

"Wish we had the pump that came with the thing," Nick said, "but it busted last year."

"That's how they do it. They don't make them to last because there's no profit in it."

"I guess not," Nick said.

The boy's cheeks were red and he was still blowing into the tab.

"You want help, there, son?" Ernest asked.

He looked up at Ernest and took a breath. "My jaw's getting sore. I think I'm dizzy."

Ernest chuckled. "This heat don't help." And he added, "I'll get it done for ya."

He took the rumpled boat in his hands, wiped the spit from the tab and pinched it so the valve would open. It took about fifteen minutes to finish.

"There you are," he said, tossing the dinghy a foot ahead of him. The boy had been sitting on the end of the picnic table with an oar pretending to row, or practicing, as he watched Ernest's progress. He jumped inside and thanked him and excitedly slapped the side of the dinghy with his hands.

"We ready to go?" he asked his dad.

Nick said, "I guess so," punching the last word to say *You're the boss*. "But watch yourself. You don't want to bust it."

Ernest half-wished there was room for him in the boat. But he knew better and didn't want to be out in that sun on the river.

"Where you going with it?" he asked.

"I thought I'd take him towards the island and back," Nick said with a gesture east to the river. There was a small patch of land with a couple dozen trees or so on it about a mile out.

"You're just gonna launch it from here then?"

"Yeah."

"I'll sit and watch you in case you sink," Ernest said with a grin. Nick picked up the dinghy and his son took the oars. Ernest grabbed a lawn chair and then a beer from the cooler in the truck. They walked the short narrow path through the few trees and shrubs. In a second, they were facing the water, standing on a grassy ledge about five feet wide. Ernest set up his chair and sat down while Nick placed the dinghy in the water. They left their shoes with Ernest and then both climbed in. Nick gave a final shove out to make sure they were deep enough so he wouldn't puncture them on the bottom. Water leaked in over the side and the boy gave a small shout of surprise. Everybody laughed.

Ernest waved and said, "So long." They didn't turn back after that to look, what with the boy at the bow leaning over the bloated front paddling and Nick doing all the work in behind. When he lifted the paddle to change sides, water dripped from the end landing down the boy's back. He made a commotion, something like a giggle.

With the beer in his belly and all the heat, Ernest fell asleep for a short while.

Inevitably, he had the same dream again. He was standing at the bottom of the stairs. There were no windows or doors, so he had to climb the steps to get out, only his feet were very heavy and the boards were rotten wood. Why did his feet weigh so much? Each step creaked and snapped under him. He was sweating.

He glided his hands along the walls to support some of his weight. With six steps left, he heard a man's voice shouting. *Was it Todd*, he wondered in his dream. *Is that Todd?* He felt a wave of shame run cold down his back. Five steps left, four, and there was the pounding of feet approaching the other side of the door. Two steps. The door swung open. One step. Aaron jumped into Ernest's arms.

The weight was too much. The board cracked underneath

him. Ernest felt his foot slide right through the wood. His stomach gave out as they fell. *No!* he yelled. *No!* he yelled himself awake.

The sun felt like it was burning through his eyelids. He blinked, and found his face was covered in sweat. He was at the campsite, by the river. He was with Nick and the boy. He'd had another of his dreams.

He looked out at the water to find the dinghy to gauge how long he'd been asleep. "What the fuck," he said under his breath.

Nick was alone in the dinghy, about half-way to the island, with the boy sitting six feet away from him. He looked to be sitting there on the water, dangling his fingers and splashing, until he moved and Ernest realized he was walking with the water nearly waist-high which gave the impression he was sitting. It frightened Ernest to see him out there, even with his father floating nearby. The two of them were more than a few hundred feet from land, and the kid was standing up, on what, Ernest didn't know.

He didn't think of shouting, though they'd have heard him, and could have answered back. Something about the look of the two of them out there kept him watching, something about how precarious they seemed, one floating, the other so casual moving through the water, waist-deep, small. Both of them likely burning in the sun even more than Ernest was on shore. He tossed his empty beer bottle in the river and it bobbed for a second, then sank slowly, disappearing into the brownness of the water.

He felt something for the boy, for how vulnerable he seemed, small for his age and his mother gone, and how the boy never mentioned her, or didn't seem to, not while he was around.

Maybe they talked about her at night, alone, but Ernest couldn't imagine that. The boy seemed closed off. He seemed private for a kid his age, too quiet. Ernest had the feeling Aaron was carrying around a great secret about all of them, he had a great secret he wouldn't tell. Always the boy would look at him when Ernest wasn't quite paying attention, and Ernest would look over and see him with an expression on his face like he was wanting to tell him something, but wouldn't.

Nick paddled over to the boy and Aaron climbed in with some help from his dad. Then Nick turned them around and paddled towards the campsite. Ernest felt too hot in the sun to watch anymore. He walked back through the bit of bush onto the site to clean up before they got back.

With a click, the phone went dead. Amanda turned around to see what was wrong and Alphie was standing with his finger on the button. She hadn't heard him, again. She hated how easily he could get to her. Normally she'd have yelled at him, but today she wasn't going to play the game she had before. She wouldn't give him the satisfaction of getting under her skin.

"Good morning, Alphie."

"Who ya calling? Stefan's just over there, you don't need to phone him. You can just walk over. I hear he's single. Is he still single?"

"Why?" she said sweetly. "You looking to date him?"

He grinned, not too happy. "Very funny," he said, then glanced down at her robe, and the bag in her hand, and her open neckline. "I want to talk to you."

She pulled the robe further closed. "Not now. I'm kinda busy."

"On the phone? I don't think so. It can wait." He put his finger in the slot to retrieve the quarter.

"There's no change. It was a free call." She stepped off the concrete onto the grass, heading for her site. "I'll see you around, Alphie."

He stepped in front of her. "Hang on, I want to talk to you."

"And I don't."

She tried walking around him, and he dodged in front of her, so she went the other way and he did it again. She stopped still, closed her eyes a second to stay calm — she wasn't going to yell at him — then snapped her eyes open to see him grinning at her. He knew it was bothering her. Whether she lost it or not, he was pulling the strings. Furious with him, and herself, she turned on a dime and marched in the other direction. She'd go around the building.

"I'll walk you back," he offered. She could hear in his voice that he was trying to be nicer.

"No, you won't," she said firmly, without looking back.

"Amanda? Amanda, wait!" he called.

She kept walking. She was a good twelve paces away, and he called again, which she ignored. Then there was the thump of his footfalls racing after her. She ran too, in her flipflops, around the side of the building. She didn't want to be followed. "Fuck off," she yelled, embarassed to be chased out here, in the park, in her pink robe.

Approaching the door to the women's washroom, she looked over her shoulder to see him catching up to her, so she ran through the bathroom door, panting. He followed her right in.

"Get out!" she yelled, mortified. Was there somebody in here? She was terrified he'd get caught in here and they'd assume the worst about her. "Alphie! Get out! You can't come in here."

"I just want to talk to you," he said, stepping towards her.

"You keep saying that and I don't want to talk to you. Get it?" She backed away and spoke again, pronouncing each word slowly and clearly, "I do not want to talk to you."

"But I love you, Amanda. How can you ignore that?" He waited for an answer, but she didn't have one. She thought of ten different nasty things to say and wouldn't bring herself to say them. He pleaded, thinking he'd hit a nerve, "I love you, and if you just give me another chance we can go back out."

"No, Alphie, it's not gonna happen."

"But why?"

She said, as nicely as she could, "'Cause you're screwing another woman, for one."

He took a second, thinking what to say next, screwing up his face and wiping the expression away with his hand. "She don't mean nothing to me, Amanda. I just want to hold you. I only want to hold *you*," he repeated, taking another step towards her.

She backed away again, and had herself trapped against the row of sinks. She could feel the sweat under her arms, dripping into the terrycloth robe. When would someone come in and find them here? They were bound to be caught any moment.

As he closed the gap between them, she said, "Don't, Alphie, I mean it." He tried to wrap his arms around her and she blocked him with her own, pushing at his chest, but he didn't budge. He bent over, cocking his head to kiss her. She turned her face and he got her by the ear. "Come on," he said. "I just want to hold you."

"Alphie, don't," she said. He didn't stop. "I'll scream."

"I just wanna hold you again, okay?" He rubbed his body against her, reaching for her robe, which she quickly grabbed closed, with her hand holding the bag between them.

"For fuck's sake," she said. Since her chest was blocked with the bag, he grabbed her by the waist instead, trying to move her hips back and forth, and moving his, pushing their pelvises together. She could feel him hard in his pants. She looked at his face, with his eyes closed and his skin gone red. "Alphie," she said as harshly as she could, but he didn't flinch or look at her. He rubbed himself harder against her, pinning her tailbone against the sink, with his grip strong on either side of her. "You're hurting me," she said. "You're *hurting* me, Alphie."

"Shhhh," he whispered in a voice she recognized, "Don't talk." He stopped rubbing himself against her.

"Look at me," she said, but he wouldn't open his eyes. She kept her voice low and threatening. "Is it just sex you want, Alphie? Eh? Is that it?" she asked, opening her robe herself. Her heart ran in her chest, pounding against her ribs. "Is that all you want out of me, you fucking pig? Come on, then, let's fuck in the stall, okay? You wanna fuck me in the stall? Do ya, Alphie?"

"Don't," he said, squeezing his eyes closed tighter. A tear ran down his cheek. "Don't talk, please, don't talk."

"Look at me," she said, pushing him backwards. "I'm ready for ya, Alphie. I'm ready to go. Come on, let's get it over with, if that's all you want from me. I love fucking, it's no skin off my ass. But you won't mean *shit* to me," she spit at him, "before or after, just so we're clear. Are we clear on that?"

He was sobbing now, and holding his arms around himself. He crouched over, wailing like a preschooler, which killed Amanda to hear, but he'd asked for it.

"Why won't you *love* me?" he howled. "Why won't *anybody love* me?"

She nearly held him, he nearly got her to, but she knew too well where that would end up, and she wasn't going there again. They were done the game. Last round over. *No winners,* she thought, and closed her robe on her way out the door.

చా

"Why can't I go?"

"Because I'm just going to take her into town and then I'm coming back."

"I want to go too."

"Well, you can't. Amanda's had a rough morning and we're going to talk about adult stuff, so you can't come. Who's going to keep Ernest company here if we both leave?"

Aaron wanted to say he didn't care, but Ernest was within earshot and his dad would kill him if he said that. Aaron couldn't believe that his dad was leaving their camping trip to see Amanda. He wondered if his dad had planned it this way. Maybe they had asked Ernest all along to babysit so they could have time alone together.

"Maybe he'll take you out on the river later. You can check out the island this time, if he's feeling up to it."

Aaron tried to look like he wasn't pleased, but his dad was ignoring him.

"Hey, Ernest? How about going for a row out in the dinghy later? You want to take the kid to the island?"

"Sure," he answered. "Why not?"

As much as he didn't want to hurt his feelings, Aaron couldn't bring himself to be satisfied with that. Ernest asked him if that would be all right, if he'd do, but Aaron could only shrug.

Almost whispering, his dad said firmly, "Don't be a spoilsport," and stared him in the eyes. "Ernest is offering to take you over there. You can't go alone, and it isn't a chauffeur service. You're lucky he's willing to go." Then he gave him a friendly slap on the shoulder. "Come on, you'll love it."

Aaron looked over at Ernest, who winked, which caught him off-guard and made him smile despite himself. He looked at his dad, who was also smiling, and Aaron breathed a huge sigh, to say it was worth a shot.

With everyone out, Bea went home and cleaned the apartment, top to bottom. She started on the bathroom, then the kitchen, clearing out all the cupboard shelves and wiping them down. She was about to take a clean rag to the walls and attack the worst of the finger marks around the doorways when she got tired. It was after lunch and she realized she hadn't eaten. *Eating for two*, she thought. If her period hadn't been so regular she might not have known she was pregnant. Even when she was younger, she knew girls who'd only found out in the fourth month, or the fifth, when it was too late. How far along was she? She hadn't gained weight, not really, maybe five pounds. That could be from anything. That could be the potato chips Ernest liked to buy.

He was expected back tomorrow already. Three days to make a decision. That wasn't long enough. Bea needed two weeks. Here she was, forty-three years old in a two-bedroom apartment. She'd wanted a house for years. Instead she was living in a shoebox: no yard, no view, no privacy. She was one step up from a girl of seventeen, though now she was pregnant, and even Amanda wasn't stupid enough to get into trouble like that. Though maybe she had. Maybe she'd already dealt with something like this. Amanda had a stronger will than Bea. She didn't flinch when it came to getting what she wanted. If Bea could only figure out what that was, what she wanted, maybe the whole thing wouldn't seem so unbearable. If she decided to keep it, would she feel this way the rest of her life?

❧

In the middle of the open water, Ernest was standing on part of a highway that he'd seen flooded more than forty years ago. Everything was green and slippery underneath him, all the rocks piled up and gravelly but with a thick coat of muck and growth over top of them. It felt like wet carpeting between his toes. The water was over knee-deep and again the boy waded along with it covering his legs. Ernest wanted to hold his hand but he seemed fine. Nick hadn't done so: he didn't want to squash the boy's nerve. But it was slippery, and Nick likely didn't realize that. And then from the edges of the pavement the sides just dropped off four feet, then gradually to five, and six, and however deep it got out there.

They walked the length of it, about hundred feet, Ernest holding the rope which made the dinghy trail along behind him and occasionally bump the back of his leg. The last ten feet the road began to dip slowly. Ernest was halfway to his waist and got uncomfortable, especially with the boy looking like he was sinking. The water rose above Aaron's bellybutton and he held his arms out at his sides to keep them above water.

"Whaddya say?"

The boy shrugged.

"You want to get going or are you doing okay here still?"

"We can go." He looked up at Ernest, squinting with the sun, and pulled his cap down further over his eyes.

"Guess we better, eh," Ernest said. The kid lifted his arms and Ernest picked him up again and tried setting him in, though it was trickier with the road slimy and the dinghy not holding still. The boy used his toes to bring the dinghy in line and Ernest held him till he had it close enough to set him down gently.

He stood at the edge of the roadway, put a knee in and gave a shove. They slid clear. Pulling his body in, he barely let any water over the side.

"How's that?" he said and the boy and he laughed from the little rush of the momentum and jostling. Ernest took his paddle and steered them around and away they went in high spirits.

He was tired by the time he rowed them up close to the island, but the boy was all excited and jumpy. He bounced out of the dinghy like a dog from an opened door and bounded through the water onto the beach.

"Hey, there, slow down," Ernest said with his tone too firm. The boy was having fun. It didn't mean he was being careless. Trying to make up, Ernest gave a big laugh, then splashed the boy and ran onto the beach with the inflatable under his arm. He dropped it on the sand far enough up the beach that it wouldn't get picked up and carried off.

"So what do you think there is to see?" he asked.

"All kinds of things," the boy shouted and raced off in an arc towards the trees in behind Ernest.

The boy was gregarious, louder than Ernest had yet heard him, more like how he'd expected the kid to be from the outset. He was glad they came.

"Come on," Aaron hollered, "I'll show you," and disappeared into the tall grass and weeds.

The island was about two hundred feet in diameter, with a dozen trees in the center and long grass surrounding them. The far side, hidden from the campsite, was rocky. Walking the circumference wasn't really feasible, not without some difficulty. The rocks lay awkwardly on top of one another, spotted with white bird droppings. The trees in the centre grew in clumps of two or three.

As Aaron climbed over the rocks, he periodically glanced at Ernest to see if he was watching. It was like he wasn't sure of himself and wanted to be certain Ernest would notice if he fell, or did something great. The boy reminded him of himself at that age.

He called to him, "You take it easy, Kelly," and Aaron looked up.

Kelly. Oh fuck. *Kelly*. It wasn't just a slip-up; Ernest hadn't just gotten their names confused. For a second, for a brief window, he thought the boy was Kelly and they were fine. Kelly was twenty-odd feet away walking across the rocks, giving Ernest a flash of concern in case he got hurt.

Amanda stood at the entrance to the campground, with its little wooden cabin for checking in and out behind her, staring down the roadway for a sight of Nick's truck. She wished she had makeup with her. She felt exhausted.

A few trucks passed that looked like his, then finally it was him, and he pulled over onto the gravel. He had the windows rolled down. She opened the passenger door and crawled in.

"Thanks so much," she said. "You're a life-saver, Nick." She buckled herself in as he did a u-turn across the two lanes.

"You sure get yourself into some awful scrapes."

"I know," she said. The wind was whipping her hair around, so she rolled the window three-quarters of the way up.

Nick scratched his jaw and asked, "Did you go there with him?"

"No," she said, a little annoyed that he didn't give her more credit than that. "He just showed up. Maybe he's following me. I can't be sure. But I think I got rid of his bad habit, finally."

"So how'd you get stuck out there if he didn't bring you?"

They were approaching the exit to the causeway that connected the various island parks. Amanda looked at the eight-foot map of the area on the back of the information station. It was printed in greens and blues, with a big red You-Are-Here arrow.

"Oh, I was with Missy, but she's not leaving until tomorrow. And it would be stupid to stick around with him so close, right?"

"Well, you've got to get your own car if you keep fighting like this. That's the second time." Nick put his blinker light on, to signal the turn.

"Yeah, I know," Amanda laughed. She took a breath and said, with her heart racing, "But it's all your fault."

"My fault?"

"The last two fights with Alphie have been over you."

"Me?" he asked. "Why me?"

"Well, he's jealous." Amanda watched him taking that in and felt very comfortable around him, for the first time really, and very wound up. *All or nothing, Nick, here we go*, she thought.

The truck slowed as it turned into the highway's merge lane. "Why would he be jealous of me?" Nick asked. He glanced at her, then looked over his other shoulder for traffic.

She rubbed her palms together, slowly, in her lap. "I don't know. You tell me."

"Tell you what?"

She held her breath. "Should he be jealous?" she asked.

Nick looked at her quizzically. "Of what? Me?"

Me? rang in her head on replay. *Me?* Her stomach sank a notch or two.

"Why would he be jealous of me?" he continued. "Amanda?" She wanted to grab his hand and ask him not to talk, but they were in the car. If they'd been in the house, on the couch, like she'd imagined it would happen . . . "Can we stop at Lamoureux Park?" she asked. "I want to go for a walk." That would be a better place. She should have held off a little, until they'd got home. She didn't want to say it in the car.

"I've got to get back to the campsite. Aaron's mad I didn't bring him with me. I don't really have time."

"But can we pull over?" Nick didn't look like he was going to say yes. "Can't we just do that?" she asked.

They pulled into the parking lot for the big green Combustion Engineering plant, which was called something else now, only it hadn't put a new sign up.

As soon as Nick put the car in park and turned the engine off, Amanda felt she might cry. Nick was nice and didn't say anything right away, waiting for her. She knew she had to get something out while she could, but hadn't any idea what would work. How could she break the ice and get through to him?

She took his right hand in her left and held it. "Alphie's jealous because he thinks I'm in love with you."

"Why would he think that?"

Amanda blinked. She couldn't not answer, but she had no idea what to say to make things go the way she wanted.

Nick pulled his hand back. "Amanda, no more games, okay? I like you, you're a good kid, but don't push me here."

"I'm not pushing you into anything."

"I mean don't push my limit. Look, why are you doing this? You're just a kid. You're seventeen. I was out screwing around having a good time when I was your age. I was having fun. Why would you want to get hooked up with me? A man with a kid?

You're too young for me."

Amanda scoffed; it slipped out before she knew she'd done it.

"That's not an insult," he said firmly. "You're very mature for your age. You're a great kid that way. I admire your oomph like that. But dammit, you're only seventeen."

Trying not to be upset and bawl, she got really pissed. "If I'm living a grown-up life, then aren't I grown up?" she asked, trying to show she was angry, only her voice came out wrong. She sounded as young as he said she was.

"You're right. That wasn't fair. How can I explain this so you'll understand?" He drummed his fingers on his knee. She had the stupid thought in her head that she even loved his fingers.

"You see this building?" he asked. "Ernest worked here when he was a teenager, with his best friend. Has he told you this story?"

She shook her head no. Where was this going? The momentum she had felt was disappearing. She didn't want him to talk because the more he said, the farther away she felt.

"His friend wasn't legally allowed to work in the mill until he was eighteen, but Ernest got him a job and within a month Ernest watched the guy burn to death. What did he say? 'He went up like a marshmallow at a camp fire.' The kid was sixteen or something. His whole life over at sixteen. And why? Because he was anxious to get a job in a mill. He was dying to grow up."

Amanda could feel her stomach turning, with her heart in her throat. She watched the cars passing on the highway, listening to him, and imagining she was in someone else's car, going somewhere, in love.

"You've got to relax a little. Let yourself be a kid for a while.

You're going to make mistakes, sure, all your life, but don't make the wrong ones. Some mistakes you learn from, which means you get on with your life, but some you never get out of. Some trap you. Next thing you know, you're forty and you haven't got a friend in the world and a husband you can't stand to be with because he's too boring. Or a job you can't stand but you need it to pay the bills. Or you're sixteen and dead already. Some of it's luck. But some of it's just plain being smart."

She couldn't help herself from crying. The tears welled in her eyes, she couldn't blink them back. "So why can't I be in love with you? Why isn't that smart?" she asked.

"Because I've already been in love, Amanda. I still *am*. My wife was the best thing that happened to me. And I won't find that again, not something like that. And you won't find it with me," he said. "I love her way too much still. You don't find someone like that by looking. Go out and enjoy yourself and figure out a life for yourself. Go to school. Get a good job. Take trips. And maybe you'll run into the right guy. But don't go looking for it. You won't find it by looking."

He said that delicately enough that it wasn't mean, but still hurt. He started the engine. "We've got to get going, here, okay?"

She tried to smile but her face felt like it would crack. She got out a weak one, and sniffled, and wiped her face with her palm. Nick had the 4X4 running but wasn't putting it in gear. He turned to look out the side window, facing away from her. He stared out for a long time while Amanda waited, trying to think of what she was supposed to say. "I'm sorry," she said finally. It was the best she could come up with.

Nick didn't look at her, but his voice was soft. "Don't worry about it," he said, putting the Rover into gear. He turned, then, to back out, and she noticed his eyes were damp. "You'll do fine," he said, smiling sweetly. "You're a smart kid, Amanda. Your parents didn't raise a dummy."

⌒

Aaron didn't know what was happening. Ernest dropped to the ground, disappearing in the long grass. When he'd climbed back over the rocks and waded through the tall grass, Ernest was there crouched with his head hung low. Aaron thought maybe he'd hurt his leg, since he was staring at himself, but when he laid a hand on the man's shoulder, he noticed his eyes were closed. "What's wrong?" Aaron asked.

Ernest tried to talk, then cleared his throat and said he was fine. "I'm just feeling a little sick. It snuck up on me."

"Are you going to throw up?" Aaron asked.

Ernest closed his eyes again and didn't answer. Maybe he was angry. "Is it because I was on the rocks? Did I scare you?"

He shook his head no, but didn't look up right away. When he did, Aaron could see tears pooled in his eyes. He must be in pain. "We got aspirin back at the campsite. My dad has a whole kit in case of emergency."

"Sorry, kid," he said. "I'm okay." The man gave his face one more squeeze and looked up at him. Aaron thought he was better; some of the wrinkles in his forehead were gone.

Ernest cleared his throat. "I had a boy your age," he said. "He was six actually. Almost seven."

Aaron didn't understand. "He lives with his mother?" he asked.

"No," Ernest explained. "He died in an accident."

All Aaron could think was *Oh*. Ernest was still tearing. Aaron didn't know what to look at. The trees over the top of the grass, the moss covering the big rock at his feet, Ernest's grey hair in the breeze. His floppy earlobes. He met his eyes again. Ernest knew what death was like, Aaron and he both knew what it was like to go to a funeral and never see someone again. "Sorry," he said.

"You got nothing to be sorry for."

Aaron smiled a little, nervously, which made the corners of Ernest's mouth curl up. He looked tired, but better.

"I bet you got a lot of secrets too, don't you kid?"

Aaron's heart ached to say something real. For two whole days he hadn't thought about Fletcher. "Me and a friend are doing bad things," he said.

Ernest let out a small short sigh. Aaron could see his shoulders relax. "Which friend?" he asked.

"A boy in my neighbourhood."

"Are you hurting someone?"

Aaron shook his head no.

Ernest sounded more serious. "Is someone hurting you?"

He paused, and shook his head again.

"Sit down, Aaron." Ernest pointed to the big stone. "Have a seat."

When he settled himself on the rock, he pulled out a bit of grass that tickled the back of his legs. Ernest took a blade of the grass from him and held it between his fingers. He placed his hands to his mouth. A high loud whistle rang out. *Bleee, bleeeeee*, it trilled between his hands.

"You know how to do that?" Ernest asked.

Aaron shook his head no.

"Pinch it between your fingers like this. You want to hold the ends tight, but leave the middle a bit slack. No, no, look, like this." Ernest held his hands out to show him.

"Okay," Aaron said.

"And then you blow. Hard."

Aaron gave it a go, but it didn't make a noise. He tried again and got a short low twitter, and again, and it squealed. "I did it!" he shouted.

"Damn right," Ernest said. He wiped a hand across his sweaty forehead. "Hey, kiddo," he continued, his voice softer, but not quite whispering, "you're a good kid. Your dad knows that, and I know that, we all know you're a good kid. And if you're not hurting anyone, then how can you be bad? Right? But if someone's bothering you, then that's different. You tell someone, and you tell the person bugging you to leave you alone. You understand? And if you don't want to do something with a kid, hang out or whatever, then you tell them as much. *Leave me the fuck alone.* Though you might not want to swear."

Ernest patted him on the back. Though Aaron didn't know how to go about doing it, he wanted to hug him. He held up his hands and blew into the grass again, but couldn't make the sound. He smiled, embarrassed, then squinted at Ernest, who asked, "Can we go back now?"

Aaron handed him the stick of grass and said, "One more time, then we'll go."

They jumped in the boat and were coasting along smoothly. Ernest's arms ached from the paddling but it was a dull pain still. He knew he'd suffer by the time he got them to the other side. It was hot and they were both burning a little in the sun despite the lotion they'd put on when they left. While he was thinking how he should have brought that with him too, he felt a small tug, as if they'd begun to drag something. Then he sank backwards and had to grab at the sides to hold himself up, only they shrank a little as well.

The back of the dinghy was giving out. It had split at a seam and was crumpling and bubbling underneath them. The boy slid down against his chest, giggling at first, thinking Ernest was playing a game. Then he saw the sides of the dinghy deflating and shouted.

Ernest slid his legs out from under him and told the boy to hang on to the front. He bunched up where the seam gaped open and held it in a fist. Ernest was in the water halfway to his chest. He was kicking them over toward the swallowed part of the highway. It had to be thirty feet and the body was collapsing too quickly.

"Can you swim?" he asked the boy, who was trying not to scream but mumbling and shouting loudly and at random.

"Can you swim?" he asked firmly. He had to catch his breath.

"I'm scared," the boy said in a cry with his face dripping in tears, his legs in the water now too and his body bent over the swell of the bow.

"Get on my back," Ernest said. "Take it easy," he forced his voice to be more calming and relaxed. It sounded like a whisper to Ernest though he knew he'd said it aloud.

"Just take it easy, son, and get on my back and hang on. We're going to swim to the road there."

His hands grabbed too roughly round Ernest's neck as he dropped onto his back with some help. Ernest let go of the dinghy and he sank. Just for a second, his head went underwater and up he came with a gasp and a flood of pain tight and curling around his heart pounding madly in his chest. It was the water and the weeds like hair or hands at his legs and the boy's arms on his back clutched like that dead girl he'd seen and crying as the voice he heard, Ernest? Ernest? his sister was shouting at the shore as he swam roughly for the point where she was and the horror in the water that he was in and moving over top of, the little girl's voice in his head like the boy's was now, the little girl bloated as her mother with their eyes gone, their fingers swollen and crooked around each other.

Ernest's arms ached, his whole body ached and froze in the water as he pulled them onto the slippery pavement of the highway. The boy wouldn't let go his grip round Ernest's neck so he swivelled him to the front saying, "C'mere, c'mere," and held him there wet and shivering as their chests heaved against each other like two men after a race.

Ernest faced the island where they'd been so the boy could see the campsite over his shoulder. "I'm sorry. I'm so sorry," he cried, holding the boy next to him. "I'm so sorry," he cried until they both calmed down.

Aaron just shivered a little and said he could set him down, though Ernest could tell he didn't much like having to get in the water again. He asked if the boy was okay and he nodded.

The boy looked up at him, squeezing his hand. "It's not your fault," Aaron said. "You didn't make it happen." And Ernest wanted to hold him again, but wouldn't.

Some men in a boat found them standing there in the middle of the river. They picked them up and took them back to the campsite. Ernest was spooked. Aaron and his dad decided to head back right away. They packed up and drove Ernest home. Aaron sat in the seat between them, wishing he could say something to Ernest to make him feel better. The man was awfully quiet and it unnerved him.

When they dropped Ernest at Bea's place, Aaron considered telling his dad about Ernest's son, but that didn't feel right. What would he say? So Aaron figured he'd keep it a secret until he talked to Ernest next, and then he'd ask if he could tell his dad.

No sooner had they pulled into the driveway than Fletcher came hopping their fence from the park.

"Does that kid not know anything?" his dad asked aloud.

Aaron wished he'd go away. He thought he'd ignore him, hoping that would work. His dad put the Rover in park and turned off the engine. As Fletcher approached, Aaron pretended to be too busy unbuckling and gathering up his stuff from the back to notice him. But Fletcher wasn't going away, that was made clear. Fletcher stood right by his door, waiting for him. When his dad stepped out of the truck he called over the hood, "Fletcher, don't hop our fence anymore. Come around the front like everybody else."

Fletcher said, "Sure," brightly, like he didn't even know he was being criticized. Aaron's dad walked to the side door of the house and unlocked it, propping it open.

Rooting through the stuff in the back seat, Aaron tried to stall as long as he could, but Fletcher opened the passenger door. "Hey, hey, hey," he said. "I got matches. Want to go make a campfire in the bush?"

"No," Aaron said crossly, looking to see if his dad had heard.

"Come on, it'll be fun," he coaxed. "I didn't get to go camping."

"I gotta unpack."

"I'll help," Fletcher said.

Aaron's dad came to the back of the truck and lifted the door. Fletcher snatched up a sleeping bag. "Where's this go?" he asked.

"Just put it at the bottom of the steps in the basement. I'm not going to store them away right yet."

Aaron crawled out of the car and his dad handed him the other sleeping bag. "Can you handle that?"

"Yes," he said, insulted, and followed Fletcher to the door. Standing on the landing inside, Fletcher pitched the bag down the stairs. Aaron scowled at him like he was stupid. "You were supposed to *carry* it down."

"This was faster," he said, grinning to show his chipped tooth. Aaron walked his bag down the stairs and set it around the corner, then placed the other bag right beside it. As he came climbing the steps, Fletcher shouted, "Catch" and Aaron had just enough time to look up and see a pillow coming for him. It hit his face and he caught it there before it fell.

"These don't go down there. We use these."

"I know that."

Aaron reached the top of the stairs but Fletcher wasn't going to let him pass. He stood still, in the middle of the entrance. "Move," Aaron said.

Fletcher laughed and put his hand on Aaron's forehead. "Try to move," he said.

Aaron hit his hand away, making Fletcher pretend-punch the pillow at his chest. "Hey, watch it. I'm on the stairs," he shouted. He grabbed the handrail. Fletcher punched harder, fast, bouncing on his toes. His dad appeared in the entrance and frowned. He couldn't get past Fletcher. One arm was loaded with a box and the other hand held a big bag. Aaron recognized it as Amanda's, from all the times she'd babysat. Why was his dad bringing her bag into the house?

"If you guys don't want to help, then you can at least get out of the way. Go play in back or something," he said.

Jumping alert, Fletcher stood on the stairs beside Aaron and let his dad go by. He turned to Aaron. "Well, let's go."

Aaron wanted to follow his dad and see what he did with Amanda's bag. He felt his stomach tightening up like he was sick. "I'm going to help unpack," he said, trying to get past Fletcher.

"Your dad just said to play in back. Come on." He wouldn't let Aaron pass, and poked him in the ribs, which tickled.

"Don't," he said, but Fletcher did it again. "Don't!" he said through his teeth. And again, Fletcher prodded him, only from the other side. Because he couldn't get around him, Aaron walked out the door with Fletcher in pursuit, wriggling a finger in his hip. He sped up, then ran, with Fletcher following right behind him.

Racing to the back, Aaron called behind him for Fletcher to cut it out, but he kept right on his tail. The panic swelled up in him again and he charged for the left side of the yard, then around the picnic table where Fletcher stopped dead on the other side, with Aaron only half-way around. He was between the table and the house, meaning he could only go left or right. Fletcher had him trapped in a game of cat and mouse.

"Fletcher, I'm not playing," he said.

"Sure you are."

"I'm not. You have to go home."

"Oh, come off it." Suddenly, Fletcher made a deek for the left, but Aaron matched him, stopping when Fletcher stopped. Then another deek, and a third.

"I mean it. Go home." Aaron tried to think of something threatening. "Take off, or I'll tell my dad."

Fletcher's face sort of jumped back in mock shock. "What?" He lifted his arms up innocently. "We're just fooling around."

"I don't want to play anything. I want you to go home."

Fletcher grinned wickedly and grabbed either side of the table. With a jump he was on top of it and coming for Aaron, who took off to the left, his heart racing and the sound of Fletcher's feet pounding on the grass behind him. He couldn't let Fletcher catch him. He couldn't let his father see Fletcher tickling him. He raced as fast as his legs would go for the back of the yard, but Fletcher was almost on top of him until he dropped to the grass and the boy tripped over him, flying to the ground with a crash. Aaron stood with the adrenaline going in him and let loose, "Fuck off!"

Fletcher sat up, looking sore, only he wasn't looking at Aaron, but over more, to the driveway. Then he heard him. "Aaron, get in the house," his dad said, cross.

Aaron turned around to see him looking real mad. Fletcher would get it now. "What the hell did you think you were doing?" he called, marching over. "Look at him. I said look at him, Aaron, he's bleeding."

Aaron snapped his head around to face Fletcher again, who cradled his elbow. There was a friction burn across it, all red and pink, a good four inches long. The lower end had a trickle of blood running down which turned Aaron's stomach in disappointment. His dad was there beside him.

"Are you okay, Fletcher?" he asked, bending over. "That doesn't look too nice. I'll clean you up, okay?" Fletcher nodded. His face read that it smarted, but Aaron doubted it was that bad.

"Aaron, go to your room," his dad said. "I'll deal with you later."

"But he was chasing me!"

"So that means you can try to kill him? Go to your room!"

Aaron hesitated, trying to find something else to say. His tongue felt trapped.

"I said go!" his dad shouted, pointing, making Aaron jump.

At the outset, Bea had only wanted the trial and error of match-making to be over. She'd looked forward to the day when she could settle down. Not to have to chose, to have chosen, to decide that *this* is the lover she'll have for the rest of her days, that *this* is the body she'll make love to, who'll please her in return. But through everything she forgot how fickle people could be. One sigh, one belch, and the picture is ruined.

When she heard his key in the door, she didn't believe it was him. Her first thought was that Amanda was home early, and her heart sank. Seeing Ernest walk through the door instead, Bea was caught totally off-guard. She felt violated, and cheated somehow. She deserved more time to think. Here she was getting ready for work, thinking she had another full day alone ahead of her. She wasn't even sure if she wanted him back.

He scooped up Brutus immediately, before kissing her hello, which was fine, but curious.

"You're home early," she said before she had time to think. She felt aggressive, but tried to keep the irritation out of her voice.

"We had a little accident," Ernest said, making Bea's heart leap into her throat.

"Who?" she asked.

Ernest still hadn't looked at her. He was staring at the cat, rubbing her belly as he cradled her in his arm. "Me and the boy."

Bea's voice came out weak with surprise. "Aaron?" she asked.

Ernest looked at her now, puzzled. "He's fine, Bea. We went out in the dinghy and it fell apart underneath us, but he's fine. We're both fine."

Bea's stomach was a knot. She felt she didn't know who he was. Ernest was a stranger, wasn't he, standing in her living room, holding a cat? The world got so much more complex as she watched him, unclear what he was thinking, now, or this afternoon, when she wasn't around him. She would never know what he'd done, couldn't know, any more than she could be sure what was going on in his mind. She hated to even consider it, but what had happened to his own son? What had Ernest done that his son was dead and a woman she didn't know had made a point of telling her to keep children away from him?

"Ernest," she said, calmly sitting down at the kitchen table, "I have to know what happened."

"I just told you. The damn boat gave way. We hit something, I think."

"No," Bea said, "with Kelly. With your son." Saying the words, speaking his name aloud, Bea felt she had more control over herself. Though Ernest looked like she'd slugged him with a bag of bricks, seeing his face drop, seeing his hand stop on the cat's belly and tremble there, vulnerable, comforted Bea.

"Okay," he said. "Okay, Bea." He put the cat on the floor and sat at the kitchen table, looking suddenly haggard, like a hospital patient. "What do you want to know?"

"How did it happen?" she asked, decisively.

☙

Aaron's dad called him into the dining room.

"What are you doing?" he asked. "Why would you trip him like that? Were you trying to hurt him? Because you did a good job of it." His dad paused, but when Aaron didn't say anything, he continued, sounding frustrated. "I don't know what to do with you, Aaron. Are you freaked out about the dinghy because I take you camping and you come back acting like this? What is that? Is there something wrong?"

Aaron couldn't bring himself to talk. He wanted to throw his arms around his father and cry, "Don't leave me, Daddy." But how could he? It was stupid. He was so stupid. He was better off not saying anything. He felt his eyes watering up.

"Why aren't you talking to me? Eh, buddy? Aaron? I asked you a question." His dad squatted in front of him and placed a hand on either knee. Aaron couldn't look him in the face. He couldn't tell his father what he'd done, what Fletcher had forced him into.

"If you don't tell me what's wrong, I can't help."

The tears spilled over his lids. "I want to live with Aunt Lue," he said impulsively.

His father paused without blinking. Aaron could tell he was registering what he'd said. "What do you mean? Have you talked to her about this?" His dad's voice grew firmer. "Aaron, answer me."

"No."

"No, what?"

"I haven't talked to her."

"Why do you want to do that?"

Again, Aaron didn't speak. He tried to think of something

else to say that would get him out of this. He couldn't bring himself to wipe the tears running down his face.

"Why do you want to live with your Aunt Lue?" his dad asked again. He had a shortness in his breath, as though he'd been punched in the gut. "Aaron, why? Why? I asked you a question. Answer me."

"Because you don't love me!" he screamed, his mouth out of control. He couldn't feel his lips they trembled so much. "You don't love me! You don't love me like my mother did!"

He didn't mean it. Or he didn't think he did. He hadn't known he felt that way at least. The sound of the words still in his head made him shake as he stared at his feet through blurry eyes. He didn't dare look at his father's face.

As soon as Aaron had said it something drained from him, some emptiness leaked out like air in a balloon, and the cavity in his chest swelled with pity for his dad, and shame for himself. He loved his father and didn't know how to tell him after what he'd just said.

"Fuck you," his dad whispered, his voice broken up.

Aaron's stomach seized and turned right over. He started for the bathroom only to have his dad grab his arm and yank him back.

"Where are you going?"

Then Aaron's stomach heaved again and he threw up, right there at their feet. An ugly yellow puddle sitting on top of the carpet.

"Look what you made me do," Aaron spat out, ashamed.

His father blanched. His whole body looked slack as his arms dropped to his sides.

With the grip released, Aaron took off out of the room and the house, and ran without his father calling for him even once.

❧

"He tripped on his shoe laces," Ernest began. Bea sat across from him. If she wanted to hear it, he'd tell her the whole thing.

All day he'd told Kelly not to walk around with them like that. It was very hot outside and the breeze wasn't blowing in through the kitchen windows as it usually did. Ernest had sat himself down at the table in the late morning to rest and cool himself down with some beer. He and Claire had fought over bills he'd said he paid but hadn't, and she wanted to know where the money was. *I bought your fucking Christmas gift okay?* he'd shouted at her, but she didn't believe him. *I bought it early.*

In July? she'd screamed back.

Yes in fucking July. There was a sale.

She was still yelling when she asked why the hell would he have spent so much if it were on sale? And didn't he think bills were more important?

So the money was gone. He'd bought rounds with it, and food, stuff, without letting her know, and the numbers had slipped by till he was caught. His guilt made him defensive, then angry.

For the half-hour they'd been fighting Kelly was practicing on a toy xylophone outside on the small back porch, banging on the keys. Ernest hated the xylophone. Kelly played it all the time; he tried to take it to bed with him. It was a girl's instrument, wasn't it? Stupid. Ernest was stupid-crazy about how much he hated Kelly playing with that toy.

So Kelly came in the door banging on the xylophone to drown them out or stop them or whatever, and Claire was still shouting as she left to do laundry in the basement. Ernest yelled at Kelly to stop playing. The boy stood staring up dumbly at him with the instrument in one hand and the sticks to play it in the other. Ernest couldn't stand how the scared soft look on his face made him feel. Angry, in one gesture, he grabbed the xylophone from him and tossed it out the side window, which he hadn't known was closed, and through the glass. When his mother heard the crash she ran up the stairs and around the corner. She suspected the worst. She yelled, *Run, Kelly, run from him!*

The boy took off. Claire charged at Ernest, wrestling with him, as Kelly ran. Kelly ran from him.

"He *ran*," Ernest said through gritted teeth.

His own son didn't trust him and that more than anything nearly killed Ernest. That's what he couldn't forget. In his head everything fell apart in a split second. Ernest broke free of Claire and was only four paces behind the boy wanting to catch him up and say not to be scared of him.

"Don't be scared of me," he sobbed as Bea stared dumbly at him.

Claire hadn't closed the cellar door. Kelly went for the stairs.

He'd been mad is all. It was so easy and harmless. *Not the stairs, not the stairs*, he remembers saying in his head. The boy's small arms and body dropped like chopsticks tied together. He cried out once as he fell but his head hit the step and he made no noise on the way down other than the clunk of his bones on wood.

In his nightmares, Ernest stood at the bottom of the step with the boy falling towards him. He raised his arms and caught him when he came to the bottom. Ernest felt the breaks in his bones and the soft parts of bruises. Every night he'd have the dream standing there, waiting for the inevitable, for gravity to drop him in his arms, for the smudge of blood on his lip to wipe across Ernest's shirt cuff, for the weight. Waking, Ernest saw the real thing again, his son falling away from him. He only caught up to the boy when he was already dead.

"That's it, Bea," he said, crying. "Don't make me say any more."

"I'm sorry, Ernest."

"It wasn't good," he said, shaking his head. "I didn't do so well through the thing. My wife wanted new shoes for the kid's funeral, he didn't have any good shoes that fit him and I'd filled up the credit cards so we had to ask her mother for the money. We had insurance, but the money was spent on the casket and everything before we realized the shoes wouldn't fit. They sent them back to us tied together."

Ernest coughed. "Four days, I didn't eat a thing. The day of the accident, two days of wake and one of funeral, I didn't go anywhere near food, nor the bottle, and everyone saying, 'Eat, Ernest. Or have a drink, it'll settle you. Calm yourself down. Take this to sleep tonight.' You don't know what that did to me."

"I'm sure it was awful, Ernest."

"It was awful. It was fucking awful. It's the worst fucking thing of my life. The cops came and asked questions and it was all settled. An accident. It was an accident. But the wife and I knew. I did it, like I'd done it with my own two hands."

Aaron didn't know how far he'd go or where, but walked for a good hour and a half towards the Zeller's mall, as best as he could figure. The city was so much larger than he'd thought it was. He never walked anywhere and the blocks added onto blocks surprised him each time he came across another landmark he recognized. The place they bought hubcaps was four blocks from his place and the nurse's residence from the college was a lot farther than that. The flower shop was in there, then Second Street which took a good part of the hour to get to, and the funeral home, beside the 7-11 which he wished he had money to go into. He was hungry.

When he stopped briefly to check his pockets for change, a man with red hair came out of the store and saw him. He gave Aaron a smile and did an about-face, which made Aaron do a straight line for the corner to cross at the light.

Aaron looked over his shoulder. The guy was getting into his rusty brown car. Aaron turned up the first street he hit, just in case the guy was reporting him. He didn't want to go back with the police. Did he look like a runaway? He must have looked guilty. He felt guilty. He was a criminal, wasn't he? Weren't runaways criminals? He was ready to go home, before he got in trouble with the police.

He stopped to turn around when a voice called, "Hey, how are you?" The guy in the brown car had pulled up alongside him with his window down. Aaron was the perfect height to look right at him from where he was. "You lost?" the man asked. He looked very concerned.

"No."

The guy nodded. His engine was still running, with his hands resting on top of the steering wheel. "You need a ride?"

Aaron shook his head no.

"You look a little upset. I thought you might be lost. Do you need any help?"

"No, thank you," Aaron said, trying to be polite and send him on his way. Maybe this guy was a policeman without his uniform.

"You look like you might have a problem. So I thought I'd ask." He paused to look in his rearview mirror. Aaron could see a mole on his neck. "Why don't you have a seat and rest yourself." He reached over and lifted the door handle so it swung loose. "Come here," he coaxed. "Come over here. I want to ask you something."

Aaron took a step closer to the car. He didn't want to talk to this guy, but he didn't know where he was either.

"You like chocolate bars? I bought a few extra but I'm on a diet. I shouldn't be cheating, eh?" He gave his belly a squeeze, then ran a hand across his mouth. "Maybe you could eat one for me? What kind do you like?" From his coat pocket he brought out an Aero, a Snickers, and a Big Turk, which Aaron hated. "Here, have one," he said, thrusting them out to him. "You can sit in the car and eat one if you like."

"I'm gonna eat supper," Aaron said.

"You live near here, then."

"I'm late."

"Well, I'll give you a ride home. I made you late, didn't I? Come on. You can save the chocolate bar for later." He gave the door a push wider, but it wasn't far enough to catch so swung back with a click shut.

When Aaron had gone two houses down the road, the man pulled his car out and eased it over to the curb again at the end of the block. The man looked at him from the rearview. Aaron crossed the street as if he'd been meaning to and hit the corner without looking over at the guy, then turned left to double around the next block. He thought it would be too obvious if he turned right around and went back the way he came. When there was no sign of the car and he'd gotten halfway down the street, Aaron looked over his shoulder. Both man and car were gone. Aaron picked up his pace, determined to get home and face the music. His stomach sank at the thought of seeing his dad. Which one of them would speak first? What Aaron would say weighed like a stone in his guts. *Sorry.* He wasn't. He'd been cheated. By Fletcher, by his dad, by his aunt and uncle, by his mother.

Aaron was a few paces from the corner, ready to turn it, when the rusty car pulled up in front of him. The man smiled out from the interior. "I just couldn't leave you walking home. Not when I'd made you late. Here, climb in," he said, and again reached across the seat and opened the car door.

"I'm almost home," Aaron lied, feeling sweat collect on his upper lip. His temples throbbed with blood. This was bigger than Mike Fletcher. This man wasn't going away.

"No, no, I insist. I'll take you home and explain why you were late for dinner. Are you late for dinner? You must be by now."

"I want to walk."

"Why would you want to do that?"

Aaron could only shrug. He had to swallow a gulp but didn't want the man to see him do it.

"Why would you want to walk when you can ride, hm? Come on, get in. It'll be fun."

"I want to walk."

"Okay then," he turned off his ignition, "I'll walk with you."

As the guy opened the driver's side door, Aaron yelled, "Stay away from me!"

Just then, from the house behind him, Aaron heard a woman's voice calling him. "Hey, what are you doing?"

It was his mother. His mother had finally come back. His mother was here to save him, not from Fletcher, but from this man. Aaron looked to the where her voice had come from and saw her pass behind an open window.

The front door swung open and the woman stepped out onto the porch. She was bigger in the chest than his mom, with a tiny waist and short brown hair. "What the frig are you doing?" she called out to them.

Aaron's heart dropped into his stomach. *Where was his mother? Why wouldn't she come save him?* he thought, racing again down the street, trying to see the sidewalk turned blurry through his tears.

Once he came to the end of the block, he looked back up the street. The man's car was nowhere in sight. As Aaron turned the corner, he spotted the big sign of the movie theatre. Finally, he knew where he was.

The summer was just starting and everyone Amanda's age was finishing school. They were going to get their contract jobs for the summer and leave for university in the fall, or at least go to the college here. And what was she doing? Waiting on people. Stupid. That's why she left her mother's house, wasn't it, so she wouldn't have to take orders? Amanda hadn't had the strength to face Bea and the apartment — her love nest with Ernest — after the ordeal with Nick, so she said she had some shopping to do. She'd asked him to bring her around to the Cumberland Square instead of home. He'd let her leave her stuff in the back of the Rover and had dropped her off, sweetly.

She wandered through the mall eating ice cream, looking at all the stuff she couldn't afford in the stores, trying to figure out what she wanted to do, which wasn't easy, until she couldn't stand it anymore and thought, *Get it over with.* She walked to the payphones and called Bea to warn her she'd be back.

"Did everyone come back early?" Bea asked. She had a funny tone to her voice that Amanda couldn't peg. "Ernest just got in not half an hour ago."

"Really?" Amanda said. That meant Nick must be home. "That's funny," she said, trying to make Bea continue.

"Ernest and Aaron had a bit of an accident. Everyone's fine, they just got a little wet and it spooked the poor kid."

"Oh," Amanda said.

Bea cleared her throat. "Will you be home for supper?" she asked awkwardly.

So that's it, she wants alone-time with Ernest. "No," she replied, feeling bitchy. "I can take care of myself."

"Oh, okay," Bea said. There was an awkward moment until Amanda said good-bye and Bea hung up.

Amanda held her finger on the connection switch. She knew she had another quarter in her pocket from the ice cream's change. Without dwelling on the idea, she dropped it in the slot and dialed. It rang once, and a voice said hello.

"Mom?" Amanda said into the receiver, and just the sound of that word made her want to burst into tears.

"Hi," her mother said. "Where are you?"

"I'm at the mall. Downtown." They chitchatted, but Amanda knew there was no other way to get what she wanted. She had to come right out and ask. She took a deep breath. "Can I come home?"

Her mother, matter-of-fact, said, "Sure," like she'd been waiting for her to ask all along. Then she added, "You mean for a visit?"

Amanda's heart sank, thinking her mother had misunderstood. Maybe the college-help was just that, she feared, and no more, no invitation to come home.

"Or for good?" her mother finished.

"For good," Amanda said.

"For good," her mother repeated. "Yes. Please."

Amanda said she'd be over soon. She didn't have any of her stuff with her, but tonight she wanted to sleep there.

"Do you want me to come get you?" she asked. "Georgie can finish cooking supper."

Georgie. She hadn't thought about seeing him. He didn't figure into the equation as nicely as she'd have liked. She and her mother both knew that. She hadn't been very nice to him, or he to her, for that matter. "Georgie's there?" she said, and knew it sounded obvious.

"He's going to darts at seven. You wanna come over when it's just the two of us?" Her mother's voice sounded scared. She sounded as scared as Amanda felt.

Amanda could feel her hand relax on the receiver — this wasn't easy — and she warmed at the idea that her mother knew her so well. She told her she'd be there after seven, and could take the bus, would prefer to take the bus. She wanted to get there on her own.

As soon as he walked up the steps to the front door, Ernest could hear the sister-in-law sobbing, and Nick too. They'd been out driving trying to find Aaron, but no luck, and had come home after an hour to call the police. The sound of Nick and Lucille crying together, choking out bits of words like a pair of drunks, was ugly. Gary was trying to soothe them.

"Hush, now, Lucille, he's only been gone a couple hours, right? There you go, drink this. You got to drink this down now so go ahead." Ernest figured she was getting nerve pills; he'd been on them for months after Kelly's accident.

He stood at the open door and didn't need to knock. Nick looked up and came barreling towards the screen. As a reflex, Ernest took a step back, scared momentarily.

Nick flung the screen door open and grabbed him by either arm. His hands gripped hard around Ernest's biceps. "Why?" he yelled at him. "Why, Ernest?" His mouth was large and distorted with each word. Gary came to the door and watched them, wondering if he should interfere. "I lost my wife. I can't lose any more. I got nothing left. Why would he do this?"

Ernest wondered if he should tell him. He figured he knew why the kid ran away, though this wasn't the time to say anything. Nick wasn't in any mood to listen, and wouldn't understand, or would overreact. He might walk over to Fletcher's house and kill the fucker.

The cops came and took a full report, though Ernest could tell they weren't too worried yet. Kids run away, and for the most part they come back. The police didn't know about this other kid, or about Nick's wife, so what did they care? Nick and the others had already checked with neighbours and friends, but to be nice the cops said they'd ask again and took names and addresses. Nick held himself together for that, but the second they closed their notepads, he collapsed in tears at the kitchen table. The guy cop turned his back to be polite, but the woman put her hand on Nick's back and rubbed a couple times. Ernest wondered if that's why they'd sent a lady cop. Nick only cried harder.

Seeing the policewoman with Nick reminded Ernest of when the cops came to his house after Kelly's accident. Wild with rage, Claire had screamed at him in front of the police, "You *killed* him! You killed my son!" Ernest could have burnt the whole city to the ground, he could have slit the throats of everyone on his block. He wouldn't face that sort of ugliness in himself again.

Ernest wanted to feel Nick's arms around him, he wanted to feel him grab him close and whisper comforting things in his ear. He was powerless, he and Nick, they were powerless to stop their lives from happening. They were small in the face of their fears and the world's potential for harm.

Bea was just setting her tray on the bar top and reloading when she saw him standing in the window, staring at her like he'd been there for hours waiting for her to look over and recognize him. She glanced at the door, across the street and at the other windows to double-check Nick wasn't with him, but from the look on his face she doubted she'd see his father nearby.

She ran to the door and stepped outside. It was still too warm although the sun was going down. Aaron's face was wet and his body was visibly shaking.

"Aaron? What are you doing here, Sweetheart? Where's your father?"

The boy didn't answer. A shudder ran right through him. Bea squatted down and frowned. "Is everything okay?" She put a hand on his arm. He was cold. "Has something happened to your dad?"

Aaron nodded.

"Where is he?" she asked.

"At home."

Bea tried to sound as comforting as she could. "What's happened?"

His face squeezed itself small. "I ran away."

"Oh, Sweetie. Comeer." Giving a gentle pull on his arm, she brought him to her breast and wrapped her arms around him in a hug. He began to sob. His little body shook and made Bea's shoulder wet with tears. "You guys have a fight? Shh," she said. "It'll be all right."

Over his shoulder she glanced inside to see the customers in the bar, and Hank, staring at them. She grimaced and every head turned away at once. "Why don't you come inside? Okay? We'll fix things up."

Aaron shook his head no.

"If you give me a few minutes, I can take you home. Why don't you wait for me inside? You'll be a lot more comfortable in there," Bea coaxed, though that didn't convince him either. "I don't know about you, but I'm hot out here." She gave her arms a little shake. "What do you say?"

The boy looked from her into the bar and back again, then sniffled his consent.

With her hand on his back, she walked them to the door, and held it open. Aaron walked gingerly in. Bea hoped to God the guys wouldn't all turn again and look at the poor thing, not with his face a mess of tears and she not knowing him well enough to put him at the ease he must need right now. *Don't look, don't look, don't look*, she chanted in her head. They did pretty well. Larry at the end of the bar stared, but the rest of them got the hint from her grimace outside and only turned after he'd passed.

Hank gave a nod from behind the bar and went to the back.

When Bea passed through the doorway, she saw he'd set up a chair for the boy. He was getting a popsicle out of the freezer. "You like banana?" he asked.

Aaron wouldn't answer. Hank handed the popsicle over to Bea and left them alone. She split the thing in two against the edge of the counter, then opened the wrapper. "You want to share this with me? I can never eat the whole thing."

The boy nodded and held out his hand. "I'm hungry," he said in a small shy voice.

"Have you been gone since before supper?"

Another nod.

"Why don't I go across the street and get you some french fries and a hot dog? Hm?"

She nearly cried when she saw the look of him. He stared around the tiny room as if it was a cage, then glanced out the door. He shook his head no.

"Are you not that hungry? You must be, eh, Sweetie?" She rubbed his back with the flat of her hand. "You want to tell me what happened? No?" When she leaned in closer to talk, he turned to her with his arms outstretched. She hugged him again. "You don't have to tell me if you don't want to," she said, holding him tight.

And God if he didn't cry. He let everything in him loose. You'd think the world was coming to an end, and he was the one responsible. Holding tight, she rocked him for a while, until he sniffled twice and she thought she should get him a tissue. Gently she pulled away. "I'm just going to get you a Kleenex. I'll be right back."

She stepped through the doorway and into the larger room, with part of her surprised to find people there. She went behind the bar to her purse and looked inside for the small package of tissues she kept in the outside pocket.

From the end of the bar, Larry slurred out, "I want another beer, Bea."

"Hank will get you one, Larry."

"No, Miss Beatrice, I request the pleasure of *your* beer." He looked up at her moony-eyed.

Figuring it better to pour a quick draught than stand arguing, or get him shouting, which he sometimes did, and scare the boy, she grabbed a glass from the shelf. "You're a handful, Larry."

"Me?" He put his floppy hands to his chest in mock protest. "I'm no handful. You're having problems of your own, ain't ya?"

"Nothing I can't handle."

"You got it under control?"

"Don't you worry, Larry. I'm fine."

Bea turned the tap off and set his beer on the counter top. "There you go."

"Thank you, darlin'," he said with a wink. Then he leaned in close and made like to whisper, "You're a good mother. I can see that."

With a lump in her throat, Bea felt her hands go numb. Her skin tingled around her eyes. "That's not my boy," she explained smoothly.

"Isn't it? You *look* awfully close."

"That's someone else's son, Larry." She gave him a weak smile and walked quickly to the back room.

Aaron was eyeing her half of the popsicle. "You want to have that too? I'm full," she said. Aaron nodded. "Go ahead." He picked it up by the stick and popped it in his mouth. "I have to make a quick phone call, okay? I forgot something, I'll just be another minute." She could have used the phone behind the bar, but didn't want more questions, so she went to the pay phone in the hall.

∽

When they were coming up to the house, Aaron could see his dad on the front step, and his aunt and Ernest inside through the picture window. His uncle must be there too. And there was a cop car parked right out front. His stomach turned over and instantly his whole body flashed hot, making him catch his breath. Bea took hold of his hand. "You'll be okay," she said.

He tried to keep his eyes from watering by blinking, but it wasn't working. When Bea let go of his hand, Aaron felt that too. That stung. Something enormous was happening, something the size of his mother's death was rising up in front of him the closer they got to the house. He was lonely, his insides were empty and aching, his hand felt cold without Bea's around it and he wished she'd grab hold of him again. He felt like he'd moved away and his home was all packed up with nothing left to remind him, or to remember him by. His mother had left first, and now he'd gone away without his dad, and he felt guilty about that. He realized just how easy it could be to lose his father too. What if there was an accident? A car crash. Or a fire. When he'd lost his mother, something of his life disappeared, something of who he was. He hadn't realized he was different, but he was, returning after running away. He was sick in his gut. He didn't know how to make it up to his father for leaving. How could he have done that? How could he have left him alone?

∽

Bea wouldn't let herself cry.

Ernest, Nick, this other woman who must be his sister-in-law, the three of them were red around the eyes from crying and Bea didn't want to be part of that. There was nothing sad here. She was the hero, wasn't she? The heroine. Maybe none of them would notice, or think that way, but Bea felt a sort of courage in her chest, a pride. Yes, it was coincidence that brought the boy to the bar, and she was only lucky that she was the one who saw him standing outside. It was only chance, but the luck fell on her. That much was intentional, wasn't it? Who got picked? Everything happens for a reason, she often told herself when things went sour.

And then the thought fell inside her. She was pregnant. Wasn't she pregnant for a reason? The look of Aaron outside the bar's window, staring in, struck Bea again. This was the look of a child waiting to be loved. Her skin prickled up and down her arms, down her spine into her legs. She had a child inside her, looking in through the glass. She couldn't turn her back on that. She wouldn't. Not when she had so much love still left to give. Ernest could do without her. Though this was his kid too.

She turned the car into the driveway. Nick was out on the step in a second, bounding down the stairs and to Aaron's side. He whipped open the car door and grabbed the boy still in his seat belt and held him.

"I'm sorry," he said sobbing. "I'm so sorry, Aaron. Don't ever leave me again, please, I don't want to lose you too." They held each other for a long time. Bea didn't want to move and disturb them. She couldn't get out of the car until they were done. When Nick unbuckled the boy's seat belt, Aaron stepped out, freeing Bea. Everyone was out of the house by then. The boy's aunt and uncle came over and hugged him, while Ernest stood back at the bottom of the steps holding onto the rail.

Aaron was crying quietly. He was a trooper. Breaking away from his aunt and uncle, he peeked over at Ernest. Bea could see Ernest was trying not to cry. This must be very hard on him.

Aaron walked over and lifted up his arms to hug him. As soon as he'd wrapped enough of himself around the boy that he couldn't see his face, Ernest broke down in tears.

Bea couldn't ignore that, could she? How could she ignore that?

୶

Coming up Vanier Drive to Second where the bus routes crossed, Amanda got to wondering. Maybe she'd just drop in quickly and get her stuff from Nick's; then she'd have a change of clothes. She could ride back and get on River Heights route after. It's not like her mother would be waiting at the door.

She had to pass the Vanier Drive bus to get to the River Heights route. The light was red. She waited a couple seconds thinking, *Well, the door's open. It's meant to be.* Pulling out her change, she climbed on the Vanier bus, resigned to going. Nick wouldn't mind her stopping in so soon if she was picking up her stuff.

The minute the bus lurched from the curb into traffic, Amanda couldn't get his voice out of her head. *I've already been in love.* Okay, so he was still in love with his wife, sure, she expected as much. It was only a year or so. But he couldn't live in the past, could he? She'd suggest putting that wedding photo away, which would be a good start.

The bus rode past her high school, closed for the summer. Amanda's whole body tightened up inside, worrying. She wanted to finish high school, and go to the college, and not be a loser in a waitressing job until she died. *Oh my God, she thought, I don't want to be Bea.*

She rang the bell for the next stop, which was just at the end of Nick's street. As the bus passed the lights and slowed, she walked to the doors and looked up his block. There were people there, on his front lawn. Aaron. And Bea and Ernest, they weren't hard to miss. And a couple of other adults. That thought made something click in her mind, tying together a small little feeling she didn't want to look at. *Adults.* Amanda heard Nick saying again that she was too young. And she was, next to the bunch of them standing there. She was the outsider. She was the kid.

The bus came to a full stop with its mechanical sigh and waited. Amanda held her hand on the bar, feet at the step. It wasn't just a matter now of *when* she could get out of her life, but how?

"You getting off or what?" the bus driver called back.

When she saw Ernest wrap Aaron in his arms and hold him, she stepped down, releasing the doors. That's what she wanted, Nick to love her like that. Only Nick wasn't her father, was he? Like a wave running through her head, everything turned clear inside her, so she suddenly saw past the immediacy of her life, the bills, and Bea and Ernest and her mother, and Georgie, and work, and Alphie who was finally gone. Amanda knew she was fooling herself with love. She didn't love Nick as much as she wanted Nick to love her. That thought struck her in her heart like an arrow, draining blood. Her mother had tried to love her and Amanda, wanting more, had walked out.

"Hey, kid?" the driver said, "I got other passengers here. Get off or get in."

"Sorry," she said, stepping back. "Wrong stop." The doors swung closed, and the bus lurched into gear. Sitting back down, she looked around at the passengers, all of them tired. Each of them seemed pathetic and alone. Without her mom, and Georgie, she thought, this is what she was headed for. This would be her life, this here, this bus ride, in this city, with these people, and she deserved more, didn't she? Didn't they all deserve more than this?

᠅

All hot and breathy from crying, the boy whispered in his ear, "I didn't want to be bad."

Because the boy said it to him and not his dad, Ernest knew he didn't mean the running away, he meant that other kid. With the boy in his arms, Ernest knew the feeling, finally. He recognized the shame, the terrible shame ripping up your self-worth. Ernest wanted to be Nick because he didn't want to be himself, a man in love with Nick.

He wiped his hands across Aaron's face to clear up the tears. "Remember what you said to me?" he asked, looking the boy in the eyes. "Remember? Out on the river? 'It's not your fault. You didn't make it happen,'" Ernest said, and gave the boy another hug. "It's not your fault, Aaron. You haven't done anything wrong." And squeezing him close he wanted to add that it wasn't worth it, all the worry and the stress of hiding himself away. *You can't run away from yourself*, he wanted to say, but couldn't. The boy wouldn't understand. Not yet, anyway. And just that easily Ernest thought he'd be there, he'd be around when the boy was ready to talk, and Ernest could say, *I've done the same thing myself.*

Look at us, he thought. They were all like a picture standing in the driveway, like a movie, as he embraced the boy, everyone in tears. With his grey hair and potbelly, he must look like the grandfather. He was old enough. He squeezed Aaron tighter. Ernest was nearly an old man. He was an old man holding onto a boy for dear life, as the hardness in him relented, crying, finally, with pain, and with relief, *my son, my son, my son.*

ACKNOWLEDGMENTS

I would like to thank the readers at various stages of the writing who had comments and insights: Adrienne Barrett, Dorothy Bartoszewski, John Finlay, Marie Gillan, George Ilsley, Bryan McKinnon, Shan McPherson, Kathryn Mockler, Paul Moore, Jerry Newman, Billeh Nickerson, Linda Svendsen, Colin Thomas, and Peggy Thompson.

I would like to thank the Canada Council and the BC Arts Council for their generous assistance over the years. At every opportunity, I thank them. I'm most grateful.

Also, I thank Marc Coté and S. E. Stewart for their excellent advice, their patience, and their confidence, Carolyn Swayze for her tireless warmth and for her work, and anthologists James

Johnstone, Brett Josef Grubisic, Carellin Brooks, and Bonnie Burnard for including me in their books.

I would especially like to thank my friends, here, again, for their boundless advice and support. I thank my family, with a reminder, by way of apology, to disregard the small facts in my fiction.